The Helford Anch

By David J. W

Introduction

'To open Pandora's Box means to perform an action that may ᵦ small or innocent, but that turns out to have severely detrimental and far-reaching consequences.'

For My Mum

The Helford Anchorage

by

David J. Watson

Contents

Chapter One ………………………………… Embarking
Chapter Two………………………………… Navigating
Chapter Three……………………………….. Approaching
Chapter Four………………………………… Morning
Chapter Five………………………………… Diverging
Chapter Six………………………………….. Driving
Chapter Seven……………………………….. Revealing
Chapter Eight………………………………... Exchanging
Chapter Nine………………………………… Crossing
Chapter Ten…………………………………. Infiltrating
Chapter Eleven……………………………… Joining
Chapter Twelve……………………………… Compromising
Chapter Thirteen……………………………... Struggling
Chapter Fourteen………………………….. Anchoring
Chapter Fifteen……………………………… Abducting
Chapter Sixteen …………………………… Landing

The Helford Anchorage

Chapter One – Embarking

   Mrs Colarossi was seated at the helm of the classic yacht 'Moutine', clad in the brightly coloured sailing clothes that Mr Bilbi had insisted she must wear at all times when she was up on deck. She understood the importance of the fluorescent colours, from a visibility and safety aspect, but nevertheless she disliked the intense red and yellow garments that seemed to be several sizes too large for her. Mrs Colarossi had followed the skipper's instructions and strapped on a bulky lifejacket and she was now feeling like a 'Michelin' man, which was the only image that came into her head. Edward was showing Anthony the control levers for the engine and pointing out the various gauges and switches on an impressive panel that was set into a varnished wooden casing. The two men were just inside a partially covered area of the cockpit which was sheltered from the elements to some degree. Judith Berry, onboard the Helford Ferry had observed the yacht from such an angle that she could only see the bulky bright coloured figure near the stern, and therefore Judith was unable at that distance to determine who was at the helm. It was not at all obvious if the person at the helm was male or female.
   Later, as the voyage progressed, Mrs Colarossi would be glad of those warm waterproof clothes and she would gradually become accustomed to their padded comfort. For the moment she was clinging onto the long sturdy tiller with her gloved hand, while looking forward as the river widened. Neither Mr Bilbi nor Mr West seemed to be at all concerned that she might so easily steer this beautiful vessel into some other vessel, or perhaps even venture too close to the banks of the river. Mrs Colarossi shouted to them both to make them aware of her anxiety. "Mr Bilbi?" Turning to face the lady at the helm, Edward strode over to where she was sitting. She noticed that the two men were also wearing full sailing gear, except theirs appeared to fit them much better than hers. "What is the

problem Mrs Colarossi?" "Shouldn't one of you be keeping lookout in case we might hit something? This is my first time you know!" Edward found this amusing. "Imagine you are at the wheel of your Ferrari then. This river is a lot wider than any road that you would drive along." She failed to see how there was any comparison. "Yes, but I have to remember to move the tiller to the left when I want the boat to go to the right, and move it to the right when it goes to the left. I find that confusing." Edward sat close beside her and proceeded to explain that she must think in terms of starboard and port, and it was also more correct to use the term 'her' rather than 'it' when referring to the boat. He rested one hand on the tiller and demonstrated how she could steer towards the middle of the river, which then allowed her to see more on the starboard side and thus keep away from the edge. By doing the same in the opposite direction, or simply maintaining a straight course, the visibility to port was greater. "I shall send Anthony forward to get the jib sail ready, so he can let you know if we are about to collide with an oil tanker. Once the sails are set I can take over at the helm if you like?" Mrs Colarossi objected to Edward's remark, warning him that she was more than capable of sighting an oil tanker well before the point of impact.

Mr West, the lawyer turned sailor, was keeping watch from the forward end of the cockpit area. He was admiring the gleaming white sails that were stretched taught as the wind filled them. Mrs Colarossi had welcomed the offer to be relieved of the helm at such an early stage into the passage and she had gone below, where she extracted herself from the cumbersome all weather gear. Wandering in the direction of the well equipped galley, she set about preparing a light lunch for the crew. Edward was sitting at his helmsman's position with the tiller grasped firmly in his strong hand. He chose not to wear gloves unless the weather turned bad, as he liked to feel the motion of the boat through the tiller. Edward was thinking deeply about his two crew members. Through half closed eyes he observed Anthony West and wondered how far this man could be trusted. The unexpected transformation from a friend who he thought he knew quite well, into a much more assertive and devious character who had seemingly conspired with the volatile lady who was the primary shareholder of this vessel that was now embarking upon a dubious voyage. Edward had not yet lived down the shocking experience of relinquishing control to the wildly unpredictable Angelina Colarossi, and he was even more at odds with the sudden shift of authority where Anthony was concerned. To some extent, Edward had reasserted himself by assuming the role of skipper aboard this fine sailing boat, albeit at the behest of Colarossi and West of course. When it came down to the task of crossing the sea to France, responsibly and safely, Mr Bilbi was obviously the man for the job. He could take comfort in having a distinct advantage over the other two, although Edward would not be getting paid for this little jaunt until they were once more back in England and the success of that venture could not be guaranteed in reality.

And what of Mrs Colarossi? Why was she going to all this trouble in order to arrange the transportation of some highly secretive cargo? What was in that cargo? Why would they wish to use a coffin for a container, what was wrong with a standard wooden crate he wondered. Edward considered the possibility that the cargo might be drugs, but very quickly he dismissed the notion as being ridiculous, because somehow Colarossi and West weren't the type of people to get involved in such dirty business. He remembered Mrs Colarossi's words… "He is not going to France, he is going to Italy." Pausing to reflect on those words, Edward had a vision of the body of her deceased husband lying in the coffin, surrounded by bags of narcotics. Presumably the customs officers would not go as far as to open a coffin, and in any case they had X-ray machines. Maybe there was no body in there? Perhaps the box was crammed with gold bars, or wads of cash or even diamonds? Surely, if it was just Bandini who was in the box, would it not have been cheaper and simpler to use air freight? Edward was turning over these ideas in his head, but he was also thinking that it didn't really matter to him what was in the cargo. As long as they gave him the money, the cargo was not his problem… job done and go home.

From his office at Falmouth Police station, D.I. Cook was co-ordinating the aerial cover that he had requested. He was speaking to senior Naval officers about what he saw as an urgent requirement for the only resource that was capable of tracking the movements of this particular vessel. Unfortunately for the detective, his desire for urgency was not shared by the officers. They explained to D.I. Cook that the Sea King search and rescue helicopter, SAR, based at RNAS Culdrose was specifically assigned to locate marine vessels that were in serious difficulty, and to conduct the necessary rescue operation in support of the RNLI and the Coastguard. This led them to downgrade the detective's request, as the yacht 'Moutine' was clearly not in difficulty and as far as anyone knew, she was not in need of assistance. The control room at Culdrose duly passed the request to Exeter Airport, where the Police helicopter was based. Devon and Cornwall Police were responsible for covering a large area, that included not only Devon, Cornwall, Dorset, Avon and Somerset but also the Scilly Isles. They had one Eurocopter available to respond to any emergencies that were not covered by the SAR helicopter or the Air Ambulance service. A further restriction was the reduced operational range of the Police helicopter, which was roughly half that of the Sea King. Consequently, D.I. Cook was told that providing the Police helicopter at Exeter was available for this task, the aircraft would be sent to the area just beyond the Helford River Estuary. It was also explained to him that the limit of the helicopter surveillance would only extend to the centre line of the designated shipping lanes, so in effect this was half way between England and France. The area of water from the centre line as far as the coast of Britanny and Normandy in Northern France would be covered by the French Police.

Putting down the phone, D.I. Cook was not entirely satisfied with the outcome, but then again he could not have expected the people at Exeter to compromise their air cover for such a large area. There were now two priorities for the detective, one would be to contact Interpol if there was to be some sort of air surveillance on the French side, and the other was to obtain as much information as possible about the suspect vessel from Mrs Berry in particular. First of all he needed to notify his superiors that he would be contacting Interpol as a matter of Police procedure.

Upstairs at the bungalow, 'Polgwyn', the phone was ringing and Judith got up to answer the call. James stood at the window and waited. He could hear Judith describing the appearance of the yacht to the detective. "Yes of course Mr Cook, she has two masts and she is all wood on the topsides. 'Moutine' is forty feet in length overall and her last known course is uncertain. She was heading East in the deep water channel on the South side of the river, that's as much as I can tell you detective, I'm afraid." Judith ended the call and put down the phone. Turning to James she related the details of the conversation with D.I. Cook. "Mr Cook needs to provide more accurate information for the helicopter that they are sending from Exeter." She realised that the chances of locating this one relatively small yacht were not great, especially once she was out into the busy shipping lanes of the English Channel. James agreed that it would be difficult for the Police in Cornwall to determine the destination of this vessel. "We don't even know who is aboard the boat. It sounds like Interpol and the French Customs authorities will be getting involved anyway." Judith wondered if perhaps they were overreacting about the whole thing, and maybe it would turn out to be nothing more than the owner of 'Moutine' simply making a routine passage across the Channel, possibly to France?

Sitting back in his chair, D.I. Cook had managed to find some degree of support from his superiors in Truro, and they had insisted upon notifying Interpol from their headquarters rather than allowing the detective in Falmouth to make the call. He did have a contact on the French side of the water who was available, should it become necessary to pool the resources of both Police forces later on. Now it was time to conduct further searches closer to home. D.I. Cook issued orders for his patrols to carry out thorough checks on the ground, which included breaking down the doors of properties that were not accessible by any other means. The detective himself accompanied the patrol car that was to visit the home of Mrs Colarossi as he intended to search the entire building, as well as seeking out anyone who might be inside the premises. Other patrols were sent out to cover the unfinished building project of Bilbi's at Porth Navas, the Falmouth office of Mr West and also his home address, the company who owned the boatyard at Gweek and a more concentrated search of the Falmouth Hotel.

Gaining entry to the courtyard of the mews house complex, the Police approached the door on the ground floor that was known to belong to Mrs Colarossi. There was no response when the detective rang the doorbell so he stepped aside while one of his officers smashed in the door with the heavy 'Enforcer', or the big key as the officers tended to call it. The door resisted the initial impact but soon gave way under the officer's enthusiastic use of force. "Nice door, Sir" They proceeded to step over the splintered woodwork of what was once a nice door that was now hanging off its hinges rather forlornly. Two officers went up the stairway ahead of D.I. Cook and moved from room to room quite quickly at first. Meanwhile, the detective descended the steps to the garage. Much to his surprise the gleaming red Ferrari was sitting there unattended. The thought crossed his mind that he would have been left red-faced if they had just destroyed Mrs Colarossi's front door and it later transpired that she had merely gone out shopping. D.I. Cook was actually adopting a heavy handed approach, and at that moment he didn't have a great deal of evidence to support his investigation. He would need more than his gut feeling to justify his actions at this stage. Returning to the main living area upstairs, he joined the officers as they scrutinised a room that was obviously some sort of office. There was no sign of a computer in the room, but this was because laptop computers had been used and then taken away. A couple of shelves had rows of carefully labelled files along them, which all seemed to correspond to Mrs Colarossi's business interests, and they noticed a metal filing cabinet in one corner that was locked. The large table had a drawer under one side, which was not locked and this contained the usual stuff such as a stapler, rubber stamps, pens, pencils, ruler, paper clips and other assorted office supplies. Leaving one of his officers to go through the files, D.I. Cook and the second officer went off to check the rooms on the upper floors. They walked into the last of the bedrooms, the one where Edward had stayed recently, before checking the only other room on the top floor. The door was closed but not locked. The detective opened the door to find that this room had no windows and it was also very cold. He ran his hand up the wall in the darkness and found the light switch. Turning the circular switch he looked up to the ceiling, but to his surprise some bright lights came on that were positioned along the edges of the floor, from corner to corner all around the room. The two men hesitated before going further into the room. Gradually the powerful white lights became increasingly intensified, until they couldn't make out the floor area at all. The glare of the lights reached a frightening level of intensity and then quite unexpectedly a single orange light doused the whole of the room, as the white lights went out suddenly. D.I. Cook and his colleague were left rubbing their eyes, while struggling to focus on what was in front of them. Nothing, it seemed. They peered through the orange gloom and saw only four aluminium poles that connected the floor to the ceiling. Hanging down almost to the floor they saw what appeared to be four metal wires that formed two slings made of what looked black rubber material. "What do you make of this Hammett?" "Never seen anything like it Sir… looks a bit strange I reckon." P.C. Hammett was thinking to himself that the scene did remind him of something he had once seen in a Hamburg nightclub and he was wondering if perhaps this Mrs Colarossi was inclined to indulge in pursuits of a slightly kinky nature? It was then that D.I. Cook interrupted the officer's lewd thoughts, turning off the light switch and backing out of the room as darkness was resumed. They rejoined the officer who was examining the files and a call came through on Hammett's radio. It was to inform the detective that a unit had gained access to Mr West's office premises in the town centre and they were awaiting orders. D.I Cook was handed the radio. "I want to know if the name 'Bilbi' appears anywhere on West's computer, or in his filing system. Let me know the minute you find anything."

Following a course of South-South-East, and taking advantage of a fairly constant South Westerly breeze, 'Moutine' was sailing comfortably with the wind almost on her beam, that is to say the wind was nearly at an angle of ninety degrees to the starboard side of her hull. Edward was gently easing the tiller away from him to port, in order to bring the boat closer to the wind. He was happy to sit there at the helm, watching the bow wave and regularly looking up at the set of the sails. Mrs Colarossi's head appeared at the companionway as she announced that lunch was served. She had gone below before Edward could respond. Leaving his position amidships, Mr West carefully made his way over to where Edward was helming. "Are you joining us for lunch Edward?" Most modern yachts of this size would have automated self steering fitted but the decision had been taken during 'Moutine's' refit not to compromise the classic heritage of the yacht, so she did not have this feature installed. "Well Anthony, one of us has to steer the ship, and I don't mind who it is." He saw Mr West's anxious glance out to sea and offered to stay where he was. "As long as one of you brings me some food up I can hold our course." Clearly relieved to hear this, Mr West wasted no time in going below to see what was on the menu. He found Mrs Colarossi seated at the cabin table with three plates of hot food ready and waiting. "Edward says he would rather not leave the steering right now, but he wants his lunch taking out." She failed to understand why Mr Bilbi was not able to join them at the table, and she had not even begun to consider the logistics of the yacht steering herself without anyone at the helm. Mr West realised he must be the one to serve their skipper with his food, as Mrs Colarossi was already well into her main course and showing no signs of getting up from the table. She didn't even look up when Mr West climbed the steps up to the hatchway, balancing the hot plate in one hand while holding on to anything solid as he went. He managed to reach Edward without spilling any of the plate's contents. "Thank you Mr West, and I shall look forward to a pudding in ten minutes!" The lawyer tried to smile as he moved unsteadily in the direction of the living quarters. Edward noticed a knife and fork had been provided on his plate, but with one hand firmly guiding the tiller he opted to use only the fork under the circumstances. Down below, Mrs Colarossi and Mr West enjoyed their meal as though they were dining in the restaurant coach on the Orient Express railway train. The motion of the boat was not particularly noticeable in the relatively calm sea state and their conversation flowed effortlessly, the pair of them unaware of what was going on above deck. Edward had finished eating and he was sighting an increasing number of larger ships on the not too distant horizon. At some point quite soon, he was thinking, it would be necessary for him to go below and monitor the movements of nearby vessels in the designated shipping lanes. Edward noticed a few yachts that were on a similar course to 'Moutine' having passed by on the port side, and making good headway. They had probably come from Falmouth judging by their angle of approach. Minutes later there was the sound of an aircraft that caught Edward's attention. He raised his head and realised that it was a helicopter, which was hovering above them at low altitude. Mr West came up on deck with the skipper's pudding so Edward invited him to take a seat. "Here Anthony, put the dish down and hang onto the tiller for a moment." As Mr West took over as helmsman, Edward dashed forward to the covered area of the cockpit and retrieved his binoculars. He leaned against the wooden roof to steady himself while he inspected the helicopter through the binoculars. It was mostly dark blue, with some yellow markings on it. Edward was sure it was a Police helicopter from its appearance. He was not unduly worried by this intrusion, but he was curious as to why they were watching their vessel. "See that helicopter Anthony? It's the Police." Mr West shielded his eyes from the sun with one hand and looked at the helicopter as it hovered above them. "What does that mean?" Edward shrugged his shoulders and took another look through his binoculars. The helicopter rose to a slightly higher altitude and maintained a flight path that matched the course of the yacht. "They seem to be following us anyway." Edward needed to check the navigation instruments in the cabin so he instructed Mr West to keep her on a straight course and not to worry. Down below deck Mrs Colarossi was finishing her dessert and Edward set his dish down next to the chart table. He flicked a few switches on various black boxes, studying the gauges with interest. Each vessel in the Traffic Separation Schemes, or TSS, showed up clearly on the plotter as a coloured icon, which included more detailed information such as the name of the vessel, the speed at which it was travelling and also the direction of travel. The screen indicated distances and compass bearings as part of the Automatic Identification System, or AIS. Edward scooped up some pudding and custard as he noted the position of 'Moutine' in relation to the nearest vessels on the screen in front of him. On the French side of the channel the vessels in the shipping lanes were moving West to East, while the those on the English side of the channel were moving East to West. The whole area resembled that of a typical motorway on land. Edward could see red icons that represented tankers, dark blue icons were passenger vessels, green icons were cargo vessels and purple icons were yachts. Tugs and pilot vessels showed up as light blue icons nearer to the shores. He scribbled down a few notes on a scrap of paper and went back up on deck to speak to Mr West at the helm. "Anything to report Mr West?" Anthony seemed to be more relaxed about his task for now. "There's a big ship up ahead, what do we do?" Edward followed Mr West's gaze to where a large vessel lay just off the port bow, moving left to right about one nautical mile ahead. "That is a tanker that's heading for the Panama Canal, at a speed of eleven knots on a bearing of two hundred and fifty degrees, West-South-West." Surprised by Edward's detailed knowledge of the ship that was in view, Mr West repeated his question. "Yes, that's all very well, but what do we do?" Edward explained to him that given the ship's speed of eleven knots, Mr West should go astern of the tanker by steering slightly to port. "Push your tiller a little out to starboard Anthony and I shall ease off the mainsheet to spill some wind. That should allow this one to pass across our bow before we get much closer." Edward made a point of warning him that later there would be more traffic, and as they approached the centre of the channel they would have to contend with vessels crossing in both directions. "I shall stay at the chart table down below when it gets busy, and I will shout instructions to you as often as possible. Mrs Colarossi can make herself useful by joining you up on deck and keeping watch. Are you alright helming for a couple of hours Anthony?" "Yes, I'm fine. We can do as you say." Edward had more faith in Mr West as a rookie sailor than he did in Mrs Colarossi. "If we get too close to any vessel I can call them on VHF radio to make sure we are visible on their radar." Edward went on to explain that there was a safety zone between the two lanes of shipping that were travelling in opposite directions, and also it may be necessary for them to change course for a short time, while waiting for a safe gap in the traffic. "We may need to use the motor as well as sail, and perhaps even use motor only in the event of there being no wind at all." Mr West accepted Edward's advice and set his eyes on the course ahead. He glanced upwards at the relentless progress of the Police helicopter. Edward returned to his station below deck.

P.C. Hammett's radio crackled and the unit that was searching the office of Edward's lawyer had something to report. "It's Ken, Sir, they've found something of interest." Taking the radio from the officer, D.I. Cook was in need of some fresh information. "What have you got Ken?" "Well Sir, as well as large folders of files concerning Edward Bilbi we have turned up a lot more that mention the name 'Colarossi'." Ken had not forgotten the crazy lady with the Italian sounding name who had confronted him at the counter that evening. "There's loads of stuff here about property transactions and some more to do with the shared ownership of a yacht. Anthony West's name appears as the legal representative for Mrs Colarossi on each document." The detective was intrigued to discover that the twitchy Mr West was not only Bilbi's lawyer, but apparently he was also representing Mrs Colarossi's interests as well. "Right Ken, let's not mess about, I want you to bring West's computer and all the printed files over here to Colarossi's house and we can go through the whole lot here and now. This is the link we were looking for."

The room upstairs at the mews house in Gyllyngvase was transformed into a hive of activity. D.I. Cook was sat at the head of the table, studying closely a bunch of manila folders, while several

Police officers were plugging in computers and running cables in all directions. The unit that was currently searching Mr West's home address was also instructed to remove all computer equipment from the lawyer's house, along with any printed documents found there and bring everything to Mrs Colarossi's property. "My guess is that our friend Mr West is helping Bilbi to leave the country. I strongly suspect that Mrs Colarossi may be involved in this escape attempt. We do not yet know who is onboard the vessel that we are tracking across the English Channel but we have all known inland locations covered." It was decided to make use of Mrs Colarossi's house as a sort of operations centre, as it was unlikely that the lady herself would return anytime soon. Following the detailed searches of West's office in Falmouth, his residence in Mabe Burnthouse and Mrs Colarossi's home, the detective's team of officers had more than enough material to sift through in support of this case. The telephone number for the Colarossi address was relayed to the control room at Truro Police station and D.I. Cook was informed of the progress of the helicopter surveillance. He was told that the yacht was about to cross the East to West shipping lanes and as soon as the vessel reached the safety zone in the centre of the Traffic Separation Schemes this would be the limit of the area covered by the Devon and Cornwall Police force. The Truro control room were now in the process of requesting the corresponding helicopter surveillance from the French side of the Channel. They assured D.I. Cook that everything would be done as far as possible to provide Falmouth Police with the intended destination port of the suspect vessel.

   The detective was not entirely confident about leaving this crucial part of the investigation in someone else's hands, so he decided to make contact with his colleague at Interpol which would not go down well with his superiors in Truro if they got to know of it. "Bonjour Maurice, how are you?" "Je suis très bien merci, Derek. What can I do for you mon ami?" D.I. Cook explained to his friend Maurice what was going on in the English Channel and asked if his French counterpart could keep an eye on proceedings for him. "Ah, you mean to say 'La Manche', Derek, we don't say 'English' Channel." "Thank you Maurice, but I shall call it the English Channel on our side, and you can call it what you like on your side. You'll be telling me next that Calais does not belong to England, I suppose?" "You are welcome to Calais if you want it mon ami?" D.I.

Cook thanked the French detective for the geography lesson but repeated his request. "Anything you can do Maurice would be most helpful." "Don't worry, Derek and what is this yacht called?" "She is called 'Moutine', two masts and forty foot in length. I just need to know where this vessel goes ashore once it reaches France." "What if I can do better than that? Perhaps my men can tell you where the people go when they get off the boat?" Smiling to himself, D.I. Cook appreciated the suggestion. "Yes, of course Maurice, that would be excellent. Thank you." After exchanging a few questions about family matters they ended the call. One of the detective's officers drew his attention to a file that was displayed on West's computer screen. It clearly showed details of the shared owners of the yacht 'Moutine' and the percentages of their shareholdings. Angelina Colarossi was the primary shareholder with fifty per cent, then Anthony West with thirty per cent and lastly Edward Bilbi with a share of twenty per cent. These figures didn't matter much to D.I. Cook but the simple fact that all three of them were part owners of the yacht was enough to establish a common motive for their actions.

Chapter Two – Navigating

Tactfully, and as politely as he could manage, Edward suggested to Mrs Colarossi that she should leave the comfort of the cabin and assist Mr West up on deck. She arose from the cabin table reluctantly. "Mr West is steering quite well at the moment, but we are approaching the busy shipping lanes and I shall have to spend some time down here at the chart table. If you could maintain a lookout for the next hour or two, then it would be really helpful." Mrs Colarossi listened to Edward's recommendations as she struggled into the waterproofs and gave him a look that revealed her true feelings. "Why can't you be the lookout Mr Bilbi?" Edward regarded her foolish question as a challenge against his authority as skipper of the vessel, and quite apart from that issue he thought the answer should be blindingly obvious to her. "Mrs Colarossi, as far as I know you are not capable of interpreting the information displayed on these screens. That is why I must guide us through the busiest shipping lanes in the World and you must keep Mr West and myself informed of which ship we are most likely to collide with, preferably before we actually make contact." She turned her nose up at this remark and squeezed through the companionway hatch in her bulky sailing garments, muttering some words to herself under her breath which Edward presumed might be in Italian. This lady was going to be hard work, Edward thought.

Fixing his gaze over the port side and across the water, Mr West became aware of an increasing number of ships that were coming into view from the East. The presence of the Police helicopter was almost forgotten and he gripped the tiller ever more tightly. As he took a brief glance towards the bow, Mrs Colarossi popped out of the companionway as though she was a fluorescent red and yellow cork bursting from a bottle of Prosecco. Joining Mr West at the helm, she was preparing to sit down when he offered what amounted to a suggestion, thinly disguised as more of an instruction. "Would you be so good as to stand near to the hatchway at the forward end of the cockpit? That way, you can relay directions to me from Mr Bilbi and also keep an eye on ships approaching from your side." Mrs Colarossi looked this way and that, before moving to her allocated position. During the next ten minutes or so there was no conversation between them. She had her back to Mr West, who was concentrating on what was happening around him. Presently, there was a warning called out from below deck. Edward could see Mrs Colarossi's arm just outside the hatchway, so from his seat at the chart table he voiced his directive, clearly and decisively. "Let Anthony know that he must go astern of the vessel that is approaching from our port beam and maintain our course to pass between that vessel and the one following." Mrs Colarossi stepped away from the companionway and waddled over to Mr West in her cumbersome suit of clothing. She hadn't quite found her sea legs yet. "Mr Bilbi says you must go behind the next ship, and then continue ahead on the same course, passing between that one and the next ship." Although her terminology was slightly different to the skipper's, the message was understood by the helmsman. Both of them could see the two ships that Edward had spotted on his AIS screen and Mr West realised they had sufficient room to manoeuvre. They observed a container ship as it cruised past at quite a rate of knots and the white lettering on the sides of the containers was clearly visible from that distance. 'Moutine' continued sailing without altering her course, passing astern of the lumbering red hulled container ship. Following behind this vessel was the grey shape of another approaching vessel which at the moment was far enough away not to give any cause for concern. The wind remained pretty constant and the swell was relatively moderate. Mrs Colarossi dutifully returned to her position at the forward end of the cockpit area, where she kept a watchful eye on the looming grey shape of the next ship in the line. Edward momentarily ascended the steps to consult the ship's compass before returning to his place at the instrument panel. Mr West looked at his watch and thought of food and drinking water.

  Barely had the gleaming white hull of 'Moutine' cleared the first lane of shipping when Mr West began to notice an increasing number of vessels out to the East, all of which were advancing steadily and they appeared to be closer together. Further out to sea there were more grey shapes but these were approaching from the West. The sudden sound of the sails flapping attracted Mrs Colarossi's attention. She was looking up at the once taught sail fabric which was now luffing loosely, and Mr West called out to her with a note of urgency. "Tell Mr Bilbi the wind has dropped!"

Edward got the message and came up on deck immediately. The wind had indeed reduced considerably. It was also changing direction gradually. The skipper started up 'Moutine's diesel engine, then he clipped his safety line on that linked his harness to the guard wire that ran along the side decks and went forward to drop the jib sail. Once the jib was stowed securely in the pulpit, Edward returned to the cockpit . "Hold your present course Mr West." He got Mrs Colarossi to help him lower the huge mainsail by winding on the winches, while the engine took over as the two of them flaked the sailcloth onto the boom, securing it with short lengths of rope. Edward swiftly descended the steps to the chart table and the navigation instruments. He studied the triangular shapes of the vessels inching across his screen in both Easterly and Westerly directions, making notes on his pad regarding each vessel's size, speed and destination. Each little triangle had a name, along with its colour to indicate the type of vessel. "Are you there Mrs Colarossi?" The lady crew member was out of position but she quickly responded to the skipper's voice. "Yes Mr Bilbi, I'm here!" He made sure that she was aware of the imminent situation, explaining in short precise terms that she must relay every instruction to the helmsman clearly and without delay. "When we reach the safety zone between the two shipping lanes I shall relieve Mr West at the helm. You can let him know that also." Edward could hear Mrs Colarossi calling out to Anthony above the noise of the engine. When Edward had been a guest at Mrs Colarossi's mews house he had not been able to assert himself to any degree, but now as the master of his ship he was naturally assuming the responsibility of skipper in order to maintain a satisfactory level of safety and morale among his small crew of limited capability. He would have had no such reservations in those days of sailing with Jack and Alberto on this very ship.

"Well James, I don't know about you, but shouldn't we be doing something?" Judith was pacing the floor of her upstairs room and James looked up from a book that he was reading. "What exactly can we do Judith, you're not suggesting we set sail across the English Channel are you?" She laughed. "No not really, it's just that we are sitting here while things are happening out there." Judith waved her hand in the direction of the open sea beyond the estuary. Standing at her window she imagined 'Moutine' braving the busy shipping lanes on some quest to reach France. Meanwhile she was waiting at home, unable to put her mind to anything useful. "What things?" James asked. "We don't know what's going on, do we James? We don't even know who is onboard .Moutine', let alone anything else." He understood her frustration and he thought for a moment. It was obvious that Judith needed something to occupy her mind until something more positive happened that would allow them to be of some use to the investigation. "Are your neighbours looking after your dog Judith?" "Yes, Pluto is still with them, he's alright there." James thought it would be a good idea to go round and pick him up. "Why don't you bring Pluto back here, and we can go for long walks along the coastal footpaths?" She considered his suggestion and decided it would be nice to get out for some fresh air and exercise. "Alright James, I'll go and see them now." He smiled and returned to the book he was reading. It was the true story of an Atlantic crossing, in which one bold sailor was taking on the mountainous waves of the great ocean single handed. James was lost in the vivid description of the forces of nature, the almighty strength of the wind, the drama of stormy skies and the sheer courage of one man and his boat challenging the elements. It was through books like these that James had discovered his interest in sailing boats, and the stories of real men and women facing their fears at sea to break free from their land locked chastity.

There was some activity downstairs as Judith returned with her dog. Bounding up the stairs, Pluto launched himself at James who closed his book hurriedly and got to his feet. "He seems to like you James!" Most dogs did like James, but the feeling wasn't usually mutual. "As long as he doesn't try to lick my face I don't mind. Down boy! Sit! Stay!" James had seen dog training programmes on TV and people always shouted out these words of command. Judith could not conceal her amusement at his antics. "You're wasting your time James, he doesn't respond to any of that stuff." She went on to explain that Pluto had been her husband's dog really, and when Jack had passed away Judith didn't want to let him go, so she took care of him. "I'm not a natural dog-person but I must admit that Pluto was good company after I had lost Jack. I do feel that I have neglected Jack's dog over the past year or two, and I have tended to let my neighbours look after him. They love dogs, and it's like a second home to Pluto." James apologised for pressuring her into fetching the dog round. "No, it's fine James, in fact when you mentioned long walks on the coastal path something stirred in me. It would be nice to do that again. Jack and I used to enjoy those walks with Pluto, after months of Jack being away at sea." James attempted to apologise again for suggesting that he might take Jack's place. "Don't be silly James, I don't see it like that at all. No-one could ever take the place of my Jack, he was a lovely man. Foolishly, I did find myself believing that Edward could be such a person, but I realise that Edward is not half the man that Jack was." They sat down to watch Pluto wandering around the room, as if he was remembering his old surroundings. The dog paused to sniff an old walking stick that was leaning against the grandfather clock. "You see that walking stick James?" He guessed the significance of the stick. "Jack would always carry that stick with him when we set off along the path to Durgan…. happy days…." Sensing that Judith was becoming a little melancholy and perhaps slipping into distant memories from her past when she had not been alone in this house, James jumped up to help her get ready. "Where's his collar and lead Judith?" The neighbours had given Judith an unopened can of dog food, which she placed in one of the kitchen cupboards. "They are hanging up in the garage James, just to the left of the door." He found them and managed to put the collar around Pluto's neck, clipping the lead onto the collar without too much fuss. James moved on ahead, pulled enthusiastically by the hound, while Judith locked the door of her bungalow and followed at a more sedate pace.

"Let's rest awhile here James." This was the familiar wooden bench that James recognised immediately. He sat down beside Judith after reading the words on the brass plaque. ' In Memory of the Old Sea Dog, John Badger of Durgan '. Both of them sat in reverent silence, looking out over the wonderful Helford River. Far out to sea there was a solitary oil tanker, barely moving. "If Jack was here now he would be looking through his binoculars to see what this ship was. He had this old tatty duffle coat that had seen better years, and a leather case for his binoculars. Jack even wore his merchant sea captain's hat when he was out walking with me." Judith smiled to herself. James did not interrupt her thoughts or seek to spoil the moment. It seemed to him that Jack Berry and John Badger were two old sea dogs who would never leave this place. Something like half an hour passed and neither of them made a move to get up from the seat. There was no hurry. "Come on James, there's an ice cream waiting for us at Durgan." Hanging onto Pluto's lead, James walked beside her towards the tiny village where apart from an old red telephone box and a small ice cream kiosk there wasn't much else. Such a joy. They saw the cluster of stone built houses and the golden sands of the beach, where a few wooden rowing boats lay peacefully, tethered by lengths of weathered rope. One or two families were setting out their beach towels and their picnic rugs. Flasks of hot tea and plastic cups appeared from basketware hampers and sandwiches were handed out from cool boxes. James and Judith chose their ice creams and strolled along the beach as the tide came in. They talked of the continuing search for Edward, which was now extending out into the English Channel and beyond these shores. Judith was not particularly concerned about whether or not the Police were able to find Edward really, but she was curious to know if there was a link to the yacht 'Moutine' and if there were any unusual circumstances of the investigation that had not yet come to light.

D.I. Cook and his team were making themselves comfortable at Mrs Colarossi's mews residence, which was quite a step up from the drab offices of the Falmouth Police station. The detective made it clear to his officers that they could help themselves to tea and coffee, but under no circumstances must they touch any wines and spirits that might be found within the property. The team was operating without having even obtained a search warrant, so the detective was keen to avoid taking liberties. He was of the opinion that it made sense to gather together all of the printed files and the computers in one place, where a detailed picture could be built up and without the need to seize the equipment, which would then have to be moved to the Police station. In this case, the officers were not seeking to obtain fingerprints as the ownership of the devices and the data was not in any doubt. The process of analysing all this information was very time consuming but as the day wore on, D.I. Cook was able to establish much of the relationship between Colarossi, West and Bilbi. For instance, Mrs Colarossi's business interests extended well beyond the U.K. into Europe, the United States of America and also the Middle East. It was noted that Mr West in his capacity as lawyer, financial consultant and general legal advisor, was closely involved with Mrs Colarossi both on a personal level and on a professional level. Meanwhile, it appeared that Mr West had been closely involved with Mr Bilbi in the past although this involvement was not quite so apparent in recent years. This did not necessarily mean that West and Bilbi had not been collaborating on some illegal activities that were as yet unknown to the Police. Presumably Mr Bilbi had not met Mrs Colarossi before their chance meeting at the Glendurgan gardens and he may not have been aware of the identity of the yacht's other shareholders. Some of the more sensitive information that had been unearthed at the Colarossi residence referred to the lady's business contacts in France, Italy, Switzerland and the Channel Islands. Other documents mentioned hotel apartments in Dubai, Abu Dhabi and Qatar that were owned, or partially owned by Mrs Colarossi, and it was evident that Anthony West's name seemed to crop up all over the place. It wasn't absolutely clear which business arrangements featured Mr West as a legal representative, which ones included him as more of a business partner and others that seemed to suggest he was actually personally involved in a particular transaction. The detective realised that he needed to bring in the experts to investigate such possible infringements as tax evasion and time-share contracts. He could see references to offshore companies with names that bore no resemblance to Colarossi or West, so the task of separating the legitimate business ventures from those that were not exactly above board was better left to the specialists in their own field.

   The yacht 'Moutine' managed to reach the safety zone that was approximately halfway across the English Channel and Edward took up his position at the helm. Mr West was thankful to be relieved of his appointed task. "Well done Anthony, you can have a brew down below now. Send one up here for me with the able sea-woman and keep a close eye on the AIS screen. Remember how I showed you what to look for?" Mr West nodded and went below without any further hesitation. Minutes later, Mrs Colarossi appeared back on deck with mugs of hot tea, which she carried to where Edward was sitting, more easily now that the wind had dropped. The boat was moving steadily through the relatively calm waters. "Here you are, Mr Bilbi. Are we nearly there yet?" He turned to look at her. Mrs Colarossi was asking the question as though she was a small child on a daytrip to the zoo with her parents. "We are halfway between England and France, so we are not nearly there, no." She sat down next to Edward and sipped her tea. "How long Mr Bilbi, do you know?" His expression was one of quiet disbelief. "Of course I know how long this next leg of the passage should take, but I cannot say with any certainty exactly when we shall arrive at our destination." Edward gazed out to sea and pretended to ignore her. Mrs Colarossi chose to ignore him also. The question went unanswered for awhile. Edward directed his attention towards the next array of shipping lanes and drank his tea. It was Mrs Colarossi who broke the uncomfortable silence. "We shall arrive in France before nightfall, is that correct Mr Bilbi?" "No, that is not correct." She waited patiently for him to continue. Presumably there was more detail forthcoming. "It is now seventeen-thirty hours, or five thirty pm to you. We have been sailing for eight and a half hours, and provided we take no more than that to cover the distance, we should be in L'Aber Wrac'h by 0200 hours but no sooner." She observed Edward studying his wrist watch and she expressed her surprise. "You mean two o'clock in the morning…. tomorrow morning?" Edward nodded as he emphasised the consequences of their passage timing. "It will be getting dark around four hours from now, so we shall have at least four and a half hours sailing to do after darkness falls." He noted the lady's worried reaction. "Have you sailed overnight before Mr Bilbi, please tell me you have?" He laughed. "Oh yes, but it was some time ago now I think about it." Mrs Colarossi was not laughing. She was beginning to realise that perhaps instead of allowing the passage to commence at the hour of nine that morning, maybe they should have listened to Mr Bilbi's advice. He had suggested a three am start, which would have been only an hour or so before dawn and they would have begun to cross the Channel at sunrise. More importantly, they could have reached France by eight pm when it was still daylight. Of course Edward was fully aware of these facts. Mrs Colarossi and Mr West had disregarded his suggestion to depart early and the realisation was now emerging slowly. She had actually made the wrong decision by having the yacht craned onto the water when the boatyard opened for business that morning, when she should have arranged to do this the previous evening, ready for an early start. There was a further lengthy silence while Mrs Colarossi considered what lay ahead and Edward thought how wonderful it would be if he could have lit up a cigar, or even a pipe at this moment of smug arrogance. Not wishing to dwell too long upon his higher ground, Edward put her out of her misery. "Don't worry, there will be well lit channels of navigation near to the port, and we can always radio for a pilot to guide us in." At this, Mrs Colarossi relaxed a little and got to her feet. Taking Edward's empty mug from him she went below to inform Mr West of this unexpected development.

While his team sifted through the files in Mrs Colarossi's office the detective left the room to wander around the house. The increasing volume of communications traffic, from both incoming telephone calls and also radio messages was distracting D.I. Cook from his innermost thoughts. He descended the steps to the garage on the ground floor, where he stood admiring the gleaming red Ferrari for a moment. Although the detective was hoping that Mrs Colarossi might return to this property at some point, he accepted that she must surely be aboard the yacht that was heading out into the English Channel for an unspecified destination. What was bothering D.I. Cook more, was that the absence of Mr West at any known locations seemed to indicate that the lawyer was very likely aboard the same vessel, which as a joint shareholder of the yacht and as a close friend of Mrs Colarossi would not be all that unusual. Then there was Edward Bilbi. The Police could not reasonably assume that simply because they had not been able to find any trace of their escaped suspect, that Bilbi might also be onboard that vessel. It was easy to draw that conclusion of course, but the detective saw no evidence of a direct connection that would put their man on that boat, and with those two individuals. D.I. Cook made his way up several flights of stairs to the top floor of the house. He looked out of a window at the seafront vista. From the beaches in the foreground out to Pendennis Castle on the headland, this was quite a view. Thinking about the last point of contact between Mr West and Bilbi, the detective went over the details again in his mind. He recalled how Mr West had denied picking up Bilbi from the public telephone box in Carnon Downs, and the lawyer had claimed not to know the whereabouts of his client. Since Mr West had gone into the Falmouth Hotel there had been no further sightings of either Bilbi, West or indeed Mrs Colarossi. The silver Mercedes Benz that belonged to the lawyer remained in the hotel car par, the red Ferrari was in the garage three floors down below from where D.I. Cook was standing and Bilbi's sports car was still in the secure Police compound. They had found no sign of anyone at Mr West's home address, not even his wife, if he had one and his Falmouth office was found to be empty and locked up.

Seeing the brilliant white sail of a solitary yacht that was crossing the bay gave the detective an idea. He watched the yacht for a few minutes and then went downstairs to the office room. "Find out who owns the moorings on the Helford River and let's see if we can determine the movements of this vessel, 'Moutine' during the past few days." One of his officers obtained the name and number of the moorings operator and this was passed to D.I. Cook, who used Mrs Colarossi's landline to speak to the operator. The man on the phone referred to his records, and confirmed that the moorings officer had collected a fee of fifteen pounds from a vessel named 'Moutine', which was for one night only on a deep water mooring. Interestingly, he also mentioned that the moorings officer had asked a lady who was aboard the vessel where they had arrived from. The lady had revealed that they had motored the short distance downriver from the Gweek Quay boatyard. Now at least, their point of origin was established, even if their destination was as yet unknown. D.I. Cook proceeded to call the boatyard at Gweek, again on the same landline phone, and a conversation ensued that was to provide the information that the detective had been looking for all along. "Good afternoon, this is Detective Inspector Cook of Falmouth Police." The office manager was a lady called Laura and she asked the detective how she could be of any help. "What can you tell me about a vessel named 'Moutine'?" Laura immediately explained that this vessel had just left their boatyard only the day before. "We have been carrying out major restoration work for over a year now and her owners arranged to have the yacht craned onto the water several weeks earlier than scheduled." D.I. Cook then asked her for details of the owners, particularly names and contact numbers. Laura put down the phone for a minute while she retrieved the bulky file that contained a vast amount of paperwork related to the project. "There are three owners listed here Mr Cook; the lady who authorised the bank transfer payment is a Mrs Angelina Colarossi and I notice her telephone number is the one you are calling from now, also there is a Mr Anthony West, and finally a Mr Edward Bilbi." The detective was very grateful for this vital information and he confirmed that this was the telephone number for Mrs Colarossi. "I shall be on my way over to speak to you shortly and if you could provide us with all the documentation that you have on this vessel that would be very helpful, thank you."

D.I. Cook was driving from the Colarossi residence at Gyllyngvase Beach to Gweek, and he was thinking about his own shortcomings as a detective. He was actually rather annoyed with himself. It was one thing to say that in his advancing years he was getting a bit rusty, but throughout this Bilbi case he had consistently allowed fundamental errors to creep into his investigation process. All these years of methodical detective work had formed the basis of his whole routine. There were so many successful cases on his distinguished record, of which he was justifiably very proud. Hundreds of hours of painstaking logical groundwork had served him well and he was a well regarded senior detective within the Devon and Cornwall force. The D.C.I. at Truro was more than happy to let D.I. Cook assume absolute full control of the large area that encompassed Falmouth, Redruth, Helston and the coastline running all the way down to The Lizard and Land's End itself. The detective had managed to reduce the crime rate significantly in all the towns and villages that he was responsible for Policing. This is why any signs of poor judgement were simply not acceptable from his own point of view. At this moment he realised that he was talking to himself out loud, but he often did so when he was alone at the wheel of his car. D.I. Cook had wrongly assumed that the yacht 'Moutine' must have entered the Helford River from out at sea and then picked up a mooring for the night, before setting off again to cross the Channel. He thought fair enough, this was something that vessels of all sizes would do routinely when stopping off part way through a passage, and the famous pirates of times long ago would have taken shelter within the quiet waters of the Helford while they made ready to sail to France. It was this foolish assumption that had prevented the detective from even thinking about making enquiries at the Gweek Quay boatyard. He never once looked to the West at any point during his investigation. What an obvious schoolboy error to make! Usually D.I. Cook would ensure that he kept an open mind and he would never rule out the unexpected. Anyway, there was nothing to be done for now while the vessel was in mid-channel so it was a matter of gathering more detailed information from the boat repairers at the head of the river. He pulled into the yard and parked outside the main office reception. After introducing himself to the counter staff, D.I. Cook asked to speak to all members of the company staff. He was taken round the various buildings that were spread out around the extensive boundaries of the entire quayside. Arriving at the concreted area where several large mobile cranes were parked, the detective questioned one of the crane drivers, specifically regarding the launching of the 'Moutine'. The driver informed D.I. Cook that some of his colleagues had been required to load a cargo onto the yacht before she was to be craned on to the water. These workmen who had supervised the loading of the cargo were duly found and questioned by the detective also. "Hello, I am Detective Inspector Cook of Falmouth Police, can you remember anything unusual about the cargo?" One of the men came forward. "Oh yes, it was unusual alright. It was a funeral box Sir." "Funeral box?" "Well, I mean a coffin of course. It was a nicely polished bit of wood too." The detective wanted to know if there were any labels or markings on the cargo. "I saw a label hanging off it on a string but I was too busy to read it properly." "What did you see?" The man told the detective that he had seen some of the printed information on the label. "I reckon it was Italian or maybe Spanish, didn't understand it, but I noticed the word 'Garda'" Thanking the man for his helpful contribution, D.I. Cook talked with the men for a short time and made notes of what they could remember about the yacht, the three people who were there to collect the vessel and any remnants of conversation at the time.

Chapter Three – Approaching

Edward checked the fuel gauge and noted their compass bearing. They had been following a course of 140° since leaving the Helford River estuary, and it was now 17:30 hours by the ship's clock. 'Moutine' would shortly change to a course of 180° and head South to their destination port. Now it was time for Mr West to be called up on deck. The skipper shouted to his motley crew down below and in due course Mrs Colarossi's head appeared at the companionway. "Yes Mr Bilbi?" Edward explained in short sentences that Mr West's presence was required at the helm. "There is a light breeze picking up Anthony, so I shall hoist the mainsail and we can motor-sail Southwards across the French half of the shipping channels. If you would be so kind as to take the helm while I sort out the mainsail, thank you." Mr West took up his position as Edward moved towards the winches. Pretty soon they would be set on a new course, partly under motor power and partly using the small amount of wind that fluttered the mainsail. They had covered around forty nautical miles so far, which was not quite the halfway distance made good. It was at this point that Edward was able to make a clever decision. He glanced upwards and noticed that the helicopter was still shadowing their progress, so he decided not to change course until the helicopter backed off. Surely, Edward was thinking, if this was indeed a Police helicopter then it must have a limited operative range. Presumably, they would have to return to the English mainland at some point, due to having reached the limit of their fuel capacity. Edward was no expert on helicopters but this line of thought seemed reasonable to him. Sure enough, twenty minutes later he watched the helicopter bank sharply to the North and resume its flight towards the coast of England. Once it was out of sight, Edward gently eased the tiller out to port and brought 'Moutine' closer to the wind, which was holding steady from the South West. He directed Mr West to unfurl the jib sail a little more, while Edward settled into his seat at the helm. For the moment there was no longer any aerial surveillance going on, although Edward would not be surprised if they were picked up by French helicopters as they were approaching the coastline of North West France. He was slightly puzzled as to why this vessel was arousing interest as far as the Police were concerned. Perhaps something was going on ashore that they were unaware of.

With Mrs Colarossi and Mr West both down below in the cabin area, Edward decided to take a look in the cargo hold. Having made sure that the vessel was on a steady course, he lashed the tiller to keep her on the chosen Southerly heading and satisfied that the sails were set nicely, Edward quietly opened up the hatch that led down to the cargo hold. He made one last visual check on a few distant vessels that were some way off and he noted the light wind that prevailed for the moment. Creeping stealthily down a series of wooden steps he approached the cargo. Edward admired the polished walnut coffin, with its gleaming brass fittings. He wasn't entirely happy about having such a thing onboard. Some things are regarded as unlucky by sailors, such as having something green aboard, which is a common superstition. There is a term 'Coffin-Ship' which refers to a vessel that is unseaworthy or unsound, and it would be probable that all who sailed in her would perish at sea. He would be glad to see this cargo unloaded at the destination port. Hanging from a brass handle on the side of the sombre coffin Edward could see a label that was tied on with string. He grasped the label and read the printed details on it. It clearly showed the destination as being 'Desenzano, Lake Garda, Italy', and there was a specific address in Italian. Although extremely curious to know what was inside this mysterious wooden box, Edward did not linger to find out more. He retraced his steps and closed the cargo hatch behind him. Returning to his position at the helm, he unlashed the tiller and he was sitting there steering the yacht when Anthony West came up on deck to speak to Edward, who was behaving as though he had never moved. "Would you like me to take over Edward, if you need a rest?" "Thanks very much. I would like to have a word with Mrs Colarossi actually." The two men swapped places and Edward headed for the cabin below.

Walking slowly back along the coastal path that ran along the cliff tops, James voiced a thought that came into his head. "What if we did make the crossing to France in 'Relax'?" Judith stopped in her tracks and looked at him. "You're not serious, James." It was pretty obvious to her from his expression that he was indeed quite serious in suggesting such a passage. "Well, why not? She's a seaworthy boat and I'm sure that you and I could do it." Judith was flattered that he regarded her as a competent crew member for him to even consider the possibility. "Wouldn't a Channel crossing be dangerous, James?" He thought for a moment before replying. "I haven't personally crossed the English Channel in a small yacht before, but it's something I would love to try. There's always potential danger when undertaking any passage like that, especially when crossing busy shipping lanes without radar or AIS." Judith asked him what AIS was, although she understood the concept of radar. "It's a system that displays the precise movements of vessels in the immediate area on a computer screen. My yacht doesn't have any electrics apart from a bilge pump, and there's not even any means of charging the battery, which would usually be done by a connection to the engine or by using a solar panel." "But what about navigation lights, James?" He admitted that 'Relax' did not have any working navigation lights. "She has got lights fitted, but they are not working as far as I know." Judith was puzzled at this. "You mean to say that if we did attempt to cross the Channel to France, the whole trip would have to be completed in daylight hours?" James nodded. "Is that possible?" He smiled. "Providing we set off at first light of day, and assuming that we did not encounter any unexpected delays along the way, we could actually reach the coast of France before darkness falls, yes Judith." He could see that she was still unsure. "We could leave the Helford River at say 4.30am, and pick up a mooring at a French port by 9.30pm the same day." Judith pointed out that any sort of problem or delay during such a passage would force them to enter an unfamiliar harbour in total darkness, and with no navigation lights of any kind. "How would you deal with that situation, James?" He was quick to respond. "Well, the safest option would be to anchor offshore and wait until daylight the following morning, before entering the harbour." Judith asked him about the danger of submerged rocks closer in to the shore. "We don't have an electronic depth gauge, so that is always a risk of course." "Doesn't that worry you, James?" He nodded once more and smiled with the knowledge that more than likely they would not be attempting this venture. They both continued walking in silence for awhile. James was thinking how exciting the adventure might be to undertake, while Judith was more realistic about the whole thing. They reached the steep downhill path that led to the beach at Helford Passage and passed through the wooden gate, without having come to any decision.

Onboard the yacht 'Moutine', Edward Bilbi was completely unaware that although the Police surveillance helicopter was no longer following their course on the water, there was actually quite a lot going on back ashore in England. Having driven away from the Gweek Quay boatyard, D.I. Cook was now ready to take the upper hand. It was clearly time for the detective to make bold and very positive decisions. He was driving more quickly now and his thoughts were all coming together as he returned to the Falmouth Police Station. D.I. Cook realised while he was talking to the boatyard staff that a strong case was building, and this was centred around the classic yacht somewhere out in the English Channel and the vessel's unknown crew. It was conceivable that one of these crew members might be none other than Edward Bilbi, who was wanted by the Police due to his escape from Police custody while being transferred to Truro Magistrates Court. In addition to this suspicion regarding Bilbi's recent movements, there was a known link between Bilbi and his lawyer, Anthony West, who by sheer coincidence had also gone missing. Then there was Mrs Colarossi, who seemed to be above suspicion. She had been identified as the main shareholder in the ownership of the suspect vessel and this lady also had a connection with the lawyer West which was on record. The detective's team of officers were examining Mrs Colarossi's property at Gyllyngvase Beach and scrutinising every minute detail of both her computer and Mr West's computer, which had so far established many business connections and also personal links between the three suspects, all of whom were currently listed as missing persons. Furthermore, D.I. Cook was particularly interested in the mysterious 'cargo' that had been loaded aboard the yacht 'Moutine', supposedly bound for an address in Italy via some unknown coastal port in Northern France. According to one of the boatyard staff, this cargo appeared to be an ornate wooden coffin. Why would anyone wish to transport a coffin, presumably containing the body of a deceased person, to a destination in the North of Italy by way of a seagoing sailing yacht and presumably an overland trip through France? Indeed, what if the contents of that coffin bore no resemblance to human remains? The detective thought perhaps drugs related items was unlikely, though not impossible, and he also considered the likelihood of the contents being something along the lines of gold bullion, or banknotes, or maybe diamonds or even historical artefacts. D.I. Cook ruled out stolen paintings as they simply would not fit into such a relatively small container. Surely, he thought, if a family member had passed away and was then being taken home to Italy as a place of birth, wouldn't this normally be as air freight? The detective reasoned that a lady of Mrs Colarossi's financial status could easily afford to arrange transport of this cargo by air, so why go to such lengths involving her yacht, unless there was some sort of final wish on the part of the deceased which specified a final journey aboard this vessel. He had knowledge of Mrs Colarossi's late husband and how he had lost his life at sea, so could this be his wife simply honouring the man's last wishes?

D.I. Cook was about to make his decision, and he was fully aware of the fact that a huge amount of responsibility rested upon his judgement in this matter. Should all of his lines of enquiry turn out to be nothing more than ill-informed suppositions, his distinguished career in the Police force and his well earned retirement would all go up in smoke. This was a considerable risk for a man in D.I. Cook's position to take, and he knew it. His primary concern was that once the yacht reached French coastal waters the English Police might have great difficulty in seizing the vessel, along with her cargo and occupants. The detective was most anxious not to allow this one to get away, because this might just be the most successful case of his entire career. What a marvellous crowning glory hinged on this one investigation. That was how D.I. Cook saw things at this stage of the proceedings. He wasted no time as he arrived at the desk in the main reception area. An urgent meeting was swiftly arranged in the operations room and all available officers were soon seated around the table to hear D.I. Cook's plan of action. The detective explained to them in precise detail what was about to happen. He would be speaking to the headquarters in Truro in order to request that a Coastguard vessel be launched immediately from Falmouth Harbour, and a search warrant would be obtained in order to intercept and board the classic yacht 'Moutine' which was known to be negotiating the area of water between the shipping lanes of the English Channel. Further to this, a second warrant would be obtained for the re-arrest of Edward Bilbi, if he was found to be aboard the suspect yacht. D.I. Cook went on to talk about the cargo that 'Moutine' was thought to be carrying, and this cargo had been identified by a reliable source as being a wooden coffin, contents unknown. The vessel would be searched, once intercepted, and the true identity of both occupants and cargo could be ascertained. "This vessel must not be permitted to land at any French port, under any circumstances." From this very operations room, the Police would co-ordinate all stages of the operation involving the Coastguard vessel from Falmouth, also helicopter support from Exeter and possibly RNAS Culdrose, and to some degree the coastal authorities on the French side of the Channel. The detective's team of officers were somewhat short staffed, owing to there being a small team of officers remaining at Mrs Colarossi's property, but they sprang into action following D.I. Cook's clear instructions. The two warrants were promptly arranged with senior detectives at the Truro Police headquarters and D.I. Cook discussed the details of his operation to intercept the suspect vessel with the Chief Inspector over the phone. The order was issued to deploy the Coastguard vessel without any further delay, based upon the most recent co-ordinates obtained from the Police surveillance helicopter that had been following the course of the yacht on the English side of the Channel.

The yacht 'Moutine' was now settled on her new course of due South, with Mr West at the helm. He watched Edward go below and resumed his careful monitoring of shipping movements that were approaching from the West now. Down below, in the comfort of the cabin area Mrs Colarossi looked up from a fashion magazine that she was reading, to see Edward descending the steps from the companionway. "Are you wanting to check the navigation screens Mr Bilbi?" Edward took a seat across the table from her and regarded the lady with some distaste. "Might I remind you dear lady that I am the skipper of this vessel for the duration of this passage. You will find that you are less likely to feel the effects of sea-sickness if you are above deck, rather than down here reading." Mrs Colarossi stared at him blankly. "If you want me to leave this cabin Mr Bilbi, why don't you just say so?" Edward tried a different approach. "Mr West is at the helm and I shall be 'checking the navigation screens', as you so kindly suggested. What would you like to do to make yourself useful?" Mrs Colarossi wasn't accustomed to being addressed in this manner and she took steps to put Edward in his place before she complied with his request. "Might I remind you 'Skipper', that I am the primary shareholder of this vessel for the duration of this passage, and keep in mind that I shall be paying you well for your services." Moving from the table to the navigation area of the cabin, Edward was in no way intimidated by her response. He waited for a moment while she closed her magazine and got to her feet. "I would like you to position yourself at the companionway entrance at the top of the steps, so that I can relay instructions to Mr West, and from your vantage point you can assist Mr West in whatever way he should require." Mrs Colarossi muttered something under her breath in Italian which Edward didn't catch, and she then ascended the steps to the deck above, both grudgingly and obediently at the same time.

Seated around the large table in the operations room at the Falmouth Police station, the group of officers were taking notes as D.I. Cook studied a large screen that was mounted on one wall of the room. Relayed from the Truro H.Q. to this screen there was an impressively detailed chart of the English Channel, that clearly showed Falmouth Harbour in the top left corner of the screen, all the way across to the coastline of North West France on the far right hand side. Using technology that was a mystery to the detective, a further link had been set up to superimpose shipping movements onto this chart, which originated from the Coastguard station based at Falmouth and these were being displayed in real-time. Both a senior operations manager at the Coastguard station and a senior detective in Truro were in direct communication with D.I. Cook in the Falmouth operations room, as the Coastguard manager was explaining what was happening at sea. "Our vessel is already leaving Falmouth Harbour and the Coastguard officers onboard the 'Atlantic Princess' are plotting a course to intercept the yacht 'Moutine'. We shall reach the last known location of the suspect yacht in three hours at a rate of seventeen and a half knots, by which time the yacht will have covered an estimated eighteen nautical miles, which we assume will be on a South Easterly course. This means that within around four hours or less, our vessel is capable of intercepting the yacht, and well before she reaches the French coastline Sir." The detective wanted them to be more specific about the actual course of the yacht 'Moutine'. "What if the yacht is no longer on a South Easterly course, and how can you be certain of her speed through the water?" The Coastguard manager responded with realistic answers. "Even before the 'Atlantic Princess' reaches the midway point of the

Channel they will have the yacht visible on radar, and we have information from the Police surveillance helicopter crew that the vessel we are looking for was maintaining a speed of no more than six knots. We shall be aware of the vessel's change of course and her position will be within a radius of less than twenty nautical miles." Satisfied that 'Moutine' could be found by the Coastguard, and with three or four hours to wait, the team of officers were able to leave the operations room for now. D.I. Cook directed them to previously assigned duties while they waited for further news of the ongoing operation at sea.

When James and Judith returned to 'Polgwyn' there was a voice message on the answer machine from the detective in Falmouth. Picking up the phone, Judith returned the call while James sat down. "What does he want Judith?" "He's asking me to call him for an update on recent progress on the case." James stood up and wandered over to look out of the large window. He surveyed the estuary, noticing a few yachts making their way out to sea and he remained there at the window, listening to Judith's phone conversation. "Oh hello Mr Cook, you wanted to speak to me?" James was watching the crisp white sails of the tiny yachts, set against the deep blue-green of the Helford River, and he was thinking how much he wished that he was out there right now." D.I. Cook outlined the proposed plan that was unfolding. "Hello Mrs Berry, I've just come out of the operations room where we are monitoring the movements of certain vessels in the English Channel. We have reason to believe that the yacht we have picked up with helicopter surveillance is indeed .Moutine' and she is approximately midway between the English coast and the French coast. There is a Coastguard vessel leaving Falmouth Harbour which should be on course to intercept the suspect yacht around four hours from now." Judith asked the detective what the Coastguard were hoping to achieve if they were able to intercept 'Moutine'. "We have a warrant to board and search the vessel, and also we have a warrant to re-arrest Edward Bilbi in the event of him being found aboard 'Moutine'. Two further missing persons are presumed to be aboard the yacht, these being Mrs Colarossi and Mr Bilbi's lawyer, who is Mr West." Judith detected a note of optimism in the detective's voice. "How confident are you Mr Cook that you can apprehend the crew of the yacht?" "Well Mrs Berry, I have the greatest respect for the Coastguard service and I am sure that they will do everything possible to prevent the yacht from reaching the coast of France. We are particularly interested in the cargo that is known to be aboard this vessel and our primary aim is to identify the yacht, also the crew and the cargo, and ultimately to bring them back here to Falmouth Harbour." With that, the telephone conversation was ended and Judith moved to where James was standing near the window. She waited until she had his full attention and then she began to go over the details of her conversation with D.I. Cook. Turning towards the window and the vista beyond, James thought about the Coastguard operation that was in progress, out there in the Channel, and he wondered what the outcome might be. "If it turns out to be Edward who is making for France, he is not likely to stop when challenged by the Coastguard, is he Judith?" She also followed his gaze out to sea and she had to agree that a man like Edward would not be taken so easily. "No, you're right there James, but surely he can't outrun a larger and faster vessel can he?" James replied without looking at her. "Who knows what Edward will do when he's cornered, we've seen him react desperately before in a tight situation." It was quite obvious to Judith that James was restless and she sensed that he needed to do something that might help with the investigation, if he could. "There really isn't much we can do James, all we can do is wait I'm afraid." He swung round abruptly, as though he had just thought of something important. "Judith? Have you still got any charts here?" She smiled knowingly. "Yes James, I have all my husband's charts in a drawer at the table over there, why?" He asked if he could look at them. Pulling out the wide drawer of the polished dark mahogany table, she invited James to have a look. "These are Jack's most prized nautical charts, which he had collected over the years. I think they cover pretty much all the oceans and seaways of the World." James stepped forward and began to carefully sort through the well preserved charts. He found what he was looking for and spread the chart out on the table top. Judith joined him at the table, where they pulled up a chair each. She could see that James was studying a large scale chart of the English Channel that included parts of England, France, Belgium and Holland, as well as the Channel Islands and the Isle of Wight. "I need a piece of paper and a pen or pencil…. oh and a ruler if you have one." Judith opened a smaller drawer to one side of the table at which they were seated and took out several items. "There you go Master Navigator! Where are we bound for this time?" James was not about to be distracted. "The question is not where are we bound, but where are the crew of 'Moutine' bound?" James reached across the table and picked up two pieces of sugar from a small glass bowl that he had noticed. "This brown sugar cube is the Coastguard vessel, which I shall place here, close to Falmouth and this white sugar cube is the yacht 'Moutine', you see?" Judith watched him place the second sugar cube approximately halfway between where the Helford River was, just below Falmouth on the chart, and a broad stretch of the Brittany coastline on the other side of the Channel. James proceeded to scribble notes and figures on his bit of paper, before laying the metal ruler across the Channel as it was represented on the surface of the chart and slowly moving the two sugar cubes. Corresponding to the distance moved by the white sugar cube, which was only a couple of inches from its starting point in the centre of the Channel, the brown sugar cube not only covered the distance from Falmouth Harbour to the midway point but James placed the brown cube directly alongside the white cube. "You see Judith, that is the point at which the Coastguard vessel should intercept the yacht.... roughly speaking of course." She stared at the lumps of sugar sitting on the chart and thought it best to voice an observation before James got too carried away with his theory. "Yes but James, you are assuming that 'Moutine' is on a constant South Easterly course, are you not?" He smiled to himself. "That's true.... well, South South East actually, but you have a point. According to what we know from D.I. Cook the yacht did leave the Helford Estuary on a course of South South East and we can't be sure that she has not altered course, because the Police helicopter was forced to turn back. I am simply showing you how the Coastguard vessel has a greater speed than that of the yacht, which is about three times faster by my reckoning." Judith was impressed by his maths and she understood the logistics of his demonstration. "So what you are saying is that the Coastguard should be able to catch up with the yacht well before she reaches the coast of France?" James nodded confidently. "Oh yes, probably as much as five hours before they can attempt to go ashore." They both regarded the chart and the two cubes of sugar, while considering the implications of such an operation. The detective had mentioned how once alongside the vessel, providing they could approach that closely, the Coastguard officers intended to board the yacht and take any crew members into custody, prior to examining the cargo. "How would they bring the yacht back to England if the crew were arrested, James?" He explained to her that it would be necessary to take the vessel in tow, much like the RNLI would do when rescuing a stricken vessel.

Studying the AIS screen carefully, Edward was aware of increased traffic in the West to East shipping lane. He made some notes on paper and scribbled a few mathematical calculations also. Within around three hours they would be only twelve nautical miles from the French coast, and this distance should be covered within a further two hours. Edward was working out how many more daylight hours remained, when Mrs Colarossi stumbled down the steps into the cabin area. Clumsily and noisily she made her way to the galley, where she prepared some hot coffee for the three of them. Edward thanked her for the coffee and announced the results of his calculations. "We have a couple of hours daylight remaining and then we need to lower all sails. There will be three hours of night time motoring to cover the distance to L'Aber Wrac'h, which is eighteen nautical miles." Mrs Colarossi asked if Edward was staying down below at the navigation table. "As soon as darkness falls and we reduce sail, I shall print out the up to date positions of traffic in the shipping lanes and all three of us can go up on deck to complete the final leg of the passage." Hearing this positive news, Mrs Colarossi trotted off to inform Mr West.

It was around nine-thirty pm, or more correctly in nautical terms, twenty-one thirty hours when Mrs Colarossi spotted a large vessel astern of .Moutine' and she made sure that Mr West was aware of its presence at that moment. Both of them kept a watchful eye on the fast approaching vessel. "Mr Bilbi told me that we are preparing to lower sail shortly before darkness falls, which is about half an hour from now. Should we draw his attention to this ship behind us?" Mr West got to his feet and took a long look at the vessel that was not only getting much closer, but it also appeared to be on a very similar course to their own. "Yes, you can ask him if he wants to come up and do a visual check, by all means." She shouted down from her vantage point at the companionway and Edward appeared shortly. Mr West pointed astern. "This ship is white, but it's a different shape to the others we've seen, what do you reckon?" Edward was slightly alarmed at the sight of this approaching vessel. "On my AIS screen down below it's showing up as 'Unidentified', which is unusual, unless it's a Royal Navy vessel." Picking up his binoculars, Edward took another look. "I do know what that is. This is the Coastguard." He put down the binoculars and issued orders as the skipper. Between the three of them, the sails were quickly lowered and furled, while Edward took over at the helm from Mr West. "We shall increase our speed and we are not going to show any navigation lights until we get nearer to the French coast. What can you tell me about Maritime Law, Mr West?" Hesitating, the lawyer wanted him to be more specific. "What do you mean Edward?" "Well, put it this way, if that is Her Majesty's Coastguard they are not likely to be stopping by for tea. How do we stand legally?" Mr West proceeded to explain that there was a twelve nautical mile limit to the territorial waters of both England and France. "Presently, we are in International waters and the Coastguard are entitled to board this yacht, as they would in English territorial waters." Edward gritted his teeth and pushed the throttle lever forward. "How about French territorial waters Mr West, can they board us there?" The lawyer confirmed what Edward was thinking. "No, they cannot legally do so. They would presumably have to arrange for the French Coastguard to intercept us."

Chapter Four – Morning

The yacht 'Moutine' pushed on ahead, maintaining a speed of six to eight knots, which was close to her maximum hull speed through the water. She was holding her course of due South and Edward had his sights firmly set on reaching the twelve nautical mile limit of French territorial waters, with total darkness being a further advantage. The pursuing Coastguard vessel soon caught up with the fleeing yacht, swept past her stern quarter and then slowed rapidly as it came alongside. Mrs Colarossi, Mr West and Mr Bilbi were able to clearly identify the name on the bow of the Coastguard vessel, 'Atlantic Princess', without the need for binoculars. During the next half hour, which saw both vessels ploughing through the waves on a parallel course, the light was failing by the minute as the sun dipped below the distant horizon, and dark clouds formed a foreboding mantle over the whole surrounding area. Having reduced her speed by half, the 'Atlantic Princess' was matching the yacht's progress precisely and keeping to a distance of two cables, which equates to about four hundred yards or one fifth of a nautical mile. This was a safe working distance between two moving vessels at sea. Edward noticed that there had been no attempt yet by the Coastguard to communicate with 'Moutine' and he was wondering how long it would be before they decided to make contact by one means or another. Mr West voiced what Edward was thinking at that moment. "Why don't they call us on the radio or something?" He was anxious and alarmed by the close proximity of a significantly larger vessel. "Don't worry Mr West, they will make their intentions clear before long, I'm certain of that." Edward was concentrating on holding their course and speed, while Mrs Colarossi was already fearing the worst. "Are they going to force us to stop Mr Bilbi?" Edward explained in short, sharp sentences that the Coastguard would certainly expect them to heave to, in order to allow their officers to board the yacht and presumably to conduct a search as part of their operation. "Do we have a plan, Mr Bilbi?" Edward gave her his usual look of contempt. "Yes, we do have a plan Madam, and it's quite simple really. When this Coastguard vessel orders us to slow down and heave to, as they inevitably will do, we shall do no such thing. My intention is to continue following our course to the agreed destination port. We may have to contend with the French authorities later, but my plan doesn't extend that far at present." Edward knew full well that Mrs Colarossi hated the term 'Madam' and that was why he addressed her in that way when he was annoyed with her attitude. "We shall proceed without navigation lights, although we shall be visible on radar anyway, and once we leave International waters the English Coastguard cannot intercept us as they wish to." Edward suggested that Mr West should go below, where he would be able to keep an eye on the AIS screen and also take a short rest. He asked Mrs Colarossi to remain on deck so that the pair of them could deal with the impending Coastguard action.

Quite suddenly, and without any prior warning, the 'Atlantic Princess' altered her course in a dramatic fashion. The distance between the two vessels reduced to within half the previously allowed margin, and although the parallel course was being maintained it seemed to the crew of 'Moutine that the Coastguard vessel was about to veer across the bow of the yacht. At the same time a loud hailer was activated from the bridge of the larger vessel. It was not a loud hailer of the type that would be handheld by an officer, rather it was an electronic device that was mounted on the roof of the bridge itself. The powerful and commanding voice of the Coastguard Captain resonated clearly across the narrow stretch of water, demanding their attention. "Yacht 'Moutine', Yacht 'Moutine', You are requested to reduce speed, switch off your engines and heave-to immediately. This is Her Majesty's Coastguard. We have a warrant to board your vessel and you are required to comply with this official request." When there was no immediate response from the yacht, the same announcement over the loud hailer was repeated with a sinister robotic monotony. The same announcement was repeated a further three times as there was no reduction in speed by the yacht 'Moutine'. Then a large, powerful searchlight that was mounted on the deck of the Coastguard vessel lit up with a long pencil beam, instantly penetrating the gloom over the water. This intense light was aimed first at the masthead of the yacht, before it was trained upon the area towards the stern of the vessel, illuminating the cockpit and blinding the defiant helmsman along with the lady owner of the yacht. Edward looked away from the source of the light and focused on his task, while Mrs Colarossi also turned away from the blinding white light, holding onto the guardrail to steady herself. Mr West briefly raised his head above the companionway hatch but ducked down again as he realised what was happening. Steep, choppy waves were thrown against the hull of 'Moutine' as the brightly lit Coastguard vessel held this dangerous course for a short while. It was only when Edward pushed the tiller away from himself for a moment that the Coastguard was forced to change course in order to avoid a near collision. Edward would not normally steer a forty foot yacht so aggressively, but such a desperate situation called for drastic measures. The manoeuvre seemed to have the desired effect as far as Edward was concerned, and he was able to look to his left as the Coastguard vessel doused its searchlight. He shouted to Mrs Colarossi, who jumped to attention. "Go below and get Mr West up here, now!" She almost fell down the stairway and swiftly passed on the skipper's command. Once up on deck, Mr West listened while Edward told him what to do. "Hold this course of due South and leave the engine speed as it is….. see the compass heading?" The lawyer nodded positively and took up his position at the helm. Edward dashed down below to the navigation area of the cabin, where he set about calculating the distance to the outer limit of the French territorial waters and also the time it would take them to cover the distance.

As the yacht 'Moutine' was leaving International waters, her navigation lights went out and Edward deliberately switched off the AIS at the same time. He then clambered up on deck, brushing past the bewildered Mrs Colarossi, grabbed a rope halyard that was fixed at the main mast and proceeded to lower the radar reflector dome. This was a white circular structure that was about two feet in diameter, with the name 'Raymarine' painted on it in red lettering. Satisfied with this action, Edward joined Mr West at the helm and beckoned Mrs Colarossi over to them. "We are now in French territorial waters and we are only twelve nautical miles from the coast. The AIS is off, radar transceiver is down and we are not showing any lights." There was no longer any sign of the Coastguard vessel off their port side. "I assumed that they would follow us into French waters, even though they cannot board us. They easily have the range, so I would be surprised if they stand down at this stage." Mr West asked Edward about the French authorities. "They won't waste any time in notifying the French Coastguard, in fact they may have done so already." Edward went on to explain how they would continue to feel their way in and they must only resort to electronic navigation at the last moment. "When we get a visual sighting of the lights onshore, that's when we need to avoid going aground or hitting rocks." Mrs Colarossi wanted to know more about the cloaking techniques that Edward was employing. "What are you hoping to achieve by switching everything off, Mr Bilbi?" He was happy to elaborate this time, because her question was reasonable and intelligent. "Well, you see if the AIS is not transmitting, we will not show up as an identified vessel on the AIS screens of any search vessels in the area. Also, by lowering the radar reflector we can't be picked up by radar systems, and with no navigation lights displayed we can effectively become almost invisible at night." Edward continued with his assessment of their predicament as he could sense that he had their attention. "Mr West is confident that the English Coastguard cannot legally attempt to board this vessel while she is no longer within International waters, or English territorial waters for that matter. There will be a significant delay while they co-ordinate a search operation with their French counterparts, and if we are lucky we might be able to creep into the harbour of L'Aber Wrac'h before they realise precisely which port is our intended destination." Mrs Colarossi wished to know how difficult it would be for them to enter this small harbour in total darkness. Edward admitted that the entrance could be hazardous to negotiate even in daylight, due to large granite rocks at the mouth of the harbour entrance, many of which were submerged. There wasn't much wind to worry about, but they had to be aware of strong tidal streams in certain areas of the navigation. "As I mentioned earlier, once we can see the shore lights of the village and the marina, I shall turn the AIS back on and it will be essential to follow the electronic chart plotter to guide us into the entrance. Most of all, we must have accurate depth sounder readings at all times during the approach to the marina itself. This has to be done slowly and carefully. Providing there are two of you keeping a watch on deck while I steer a safe course under minimal engine speed, we should be alright." Edward issued them both with hand torches and he stressed the importance of only using them when necessary and to keep the beam shining downwards. 'Moutine' began her approach towards the French coast quietly and stealthily, with barely a few ripples to disturb the dark waters.

The Captain aboard the 'Atlantic Princess' had received orders from the Coastguard headquarters over in Falmouth that he must not enter French territorial waters in order to intercept the suspect yacht, as such an action would inevitably compromise the good working relationship between English and French authorities. Consequently, a call was made to the Gendarmerie Maritime in Cross Corsen and all details of the yacht were passed to them, to allow the French Coastguard to pick up the ongoing operation from their side of the Channel. Of course, this was frustrating for the Captain of the 'Atlantic Princess', and copies of the British board and search warrants had to be sent by fax across to the control centre in Cross Corsen. Just as Edward Bilbi had shrewdly surmised, a certain amount of time would pass before a vessel could be launched, and this would have to make its way along the North West coastline to arrive in the approximate area where the yacht was presumed to be located, according to last known sightings by the English Coastguard.

Having driven from the Police station in Falmouth to Mrs Colarossi's mews house at Gyllyngvase Beach, the detective could do nothing more to influence the situation that was taking place just off the coast of France. D.I. Cook made himself known at the gate and his officers upstairs in the building let him in. Standing with his back to the window of the room, he addressed the small group of officers. "We need to find some evidence to show us who exactly is involved here. Specifically, we need to uncover any details regarding this unknown cargo and its intended destination. The answers must be here in this property, somewhere." So far, the team of officers had turned up a huge amount of information from examining several computers and a bundle of files, but there was nothing to help them piece together what D.I. Cook suspected was some sort of planned movement of an unidentified cargo across the English Channel by sailing yacht. He could not at this stage be absolutely certain as to how many people were onboard that particular vessel, or indeed who those people were. The detective was troubled by his own assumptions, which were leading him to think that just because he had three missing persons, whose whereabouts were demanding further investigation, then it followed that these three people must be out there on that yacht. Without more positive sightings, he could not reliably assume anything of the sort. How could these people slip through the Police net so easily? Was this operation being orchestrated by Edward Bilbi, or perhaps he is still on the English mainland? Surely, the very fact that all three suspects have part ownership in the vessel they are tracking is enough to confirm that the detective's assumptions were actually correct? D.I. Cook decided to relieve the three officers of their duties at the Colarossi residence as it was late in the day, and he replaced them with two officers from the Falmouth station who could bring fresh thinking to the existing problem. Meanwhile, he made a call to Mrs Berry at her bungalow and arranged to drive over there early the next morning to discuss things with her and Mr David.

Pouring cups of tea for the three of them, Judith sat down at the table with James and D.I. Cook, placing a plate of chocolate digestive biscuits in the centre of the kitchen table. "Mrs Berry, do you ever remember Mr Bilbi talking about properties that he might have owned or rented in France, or Italy, or Spain possibly?" He helped himself to a couple of biscuits as he waited for her reply. James looked on quietly. Judith thought for a moment. "Edward used to go to France for holidays sometimes, but I don't think he actually owned any of the properties he visited. Having said that Mr Cook, you know how complicated Edward's property dealings were, so there could be some details that he did not confide in me. We did work together for quite a few years as solicitors, and he did talk to me about most things, but I suspect not everything." The detective finished off his biscuits, took a few sips of his tea and set his cup down before he continued. "Late last night we were informed that the Coastguard have stood down the operation to intercept the suspect yacht, because the vessel is now within French territorial waters. Although we have been told that the French Coastguard will attempt to locate and board the yacht 'Moutine', this means that her crew may be successful in reaching a port on the French coast. Should that turn out to be the case, I am not optimistic about bringing the vessel, the crew and the cargo back to England, or not without some difficulty anyway. Once these people go ashore in France they might go off to anywhere in Europe, and we will have little chance of tracking them from there on." James wanted to know if there was anything they could do to help. "Well I was about to ask you for your thoughts on where a man like Mr Bilbi would choose to land his ship, if he reached the other side of the Channel?" James immediately produced his charts from the previous evening. "How do you know that Edward Bilbi is the skipper on this yacht, detective?" Smiling, D.I. Cook admitted that he was guessing. "I don't, is the short answer Mr David, but right now he's top of my list, and I would be very surprised if the man at the helm is not Bilbi." With the chart spread out in front of them, James explained to the detective how he and Judith had plotted the approximate course taken by the yacht, and where this would bring the vessel in relation to the coast of France. He indicated the area where, roughly speaking, the Coastguard from England would have been able to intercept the yacht's course. James saw that Judith was about to make a point, so he spoke up first. "This is assuming that 'Moutine' remained on a course of South, South-East all the way from the Helford River, which as Judith will tell you is not necessarily the case, detective." D.I. Cook listened with interest. "How about if I get you some accurate data from the Coastguard operations room in Falmouth, maybe we could try to determine one or two possible landing points along that particular stretch of coastline?" James agreed that it was a good idea. "Yes, we should be able to narrow it down fairly accurately with some compass bearings and positions of latitude and longitude." Judith showed the detective to the phone and let him make his call. D.I. Cook was put through to the Coastguard by his officer at the station.

Using some figures that the detective had written down during his phone conversation with the Coastguard, James set about plotting a more precise picture on the chart. Judith and D.I. Cook assisted James with suggestions and between them a series of pencil lines was established. The result was encouraging, and the most important fact to come out of the exercise was that the vessel they were tracking had indeed changed course. "You can see that 'Moutine' has taken a course directly to the South, and this alteration in heading seemed to occur shortly after the Police surveillance helicopter stopped tracking the vessel, and at about the same time as the Coastguard vessel was approaching. From these time slots, plus the compass bearing and the positioning co-ordinates, we can estimate how close this vessel is to the coast." Clearly impressed at James's calculations, Judith and D.I. Cook awaited his conclusion with some anticipation. James traced the names along a section of the shore as it appeared on the chart, looking at it from the French side, so that a vessel would be approaching from the North. "There are many small inlets and bays, and this larger inlet just here, passes between a few islands until it reaches this place, it says L'Aber Wrac'h, not sure how you pronounce that." Judith leaned over to see the printed place name on the chart and corrected James on his pronunciation. "Oh I know that place, it is well known around here. There is a yacht race that has been held for many years, in which they race yachts from the Helford River Sailing Club across to L'Aber Wrac'h at the end of June every year. They have a prize-giving and reception at the yacht club on the French side, I think." D.I. Cook was also familiar with the name, for the same reasons. "So that could be where Bilbi is making for?" James thought it was likely, unless the vessel that was being tracked changed course again and headed further to the East or the West of where they were looking. "There's no guarantee that's where they will land, but it does look ideal." The detective asked James if he would make for that harbour, in the event of him finding himself in that location at sea. "Yes, I think I would." That was all D.I. Cook needed to know. He excused himself hurriedly and drove off to Falmouth at speed.

They were moving ahead through the darkness, passing between small uninhabited islands and clusters of jagged rocks. Edward peered forward as he gently pushed the tiller to one side or the other, listening to the melodic throb of the diesel engine below decks. He could see Mr West leaning over the starboard side, and Mrs Colarossi was doing likewise on the port side, both of them positioned amidships. Their hand torches were switched off and nobody spoke. After following their present course for the next half hour, Edward decided that it was time to consult the chart plotter and the depth sounder. He asked Mr West to go below, giving him clear instructions as to which instruments should be switched on, while explaining to him the importance of the information that would be required very shortly. This was something that Edward and Mr West had discussed previously, when demonstrating the use of the navigation instruments at the chart table. Mr West took a seat at the array of instruments and switched on those devices as instructed. Next to the panel there was a written sheet of paper with details of the yacht's draught, also her length at the waterline and her beam. The amount of draught corresponded to the readings on the depth sounder, in terms of how much water they had under them at any given time during the harbour approach. Mr West settled into his appointed task and concentrated on the obstacles as they appeared on the screen before him.

With all sails lowered, Edward as the helmsman had a clear view ahead of the bow. He suggested that Mrs Colarossi should switch on her hand torch. "Hold it close to the side of the hull and below the level of the side deck. Shine the beam downwards, like this." Edward showed her how it must be done by using his own hand torch in the required manner. Satisfied that she had got the general idea, he shone his beam forward once more to identify oncoming markers. He had already established from looking at the printed charts earlier that there was an important set of coloured marks which would guide their vessel into the entrance of this small harbour. This would take the form of a red marker buoy which they must keep to the port side, along with a green marker post to be kept to the starboard side and a further white marker post that indicated a large expanse of rock that lay ahead of them as they must steer sharply to port, passing directly between the red and the green marks. Mr West stuck his head out of the companionway at one point and shouted to Edward that he should steer more to starboard in order to avoid approaching rock formations. At the same moment, Mrs Colarossi voiced her concern regarding the close proximity of some underlying rocks that had appeared in her torch beam. In this way Edward was able to avoid these obstacles and steer a safe course. Progress was slow and painstakingly methodical. The power of the engine was just sufficient to overcome the strength of the tidal current, while at the same time maintaining reduced speed through the water. Edward asked Mrs Colarossi to take a look over the starboard side as they drew nearer to the main obstruction. He picked out the red marker buoy in the beam of his torch first of all, then he swung the torch beam across to where he expected to find the second marker. He could see a stone post that was painted green, which allowed him to steer a course that was midway between the two marks. Once 'Moutine' was heading through the gate that was formed by the red and green markers, Edward moved his torch beam all the way across to the right of the green painted marker post and managed to identify the white painted stone post at the other extreme of the rocky outcrop.

Over on the English side of the Channel, the detective had resumed his position in the operations room and he was talking to the Coastguard officers on the phone. D.I. Cook informed their headquarters that a reliable source of his had suggested L'Aber Wrac'h as being the most likely destination port for the suspect vessel. This new information was received by the English Coastguard with some interest, and they duly passed this directive to the Gendarmerie Maritime officers in Cross Corsen on the French side. Their vessel had already passed through the Chenal du Four and rounded Le Four lighthouse to the North of the channel, heading due East along the coast. This would be about ten nautical miles to reach the small harbour of L'Aber Wrac'h, so all the detective and his team could do was to wait for further developments.

'Moutine' negotiated the final approach to the inner harbour and she motored slowly towards the pontoon jetties. Edward was expecting many boats to be already tied alongside these pontoons, and there would be few vacant spaces if any. It was not too difficult to pick out the white hulls of the berthed yachts but finding a space that would accommodate a forty foot vessel was more of a challenge. Mr West was summoned up on deck and three pairs of eyes peered through the darkness as they drew close to the lines of yachts. Mrs Colarossi pointed out a space, but Edward regarded this one as too restricted for the likes of 'Moutine'. They spoke in hushed voices as the engine was reduced to a tickover. Mr West spotted a large space, which he indicated to Edward with a tap on his shoulder. "Over there, next to the catamaran." Edward saw it too. With some considerable skill and precise control, he steered their vessel inside a wooden post on the port side, while a yellow hulled catamaran lay off the starboard beam. Both Mrs Colarossi and Mr West went forward with mooring lines in their hands, following their skipper's timely instructions. Edward ensured that the boat remained close to the jetty on the port side, allowing Mrs Colarossi to step off gingerly, and seeing that she was hesitating with the end of the mooring line Mr West also stepped off to secure the rope around a large cleat on the pontoon. Between the three of them, 'Moutine' was soon attached at the bow and the stern. Edward set up half a dozen fenders and cleated off the last remaining line amidships. "Alright then, I suggest we go below for hot drinks and a bite to eat."

Seated around the table in the cabin, they discussed what must be done, over a meal that was neither supper nor breakfast. Mrs Colarossi was quick to assume control once more at this point in the proceedings. She wasted no time in calling a pre-arranged courier service and she spoke at some length in Italian, holding her expensive mobile phone in one hand while making notes on a pad with the other. The two men waited patiently. Putting down her phone, Mrs Colarossi was ready to issue directions to her motley crew. "There will be a van here within the hour and the cargo can be offloaded without delay." Edward was wondering how this would be accomplished in semi-darkness and with no crane available. He chose not to mention his concerns, and in any case he was more interested in his own role while all this was going on. "Let me get this right, you are taking the cargo ashore and having it transported across France by road?" "Yes Mr Bilbi, that is correct. You do not need to concern yourself about the transportation of the cargo, as this will be in our hands from here." Mrs Colarossi left it to Mr West to explain further. "Mrs Colarossi and myself shall accompany the cargo on the next leg of its journey and all you need to do Edward is to make sure this vessel is here upon our return. You will be advised of our arrival at this harbour, probably one week from today, and we intend to make the crossing to England on the same day." Edward thought for a moment. "Surely you don't expect me to sit here and face the French authorities, how is that going to work?" Mr West leaned forward across the table and made eye contact with Edward. "That is not going to work is it Edward? You do not sit here and wait to be picked up. They would obviously arrest you and seize the yacht. What you do with yourself and this vessel is entirely up to you, and as long as you are here to complete our return trip you will receive payment for your services as we agreed. Do I make myself clear Edward?" It was indeed absolutely clear, but this arrangement would force Edward to evade the French authorities for a period of one week at sea, while waiting for Colarossi and West to hop back onboard for their Channel crossing to home port. This was a raw deal for Edward and he was far from happy about it. "You do realise Mr West, that I shall find myself out at sea single handed with this vessel that requires a crew of three and you expect me to somehow avoid being intercepted by the French Coastguard?" Both of them stared at Edward for a few minutes before Mrs Colarossi spoke again. "Come now Mr Bilbi, a man of your experience should have no trouble in concealing your movements, I mean you practically wrote the book when it comes to that sort of thing." Edward was not impressed by the woman's ridiculous trivialisation of his forthcoming situation. "We are not talking about just myself, or even a motor vehicle on land, this is a forty foot yacht that demands a considerable amount of space in which to manoeuvre….. 'Moutine' cannot simply disappear, for goodness sake." Neither of them seemed to be at all sympathetic towards Edward, which made him feel somewhat annoyed, given that he had brought them across to France without encountering any problems or delays. Mr West continued, having disregarded Edward's impending predicament. "We have your mobile number so we can give you a day or two advance notice of our return, and if necessary we can always rendezvous at a different port of your choice." Edward forced a smile. "Thanks very much, that makes me feel a whole lot better."

Chapter Five – Diverging

One hour before dawn, in the half light of early morning and shrouded in a clinging damp mist, two men in black clothing got out of a white van. The van was parked on the foreshore. Both men were tall, and heavily built too. They paused to check the vessels on each pontoon and then strode decisively along their chosen jetty. One of the men was carrying something bulky. Colarossi and West deployed a set of folding steps that led down to the jetty from the widest part of the yacht. They remained onboard, observing the two dark figures as they approached the aluminium steps. From the deck, Mrs Colarossi addressed the men, once again in Italian. Following a short exchange of words in hushed foreign voices, Edward watched the men come aboard from his position in the cockpit. Mr West asked Edward to open the large locker which for the purposes of this trip was effectively a cargo hold. Lifting up the heavy wooden lid of the locker, Edward stepped back to allow the men in black to gain access to the cargo. He had no intention of assisting them with their task. It became clear that these men knew exactly what they were doing. No time was wasted in lowering two lengths of strong webbing straps into the hold and then one of the men got into the space around the coffin. The straps were looped under the wooden casket and brought back up on the other side, so that the other could bring all four ends of the webbing to a single point. Without consulting Edward, the man reached for a spare halyard on the mizzen mast towards the stern of the boat, tied this onto the hook eyes of the straps and proceeded to run the halyard around a nearby winch. The coffin rose slowly from the hold. One man winched steadily, while the other guided the suspended cargo. Edward was quite impressed by the way they had set up a line that ran through a block pulley on the boom. Using this arrangement, they were able to swing the boom over the side and lower the coffin gently onto the wooden floorboards of the pontoon jetty. With the straps draped over the lid, the two men carried the coffin away to the waiting van. It all looked so effortless. Edward remembered quite a different scenario back in Cornwall, when this mysterious cargo had been moved downstairs from the top floor of Mrs Colarossi's house. Gathering up their personal belongings from the cabins below deck, Mr West and Mrs Colarossi bid farewell to Edward and walked off down the jetty. There was no waving goodbye, merely a parting comment from Anthony West. "Remember Mr Bilbi, look after your ship and have her back here when we return. Don't go taking any unnecessary risks." Sitting down at the helm, Edward was glad to see the back of them. He made up his mind to go below for a good breakfast and perhaps then to consider his limited options.

D.I. Cook was at his desk in Falmouth and having rushed in from Judith's bungalow he had immediately called his friend Maurice through Interpol. With a mug of hot coffee at arm's length, the detective settled into a lengthy conversation with the Frenchman. "We have a strong suspicion that this yacht we are tracking may be heading for a small harbour called L'Aber Wrac'h. My concern is that the French Coastguard will not reach the area before the suspect vessel is able to put its crew ashore, along with this unknown cargo I fear." Maurice listened with interest and surveyed a large map on the wall of his office. "Well Monsieur Cook, I do have some officers in Brest, which I can see is only twenty kilometres from L'Aber Wrac'h." Maurice assured D.I. Cook that he could have his team of men at the harbour within not much more than half an hour. Also, he offered to pass the information to the Coastguard headquarters at Cross Corsen. The detective thanked Maurice for his help and put down the phone. He was thinking that Brest was only twelve and a half miles from the harbour where the yacht 'Moutine' might be docking within the hour if his gut feeling could be relied upon. Perhaps a policy of cautious observation, rather than confrontational interception, would provide a more favourable result. D.I. Cook thought about the possibility of the cargo being taken ashore at this location. He was aware of its intended destination being somewhere in either Italy or Spain. The Police could not be certain how many people were aboard the yacht, but it was unlikely that all onboard would depart with the cargo as this would leave the vessel unattended and defenceless. Nobody was going to plan an operation of this nature and then allow the authorities to simply seize the vessel and arrest any remaining crew. It was understood that the team of officers sent by Maurice to the harbour would merely observe the yacht and any persons leaving the vessel, taking photographs from a discreet distance and not attempting to apprehend anyone at this stage.

Spread out on the cabin table, there was an assortment of breakfast delights that Edward had gathered from the various cupboards and the large fridge. He soon organised a meal that would set him up for the day. Generous portions of bacon and eggs, followed by several slices of toast with lashings of butter, a bowl of cereal with fresh milk and rounded off nicely with orange juice and coffee. Lounging on the soft berth cushions of the cabin, Edward decided that he might as well enjoy this to the full while it lasted. Here he was, alone onboard a very comfortable yacht and there was no-one to stop him from making the most of the situation for now at least. He didn't have a plan. There did not seem to be much hope of avoiding the French authorities and sooner or later they were bound to find him. Finishing his coffee, Edward wasn't really all that optimistic about his chances of returning to England and receiving payment for this crazy trip. He was by now having serious regrets about the whole thing. This foolhardy passage was inevitably going to end in tears. It would be so easy to start up the engine and cast off from this jetty, but then what? Where would he go? The very idea of crossing the English Channel single-handed with this forty foot vessel was sheer madness. Only a madman would attempt such a thing. He would be forced to stay within French territorial waters, unable to go ashore, drifting aimlessly and counting time. Edward wondered if all this was worth the money. He fixed himself a second coffee and poured some brandy into this one. Wandering over to the chart table, he switched on all the electronic navigation devices and sat down to think. To the East of where 'Moutine' was berthed there was an inland waterways system that Edward was reluctant to enter, mainly because there would not be sufficient deep water under her hull for any appreciable distance. This forced him to look outside the harbour entrance, which then raised the question of how to proceed from there. Should he turn to the South West and round the North West tip of the Brittany coastline, only to sail into the Bay of Biscay where adverse weather conditions frequently descended upon unfortunate mariners? Perhaps he should head North East and stop off at some small island where he might go into hiding? For a brief moment, Edward even considered the notion of leaving the yacht here and taking his chances on land, but such a choice would guarantee the seizure of the vessel and also he would have to abandon all hope of ever getting paid for his troubles.

Two unmarked French Police cars pulled up quietly, a short distance away from the jetties at the harbour and several officers in plain clothing got out. They advanced as far as the dunes that surrounded the gentle slope that led down to the main approach road. From their vantage point the officers had a good view of the boats on the pontoon jetties. Using powerful binoculars, the name 'Moutine' was positively identified on the bow of a two-masted vessel and a second officer attached a long lens to a sophisticated camera. All these officers were armed, but they had been ordered not to open fire unless directly threatened themselves. They didn't have to wait long, before they witnessed an object being transferred from the boat to the jetty by a group of dark figures. A long, narrow wooden box was winched ashore, slung beneath the boom at the stern of the vessel. Two of the group appeared to be well built men dressed entirely in black, while a third male was short and well dressed and they were accompanied by a female who was clothed in red and white. The woman was wearing dark sunglasses and she had an expensive looking leather bag over one shoulder. Talking to their superior over headsets, the officers described how the group were taking the box over to a waiting white van at the roadside. Maurice immediately issued the order to follow this vehicle at a safe distance with one of the unmarked cars, while the remaining car was to prepare for a direct assault on the berthed vessel. As the van slowly drove off towards the exit road, Maurice received the information that his officers were in position and ready to move at a moment's notice. One car set off in covert pursuit of the fleeing white van and three armed officers climbed out of the other car and closed in on the unsuspecting yacht, ready to set foot on the aluminium folding steps that were still in place amidships. With hardly a sound from their soft soled shoes, all three officers were inside the cabin before Edward was even aware of what was happening. One minute he was sipping his coffee and smelling the brandy, when suddenly he was faced with three men pointing weapons at him and shouting something in French that he failed to understand. They came from nowhere and there was no warning. Edward knocked over his mug of hot coffee as he instinctively raised both hands above his head.

Unable to exchange much in the way of conversation, as most of what Edward was saying was lost in translation, the French officers handcuffed him and led him away from the yacht to their waiting car. They made him sit there for half an hour while two of them searched the boat for any suspicious documents, or indeed any items that were of interest. Edward listened to the driver of the unmarked Police car talking on the radio. He was informing his superior that one male suspect was now in custody, and according to this man's British passport which was handed over during the boarding of the yacht, his name was Edward D. Bilbi. This was excellent news for Maurice, and it was confirmed that there was only one member of the crew onboard. Wasting no time in getting on the phone to D.I. Cook in Falmouth, the French detective was in high spirits following the success of his operation. "Monsieur Cook, I have some good news for you." He explained how Mr Bilbi was removed from the vessel while it was still tied up at the jetty and the suspect was being taken to the nearest Police station in Brest. "We shall carry out a more detailed search now that we have seized the vessel. Do you wish to speak to Monsieur Bilbi later?" D.I. Cook welcomed this positive development and he was keen to maximise the advantage. "Well done Maurice my friend, now we have something to go on. Yes, I shall need to speak to Mr Bilbi as soon as possible. How do you propose to deal with the four suspects in the van?" Maurice replied that he would prefer to track the movements of the white van in order to determine its intended destination, should that turn out to be somewhere in France, or ultimately into a neighbouring European country. Meanwhile, the Englishman in custody would be subject to intensive questioning before they would decide how to arrange his return to the English authorities at some point. "Now I must leave for the gendarmerie in Brest, and I can contact you from there." Thanking Maurice for his efficient handling of the matter, D.I. Cook ended the call.

The detective was going to be busy at Falmouth Police station, firstly organising the communications link with the French Police in Brest, and then arranging to bring Bilbi back to Cornwall, while continuing to monitor the pursuit of the suspect vehicle that was being tracked by Maurice's officers in France. D.I. Cook wanted to discuss everything with Mrs Berry and Mr David, but he wasn't going to have time to drive over to Helford Passage, so he called them on the phone instead. "Oh hello Mrs Berry, we have made some considerable progress with the case involving Bilby and I would like to bring you in on current developments. Would you both have time to come over to the station for a meeting?" Judith quickly checked with James and they agreed to drive out to Falmouth right away.

The meeting was informal, and it was held in D.I. Cook's office for just the three of them. James and Judith were offered a seat facing the detective's desk. "Make yourselves comfortable and there will be some tea and biscuits brought up shortly. Now then, you may be surprised at what I have to tell you." They both looked at one another, unaware of what was about to be revealed. James jokingly interrupted the dramatic build up that D.I. Cook was aiming for. "Edward and his crew have collided with a super tanker and their yacht has sunk?" Pausing to extract a notepad from a drawer in his desk, the detective was not amused. He was not to be distracted from what he regarded as a significant result in terms of co-ordinated detective work on both sides of the Channel. "We have detained a male suspect for questioning, and he is believed to be Edward Bilbi. I am hoping to speak to our friend Mr Bilbi directly, once my French counterpart has arrived in Brest." Judith brushed aside James's flippant comment, preferring instead to show some interest. "Impressive Police work Mr Cook, you must be pleased?" The detective was writing something down while it was still fresh in his mind. He allowed her question to hang in the air for a moment. "Well, yes, although this is only part of the ongoing investigation. We still have to apprehend our other two suspects in this matter and we don't yet know where they intend to dispose of the cargo, which remains unidentified." He was satisfied that he had their full attention so he continued with his summary of the situation. "The officers in Brittany were able to seize the vessel and swiftly arrest the only remaining crew member onboard, who is now being held by the gendarmerie in Brest. Other officers who are part of the same task force are following a suspect vehicle as we speak. This vehicle has been photographed from a concealed location and it is believed to contain the wooden box which we think is a coffin, along with a driver and three passengers. The detective on the French side who is supervising the next stage of the operation is hoping to be able to determine the intended destination and also the precise contents of this so far undisclosed cargo." Judith asked the detective about the identity of the passengers in the vehicle. "Shortly we shall be receiving copies of the photographs taken by the task force officers, so we can be more certain of their identity. We already know that one of the suspects is female, one is a male described as being short and well dressed, while the other two males were clothed in black." The refreshments arrived and D.I. Cook was called away to the desk downstairs, leaving James and Judith to ponder over the news. "Don't be so trivial towards Mr Cook, I mean after all this is probably his last big case before he retires from the force. We should treat this investigation seriously, as I am sure he is doing." James was suitably reprimanded. Returning to his desk, the detective strode into the room and sat down. He was clutching some papers in a manila folder. Opening the folder, he spread out a number of photographs and several official-looking documents. "There we have it Mrs Berry…. that's Bilbi alright." James leaned forward to examine the photographs in front of Judith. "Here you can see Mrs Colarossi and Mr West, there's no mistaking them, would you agree?" The images were absolutely clear and there was no doubt. D.I. Cook explained to them that he would be interviewing Bilbi by means of a video link and he asked Judith if she thought it would be worth her speaking to Edward. "Why would I want to speak to the scoundrel?" The detective had expected Judith to be less than enthusiastic about the very idea of talking to Bilbi directly, but he did have his reasons. "Well Mrs Berry, I do of course understand how you might feel towards Mr Bilbi, due to his past behaviour, however I would like to try this approach for two reasons really. Firstly, he will not be expecting you to make contact with him, so we have the element of surprise and secondly, I believe he might open up to you in a way that he wouldn't to a Police officer." D.I. Cook was thinking back to when he last had the opportunity to interview Bilbi, although on that occasion he did have his lawyer Mr West in attendance. Bilbi would be on his own this time. Judith considered the prospect of confronting Edward, albeit via a video link rather than face to face, and she decided to give it a go. "Alright Mr Cook, I shall speak to Edward for you, but don't think for one minute that it will do any good." The detective thanked her and he offered words of encouragement to make her task less of an ordeal. Judith accepted his proposed course of action and followed him to the operations room, with James close behind them.

Maurice, the French detective, pulled into the car park outside the gendarmerie in Brest and made his way up to the offices on the top floor of the building. There he spoke to the officers who had arrested Edward Bilbi and they prepared a room for the scheduled video link to the Police station in Falmouth across the Channel. Once everything was in place, Maurice asked for the suspect to be brought up to the room and they were ready to commence the conference link. "Have a seat Monsieur Bilbi and we can begin." Edward did as he was told, sitting down quietly and without any visible expression. Barely had he assumed his position at the table when he became aware of a familiar face on the screen in the centre of the large table. "Judith?" He was caught off guard, much as D.I. Cook had anticipated. The detective motioned to Mrs Berry that she should engage with Bilbi as soon as she was sufficiently composed. Judith regarded the haggard face of Edward Bilbi once more and proceeded to direct a pertinent question at him. "What exactly do you think you are doing Edward?" He was almost lost for words. He fumbled with his useless hands and mumbled something which didn't carry well across the fragile audio link. "What did you say Edward? Speak up man, for goodness' sake!" Edward repeated his garbled response. "Sorry Judith, I didn't realise that you were in France." He was confused and he believed Judith to be somewhere in the building where he found himself now. "I'm not in France you dimwit, I am in Cornwall." Pausing to allow Edward to grasp the orientation of the conference call, she continued forcefully. "I asked you what you've been up to. Have you stolen a yacht Edward?" Remaining somewhat dazed and confused, Edward tried to pull himself together. It was clearly a struggle for him. Maurice and the members of his team in Brest were watching Bilbi's antics as he fought to communicate meaningfully. "No, I haven't stolen anyone's yacht Judith, let me explain." He went on to describe in some detail, how he had been cajoled into skippering the vessel by Mrs Colarossi along with the lawyer Mr West, and how they were moving a cargo from England to some unknown destination in Europe. Judith wanted to know where they were taking this mysterious cargo. " I have no idea Judith, and that's the truth. They wouldn't tell me anything about the movement of the cargo and I don't even know what is inside the casket." D.I. Cook saw that Mrs Berry was not fooled by Bilbi's weak denial. "You're lying to me Edward…. You have that stupid look on your face. When you say 'casket', do you mean it's a coffin?" Edward nodded but he was told to answer the question vocally by the French officers at his side. Judith repeated her enquiry regarding the precise destination of the cargo, assertively and while maintaining eye contact with Edward, who was visibly shaken. "Alright, I did see a label on the coffin which said it is intended for Desenzano, Lake Garda in Northern Italy, but I don't have any idea what is inside, honestly I don't." By now, Edward could sense that the whole operation was going down the drain rapidly, and he was losing all hope of ever seeing the money that he had imagined he would receive at some point. It seemed to him that the only way he was going to return to England would be aboard a Coastguard vessel or perhaps a Police helicopter if he was lucky. D.I. Cook indicated to Mrs Berry that she should ask Bilbi to clarify what purpose the yacht was required to serve, following the delivery of the cargo to this location in Italy. "What are you supposed to be doing with 'Moutine' once the movement of the cargo has been completed, Edward?" He explained to Judith that he was expected to avoid being intercepted by the authorities, then to somehow bring the vessel back to a port on the French coast where Colarossi and West could rejoin her and consequently return to England. "Quite frankly, I didn't fancy my chances of achieving that part of their crazy plan, but there you go." Judith was instructed to close the video link and thereby end the conference call. "Thank you Edward, perhaps we can talk again when you return to Falmouth.... Goodbye." The link was also terminated on the French side. Edward was taken down to a cell where he would spend the night and Maurice duly received information that the suspect white van was by now heading due East across France, and passing to the South of the city of Paris. This confirmed that the vehicle was indeed making for Switzerland and almost certainly Northern Italy, rather than Spain, as was first thought.

 Immediately after the video link was closed, Maurice picked up the phone to speak to D.I. Cook as he wanted to agree upon a proposed course of action. Now that Edward Bilbi was in custody the French detective wished to pursue the suspect vehicle that was making its way across Northern France, more aggressively, with a view to intercepting it and bringing the vehicle to a halt. Maurice felt that by allowing the people in the van to reach their destination there was always the risk that the Police would lose their opportunity to detain both the suspects and the cargo. Time was also an issue, and not to mention the involvement of the Italian Police, when the pursuit would have to be handed over to them at the border with Switzerland or France. "Do you feel confident to pull them in at this stage, Maurice?" D.I. Cook was concerned about this sudden change of strategy. "We have one car with no markings following the van mon ami, and we can easily bring in some backup if it is needed. I don't want to lose them by waiting for them to reach Italy, if you understand me?" The detective in Falmouth thought for a moment and he decided this was not a good idea. "No Maurice, I can't let you stop the van. My superiors at Police H.Q. in Truro have given me clear orders, and my instructions are to establish where this unidentified cargo is being taken to precisely. I am sorry my friend, but we have to allow the suspects to continue with their journey so that we can determine its final destination." Not surprisingly, the Frenchman wasn't entirely happy about the decision, although he did appreciate why it was important for the English authorities to find out exactly where the suspects in the van were transporting this mysterious cargo. D.I. Cook asked Maurice to ensure that his officers must follow the white van as far as the Swiss border, or alternatively the Italian border and once the crossing point was known to them, the surveillance would be handed over to the relevant authorities on the ground.

Sitting in the back of the van, Mrs Colarossi glanced at her expensive wrist watch, while attempting to find a more comfortable seating position, but not with any degree of success. Mr West was close to nodding off, when there was a tapping sound from the small window ahead of them. One of the two men in the cab was holding his fingers against the glass to form a 'T' sign, indicating they were about to stop for a tea break. The van slowed to a crawl as it pulled into an Aire de Service. One of the courier drivers got out and opened the sliding door on the opposite side to the rear passengers. Mr West was slow to get up so Mrs Colarossi stepped out of the van and onto firm ground. She suggested that Mr West and herself should leave the vehicle in order to purchase hot drinks and whatever the drivers wanted, and that the two men should remain with the vehicle and its cargo. They were in agreement that croissants and coffee would go down well, so Mr West followed briskly in Mrs Colarossi's footsteps.

The group of four stood close by the van in the car park, enjoying hot buttered croissants and some strong French coffee, while taking the opportunity to stretch their legs and get some fresh air. Some distance away, over on the far side of the car park, the plain clothes officers in their unmarked car were discreetly surveying the movements of the four suspects as they were taking their break. Up to now the three men and the woman in the van had not been aware of the Police vehicle that was tracking them across Northern France. Having covered the three hundred and fifty miles from L'Aber Wrac'h to an area just South of Paris, which had taken them around six hours, the courier drivers were explaining to Mrs Colarossi that the second leg of their trip would involve about nine hours of driving in order to reach Lake Garda in Northern Italy. "This means we have to stop for a few hours sleep near to Geneva, at Chamonix. We can get to Chamonix in five hours from now and then a further four hours to reach Desenzano del Garda." The two drivers were changing places in the cab as the first driver had already done his six hours of driving. Now the second driver would take over for the next five hours, and after sleeping at Chamonix the first driver would complete the last four hours on the road.

Edward was making a nuisance of himself at the Gendarmerie in Brest, which he would have done anyway but the whole day in confinement was driving him crazy with boredom and frustration. He banged on the metal door of his cell until it was eventually opened by a disinterested officer who had first peered in through a small sliding window. Stepping away from the opening door, Edward voiced his dissatisfaction in no uncertain terms. "I want a cell with a proper toilet, not this stinking bucket!" Without speaking, the officer pushed Edward to one side and picked up the bucket. Turning to leave the cell with the offending item in hand, the officer was confronted by a very angry Edward who was attempting to bar his way out. The office immediately produced a menacing looking riot stick from a clip on the back of his leather belt. Seeing the officer's determined stance, Edward stood to one side and asked a further question, but this time using a lower tone of voice. "When am I leaving for England?" The noisy commotion from within Edward's cell aroused the attention of a superior officer who approached the open doorway. "What is all this disturbance?" His subordinate officer informed him of the prisoner's complaints before

Edward himself could speak. Looking his prisoner up and down, the senior officer ordered Edward to sit down. Once the other officer had left the cell and closed the door behind him, the older man stood over Edward to listen. "You are not happy here, Monsieur Bilbi?" "This cell is like something out of the middle ages. Have you people not heard of Human Rights? Why have I not been allowed to speak to a lawyer? When do I leave this stinking pig-sty? I want some food, I want clean clothes, I want to know why you haven't charged me with anything yet, and I want to see your commanding officer!" "Monsieur, I am the commanding officer of this Gendarmerie, and I would ask you to show me some respect. You will calm down and maybe I can make things a little better for you." Edward remained seated and stopped ranting. The officer tapped on the door with a metal cup that he had picked up from a shelf and walked out. Some fifteen minutes later he returned. "Come with me Monsieur Bilbi, there is someone who wishes to speak with you." Edward followed the officer out of the cell and along the dim corridor to a larger room. Maurice the detective had not yet left the building, so he agreed to deal with Bilbi's complaints without prolonging the unfortunate situation. "Please, sit down Monsieur Bilbi." Taking the chair opposite the detective, Edward rested both hands on the table and stared blankly at the wall to his right. "Would you like a cup of tea Monsieur Bilbi?" Edward nodded and said nothing for the moment. The detective uttered something in French to the officer who was standing at the doorway and proceeded to light a strong cigarette. Edward casually noticed the name on the packet of cigarettes, 'Gauloises Caporal', as the fat detective took his time in exhaling the first few puffs of acrid smoke towards Edward across the table. Involuntarily, Edward found himself smiling at the detective's manner. It was like something he remembered seeing in an old French film, with subtitles in English, and probably in black and white. "Do you find this amusing Monsieur Bilbi, may I ask?" Edward continued to smile as he replied. "Not really, but in the film the detective offers the prisoner a cigarette, that's all." At this point the French detective was reaffirming his belief that all Englishmen are usually mad. "What film, Monsieur Bilbi?" The smile on Edward's face never faltered. "I don't recall the title, it was a long time ago you see. I'm sure it was Gauloises though, I do remember that." Pushing the cigarette packet to the centre of the table, the detective leaned back in his chair, his cigarette balanced precariously at the edge of his bottom lip, saying nothing. Just like in the film. Edward did not reach out for the cigarettes and he too leaned back in his chair, almost arrogantly. Neither of the men spoke for several minutes. The detective puffed away at his cigarette, while Edward smiled stupidly and without reason. Entering the room, an officer placed a cup of tea in front of the grinning Edward and a cup of coffee for his superior. Sipping his tea, Edward regarded the fat detective and decided to make the interview as difficult as possible from the start. "Monsieur Bilbi, what can you tell me about the cargo that was unloaded from your boat this morning?" A lengthy silence ensued before Edward chose to answer. The detective stubbed out his cigarette in a metal ashtray and leaned forward, waiting with anticipation. "What would you like to know about it?" "Of course, Monsieur Bilbi, you can tell me what is in the box and where it is going to, in your own time….. we have all day." Edward took this as an invitation to settle into another long pause. Minutes passed. Finishing his cup of tea, he pushed the empty cup towards the centre of the table and assumed his idiotic smile once more. "The box is a coffin, so what do you think is inside?" The detective reminded Edward that it was he who was asking the questions, and he repeated the second part of his earlier question for Edward's benefit. "Where is the coffin going to?" More silence. "The man and the woman who got into the van, who are they, Monsieur Bilbi?" "I have no idea. Why don't you ask them?" The French detective was beginning to lose patience with the smug Englishman before him. It would be so much easier to hand him over to the British Police and let them try to extract sensible answers from this man. There was a requirement for the Gendarmerie in Brest to produce a report, which would accompany the man in their custody when he was returned to the British authorities. If it wasn't for this irritating need for standard procedure, the detective would have preferred to confine Bilbi to his cell for a few more days and then simply let him go. During the course of the interview, an officer had brought a piece of paper into the room, which the detective had examined and then slipped into the pocket of his jacket. "You are not my problem, Monsieur Bilbi, and I have other things to do with my time. Your friends in the van will be arrested in due course and no doubt they will be questioned also. There is nothing that we can charge you with at this time, as you have not committed an offence in this country. However, you are wanted by the British Police for several offences and in particular, for escaping custody." Edward looked up at him and feebly enquired about his vessel that was still berthed in L'Aber Wrac'h, as far as he was aware. "What happens to my yacht, we have to get her back to England?" The detective paused only briefly, as he walked towards the door. "As I told you Monsieur, you are not my problem, and neither is your sailing boat of any interest to me. If you have anything that you do wish to tell me, you can say it now, but if not you will be leaving for England early tomorrow morning." Edward made no attempt to respond, so the detective instructed his officers to return their guest to his cell.

Chapter Six – Driving

D.I. Cook was rather pleased to have Bilbi in custody, on the French side at least, and he would feel much more confident about reaching a conclusion to this case if he could apprehend the two suspects Colarossi and West who were somewhere halfway between Paris and the borders with Italy and Switzerland. The English Coastguard vessel was to delay her departure from the harbour until early the next morning, to allow the transfer of Edward Bilbi from Brest to L'Aber Wrac'h. The detective would not get too confident just yet, as Bilbi had not been brought back to England and the real problem was how far to let the white van go, before intercepting the vehicle and seizing the cargo. Once the four people in the van reached Desenzano, which seemed to be the intended destination according to reliable information, the matter would be in the hands of the Italian Polizia. If at all possible, the British Police urgently needed to determine the contents of that cargo before it was delivered to whoever might be waiting for it in Italy. This prompted D.I. Cook to retire to his office, where he could think more clearly. Using his large whiteboard and a selection of maps he made detailed notes to stimulate his thinking process. This whole operation depended upon the organised strategy that would now span across several European countries, involving three different Police forces and also two maritime agencies. The detective in Falmouth would of course be making his own decisions, but to a greater extent the actual arrangements on the ground required the close communication of many different organisations, all of which had their own methods and procedures.

Seated in the back of the van, Mrs Colarossi was studying the screen of her iPad, which was displaying a detailed Google Maps image. She pointed out to Mr West who was at her side, the A40 route that would take them just South of Geneva and then to Chamonix. The small town of Chamonix was inside France and it was the last stop before crossing the border into Italy. To the East of Chamonix was Switzerland, with North Western Italy lying to the South-East. "You can see that from Chamonix to Desenzano is five hundred and fifty kilometres, so three hundred and forty miles, which should take us around five and a half hours if we can maintain an average speed of fifty to sixty miles per hour." Satisfied that her maths was reasonably accurate, Mrs Colarossi went on to explain how the final stage of the journey would evolve. "We don't really want to stop for more than about three hours in Chamonix and we can change drivers one hour after leaving there, does that sound feasible to you Anthony?" Mr West saw no reason why not. "Where are we staying in Chamonix?" She confirmed that a small hotel had been booked for them in the town. "We have instructions to call a phone number in Milan, from the hotel in Chamonix as we are leaving, and someone will rendezvous with us when we arrive in Desenzano. They will arrange to receive the cargo and we shall expect to exchange this for the agreed terms of our transaction." Mr West was the only person, other than Mrs Colarossi herself, who was fully aware of the details of that transaction, and he was the only other person who knew what was contained in the coffin. The pair of them had decided right from the very beginning that the fewer people who knew of the cargo's destination and more importantly, its contents, the better would be their chances of success in all of this.

Most of the road between Geneva and Chamonix was a fast dual carriageway, winding through steep sided mountainous valleys. It was densely forested on either side of the road, with a spectacular view of snow capped mountains in the distance, rising to stark jagged peaks that were so typical of the French Alps. The two courier drivers were able to enjoy the scenery that was unfolding before them and this was an easy job for them to carry out. Meanwhile, inside the closed interior of the cargo area at the rear of the van, there was nothing interesting to see. Mrs Colarossi and Mr West passed the time talking and taking short naps, sometimes reading or dipping into a bag of chocolate bars. Further on, the dual carriageway changed to a narrow road with only two lanes, with brightly painted red and white striped bollards along the centre so that any overtaking was prevented. Now the road became a flyover that was perched high on the top of concrete posts. Bulky heavy goods vehicles sped past on the other side of the bollards, heading West, passing by alarmingly close to the vehicles on the Eastbound carriageway. Some of the company names on the sides of the trailers were in Italian, many were in French and others were English or

German. There were lots of estate cars with ski racks on the roof and a steady stream of tourist coaches that had two decks of blacked out windows and bold colour schemes. Both of the courier drivers talked in Italian as the white van made its way to the Chamonix valley. As they approached the town itself, it was late afternoon and by early evening the sun was going down behind them, casting a soft orange glow over the snow on the mountains. The driver at the wheel followed his satnav device to the location of the Hôtel Morgane, which was in the centre of the town. Chamonix was an attractive historic town at the foot of Mont Blanc, with traditional chalet style houses that clustered around charming tree lined squares and many of them had wooden balconies covered in baskets of colourful flowers. Pulling into the car park that belonged to the hotel and slowly reversing into an empty parking space, the van came to a stop. Leaping out of the cab on his side the backup driver slid open the rear side door to allow their weary passengers to step out. Mrs Colarossi took the hand of the driver as she came out into the colder air and she blinked at the bright lights of the hotel, that were set against the intense blue of the sky and the golden white snow beneath. The beauty of it all took her breath away for a moment. Mr West was close behind her, and he too marvelled at the sight. "This was well worth the long drive, I must say." Mrs Colarossi dashed his hopes of a lengthened stay. "We won't be here for more than a few hours Anthony, so take it in while you can."

   Having tracked the suspect van well into South Eastern France, the officers were able to report to Maurice that the vehicle was still in sight and it was now joining the main access road into Chamonix. They could see the white van up ahead, and there were three vehicles between them on the single carriageway of the elevated section of the road. At this point of the pursuit, the French detective was authorised by his superiors to liaise with the Gendarmerie in Geneva, who would ensure that the Italian Polizia were ready to pick up the route that the van was taking from their side of the border. There was only one crossing point available to them, which was the Mont Blanc Tunnel, and this links Chamonix in France to Courmayeur in Italy. The tunnel is just over seven miles in length and this is where the A40 becomes the N205. Maintaining a discreet distance behind the van, the officers later photographed the occupants of the white van getting out of the vehicle which had stopped at the Hôtel Morgane, where it remained parked for several hours. Waiting across the square, the officers were in position to follow the suspect vehicle to the entrance of the tunnel when it made a move. Under no circumstances were they to pursue the van into the tunnel. Their orders were very clear on this.

Inside the hotel lobby, Mrs Colarossi was having a stern exchange of words with the two drivers, in Italian naturally, stressing that they must not linger for too long at the bar. She then accompanied Mr West to the restaurant for some light refreshment before they would all retire to a couple of rooms for a short sleep. Sitting at their table, Mrs Colarossi was explaining how one of the drivers had voiced a problem, specifically with the tunnel road. "It seems that one of our drivers had an extremely distressing experience involving the Mont Blanc Tunnel, where there was a serious fire in 1999. Tragically, many people lost their lives when a truck caused a fire that got out of control and an investigation that followed the fire found that certain organisations who should have implemented the safety of the tunnel were partly to blame for the high number of casualties." Mr West was concerned at hearing this. "Does this mean that the driver won't continue with the trip?" Mrs Colarossi explained that the man would prefer to remain in Chamonix, and he would like to rejoin them when they cross back into France. "Apparently he intends to drink heavily tonight, so he won't be much use to us anyway. We have booked these rooms for one night only and I have suggested that the driver finds alternative accommodation until we return from Italy." She went on to reassure Mr West that she wasn't worried about this slight change to their plans, and she understood how the driver's troubled memories of that stretch of road would affect him if he were to continue.

Edward Bilbi was to be driven from the Gendarmerie in Brest to the harbour at L'Aber Wrac'h in a Police van, where it was decided that the Englishman should not be allowed onboard the yacht, but instead he was to be taken aboard the 'Atlantic Princess' so that the English Coastguard could oversee his return to the authorities in Falmouth. In the short term this would require Bilbi to be confined to his cell for one more night. He was sitting on the bunk which was hard and uncomfortable, thinking about the overall plan that was falling apart. Colarossi and West were unaware of Edward's arrest by the French Police and consequently there would be no possibility of them rejoining the yacht 'Moutine' when they returned from delivering the cargo to somewhere in Northern Italy. Edward no longer had his mobile phone, which had been confiscated by his captors, so they were not going to be able to contact him in order to determine the location of the waiting yacht. The way things were going, by the time Colarossi and West came back to the coast of Britanny, not only would 'Moutine' be long gone, but she would very likely be in Falmouth Harbour he was guessing. As far as he could see at that moment, Edward presumed that he would find himself back in custody on English soil, with the prospect of facing further questioning and certainly additional charges to his growing list of offences.

"Bonjour Monsieur Bilbi" The French detective was smiling broadly that morning as he greeted Edward. He was standing in the open doorway of the cell, waiting for a response from Edward who was only just beginning to waken from a troubled night's sleep. There was not much of a response from the crumpled heap on the bunk. "What time is it?" Maurice glanced at his wristwatch and announced that it was 7.00am, widening his smile as he did so. "Are we going somewhere with a decent bed, this one is impossible to sleep on?" Without replying to Edward's question, Maurice tossed a pair of shoes onto the floor. "Get yourself ready Monsieur Bilbi, you are going home!" Edward sat on the bunk and took his time putting his shoes on. He then made the detective wait while he washed his hands and face, cleaned his teeth and whistled monotonously. After some time had passed, Edward was ready to be led out of the cell. "What do I get for breakfast?" He was told bluntly that there was no time for breakfast, as there was a tide to catch. "Perhaps the Coastguard will feed you Monsieur Bilbi, if you ask nicely." Edward dismissed the Frenchman's sarcasm and brushed past him abruptly, almost knocking him over as he made for the next doorway. Two officers appeared and grabbed hold of Edward by his arms. "Put him in the van, I don't wish to see anymore of him. Au revoir Monsieur Bilbi and bon voyage!" Edward allowed himself to be hauled out of the building and shouted a mock thank you for the benefit of the detective. "Merci beaucoup Inspector Clouseau and I hope we never meet again!" The disgruntled Englishman was bundled unceremoniously into the waiting van, where he grumbled loudly about the lack of French hospitality. He was still complaining about his poor treatment several miles down the road. It was some consolation that at least he was going back to England, where even the Police usually treated you as a civilised human being, even if you happened to be a petty criminal.

It had been arranged in advance for a small motor launch to be tied up alongside the jetty in the harbour at L'Aber Wrac'h, manned by several crew from the Coastguard vessel that lay at anchor out towards the harbour entrance. Approaching the jetty slowly, the dark blue Police van came to a halt and the officers escorted Bilbi to the waiting launch. He was calmly handed over to the Coastguard crew and they stepped aboard the motor launch. Within twenty minutes or so, Edward was climbing a short ladder at the stern of the 'Atlantic Princess' before he was shown to a secure cabin on the upper deck. It soon became apparent to Edward that conditions aboard this vessel would be somewhat better than he had experienced while in custody on the French mainland. He looked around the cabin and noticed a more comfortable bunk, coffee making facilities and a small porthole window that gave him a view outside. It seemed more like the passenger cabin on a cross channel ferry compared to the harshness of the Police cell in Brest and already Edward was feeling much better within himself. Through the porthole, Edward saw the Libenter West cardinal buoy off the port side as the vessel made her way out into the open sea, leaving the Grande Chenal behind. During the uneventful passage across the English Channel which would take approximately six hours, Edward was not questioned formally and apart from having a couple of simple meals brought into his cabin, he was left pretty much to his own devices. There was a small shower compartment with a toilet cubicle and Edward almost forgot he was effectively in Police custody. He decided that he must make the most of a good thing while it lasted.

One of the courier drivers left his room quietly as the mobile phone alarm went off, and he managed not to disturb the other driver who was sleeping deeply, after the effects of his heavy drinking session at the hotel bar. A pre-arranged wake up call was sent to Mrs Colarossi's phone, leading to Mr West and herself appearing in the corridor outside the two rooms. Without a word the three of them crept stealthily down the stairway and into the reception area. Depositing their respective room keys in a box provided on the counter, they signed out. Out in the cold night air they were glad of their layers of warm clothing, pulling on leather gloves as they got into the parked van. Mr West stared at the coffin in front of him, not yet fully awake himself. Mrs Colarossi tapped on the window of the cab to alert the driver and they were on their way once more. A recent light fall of snow covered the roads which were very quiet in the early hours of the morning. Apart from an articulated chemical tanker with a Belgian registration plate, that was crawling along in front of them and one or two parked cars across the square, there was nothing on the roads at this hour. Watching from one of those parked cars were the two officers sent by Maurice as part of the ongoing surveillance operation that was about to be handed over to the Italian authorities on the other side of the Mont Blanc tunnel. The driver of the white van wasn't able to see the unmarked French Police car move out of the shadows, with its lights switched off. Concentrating on the approach road to the entrance of the tunnel, he was taking note of the various warning signs and lights, while allowing sufficient space between their van and the tanker. The queue of two vehicles stopped at the hut where passports were to be checked and short conversations in Italian, Belgian and French took place. Waiting in turn behind the tanker, the courier driver listened to the big diesel engine of the truck ticking over, as he sorted out his papers for the border checks. Some distance behind them and partly concealed by a large signboard, the dark Peugeot stood in silence, and observed the van that was leaving France. One of the French officers was speaking quietly over his radio to a base station in nearby Geneva to give them up to date information of the van's movements. He saw the lumbering chemical tanker heading for the tunnel and the target van assuming its position at the checkpoint. Finding no issues with the paperwork, the border control operative permitted the van to proceed.

Ahead of them, the heavy goods vehicles and coaches would be directed to the right hand lane, while cars, vans, motorhomes and caravans would follow the lane to the left. This was for the purpose of ensuring that all HGV's passed through heat detectors, and then to pay the toll charge before entering the tunnel. Keeping his attention on the tanker in front, the courier driver noticed the double white lines that divided the two lanes, also the white tube lights up on the edges of the roof and the orange rectangular lights spaced along the side walls. He was careful to maintain a distance of one hundred and fifty metres between himself and the vehicle in front, as stipulated in the regulations, and he was observing the minimum speed of fifty kilometres per hour with a maximum speed of seventy kilometres per hour. The regulations were extensive and included the use of dipped headlamps, also listening to the radio for announcements, no overtaking, no U-turns or reversing. Since the tragic circumstances of 1999 the safety regulations for the Tunnel du Mont Blanc were arguably among the most stringent in the world, and these rules were strictly enforced by imposing heavy on the spot fines for non-compliance. It was only a matter of twelve to fifteen minutes for the van to reach the exit of the tunnel on the Italian side of the border, but the driver was relieved to see the stars of the night sky once more, after the vaguely mesmerising and hypnotic monotony of those white lights that raced towards your screen at a constant rate. The driver's friend, who was back there in Chamonix, had once told him the story of his fateful experience involving the fire of 1999, but he had only ever mentioned the events of that terrible day once and he never brought it up again. Clearly, the tragedy had affected the man for life, and it was never talked about after that one account.

Inside the rear compartment of the van, Mrs Colarossi and Mr West saw nothing of the tunnel interior and for them there was no drama. The boredom of the long drive was no different before or after the tunnel was negotiated. Raising her head momentarily from her iPad, Mrs Colarossi reeled off some figures for Mr West's benefit. "We have crossed the border and it is now two hundred kilometres to Milan. A further one hundred kilometres will bring us to Desenzano, and three hundred kilometres is one hundred and eighty-six miles in pounds, shillings and pence!" Mr West appreciated her Imperial conversion with a roll of his weary eyes. "How long will that take us, or were you about to tell me anyway?" She smiled and trotted out the figures without hesitating. "I would say around two and a half hours to Milan, where we stop to make our phone call, and then one and a half hours to Lake Garda." Mrs Colarossi went back to playfully tapping the screen of her iPad, while Mr West wished there was a window that he could look out of. How nice it would be to see the passing scenery, even at night. He had considered asking if he could sit in the front with the two courier drivers, as there were three seats in the cab, and there was only one driver now in any case, but somehow it would have sounded childish and he didn't think it seemed fair to expect Mrs Colarossi to sit alone in the back with only a coffin for company. The woman's fascination with numbers was sometimes slightly irritating. He picked up a book that he was half way through reading and he had barely managed three pages before he dropped off to sleep. If it wasn't for the seat belt that he was strapped into, he would have fallen over. The van rumbled onwards towards Milan as dawn approached almost unseen.

Travelling West, between Aosta and Courmayeur on the twisting alpine road the pale blue Alfa Romeo had been sent from the Polizia di Stato headquarters in the city of Milan and there were no Police markings on the car. On arriving at Courmayeur the Italian officers turned around to park in a layby, facing back towards the East. These officers were in position well before the suspect white van was due to pass them. Sitting back to wait for their target vehicle, their instructions were to follow a white Mercedes van with the registration plate as notified, and observe the vehicle's movements. They had been told that the van might turn South in the direction of Turin, or more likely it would take the road to Milan. According to reliable intelligence material obtained from the authorities in Geneva, this vehicle's intended destination was specified as Desenzano del Garda to the east of Milan. Their orders were to maintain contact with the suspect van as far as the small town of Desenzano on the southern shore of Lake Garda.

Driving at a steady eighty kilometres per hour, which was fifty miles per hour the lone courier driver steered his van through a series of long sweeping bends and he was feeling relaxed and confident. He too was following instructions, which amounted to a brief stop in Milan and there he would be given specific directions to an address in Desenzano to complete the delivery of the cargo. He saw the Alfa Romeo parked off to the right hand side of the road near to Courmayeur but he didn't pay much attention to it. The car waited until the van was several hundred metres ahead, before pulling out into the inside lane of the main carriageway. During the next couple of hours there were only small sidelights showing on the pursuing car and as sunrise approached these lights were extinguished. Most of the road from Courmayeur to Aosta was downhill and there were many bends, some of which were very tight. Intimidating metal barriers ran along the outer edges of each carriageway, with a considerable drop should any vehicle manage to crash through the barrier. Aosta is famous for its Roman ruins and the SS26 road that runs alongside the E25 autoroute to Ivrea was used in the film 'The Italian Job' and this is even more winding and treacherous. Colarossi and West were being driven down the E25 road by their courier driver and the speed of the white Mercedes van gradually crept up to ninety, and even one hundred kilometres per hour as the smooth black tarmac surface carried them on the downhill slalom. The driver noted the speed limit signs showing one hundred and ten kilometres per hour as each warning sign flashed past. Apart from the odd heavy goods vehicle toiling laboriously up the autoroute in the opposite direction, there was only a pale blue car behind him, which did not seem to be gaining on them at all. Slowing to eighty kilometres per hour once more, the driver decided not to push too hard. He did not have a set time to arrive in Milan and as yet there was no deadline to arrive at the cargo's final destination.

Following the speeding van, the officer driving the Alfa Romeo became aware that the suspect vehicle was slowing down on the approach to Ivrea. He too reduced his speed to keep pace with the target. Talking on the radio, the second officer was being advised of the strategy that would be deployed as the pursuit progressed. Only the one unmarked car was to maintain close surveillance of the suspect vehicle as it passed through or around the city of Milan, and as the operation entered the second stage there would be several more Polizia backup units joining them within the immediate vicinity of Desenzano. Until all units were certain of the location for the delivery of the van's cargo there was to be no intercept manoeuvre. It was most important for them to preserve the element of surprise right up to the last minute. The E25 autoroute bypassed Ivrea heading to the south of the city before turning left to join the A4 that would take them eastwards to Milan.

From time to time, Edward looked out of his porthole window and he saw only distant shipping set against the open sea. He could not yet see any land on the horizon that would suggest the imminent arrival upon the shores of his homeland. Then he thought about what he was coming home to. All he had to look forward to was yet another cell. This time they would take him to court, and undoubtedly a prison sentence would follow. None of his offences had been serious enough to warrant a lengthy stay in prison, but even a few years would be unbearable for Edward. He knew full well that

74

the detective who had tracked him down relentlessly was going to make this arrest count this time. Perhaps getting involved with the crazy Italian woman and sailing off to France had been one of Edward's biggest mistakes. How was he to know that his friend and business associate, Anthony West was mixed up with the Colarossi woman? All this time while West was representing him as his legal aid, the man was plotting some sort of mad scheme to ship a casket to Europe, and Edward still had no knowledge of what was in that coffin. How could he have been so stupid and so naïve to believe that he could sail a yacht across the Channel and somehow return to England as a rich man? This was a vessel of which he already had part ownership. Why on earth had he not simply waited until Colarossi and West had driven off from L'Aber Wrac'h, and then he could have abandoned the whole idea and sailed the yacht 'Moutine' back to Cornwall? Edward was running all these thoughts through his head and beating himself up about the entire fiasco that had unfolded without him realising what might happen if it all went badly wrong. For a moment he imagined himself living aboard 'Moutine' while hidden away in some secret creek, of which there were many along that stretch of the Cornwall coast, tied up at some unvisited jetty and enjoying the total freedom that might have afforded the likes of a notorious pirate of old. That was how Edward saw himself really. He wanted to be a kind of modern day buccaneer, outwitting the establishment and living a comfortable life of secluded anonymity, as a recluse.

Drifting off into a deep sleep, Edward was living the dream. The magical calm waters of some quiet cove were gently lapping against the hull of his yacht…. HIS yacht, and he lay on his bunk among clean white sheets, and there was no hurry to go anywhere or do anything. Somewhere outside his bubble of warmth he could hear seagulls calling. The sun was shining in through a hatch that was half open and there was the distinct smell of sea air, wafted into his cabin on the light breeze. It was early morning, shortly after dawn. Edward felt warm and peaceful. He was as close to heaven as a living man could be. What a lucky man you are, Edward Bilbi…. Captain Bilbi…. What a lucky man….

Chapter Seven - Revealing

Having joined the A4 autoroute to Milan, the white van was making good progress and there was more traffic on the roads by now. Mrs Colarossi and Mr West had been taking frequent naps, which were usually interrupted when the van passed over a pothole or some other bump in the road. Soon this uncomfortable journey would end when they reached Lake Garda. The return trip promised to be somewhat different. Mr West wished to know what would happen in Milan. "How do we make contact with the people in Desenzano?" Mrs Colarossi raised her head slowly. "We have to call this mobile number when we get to Milan and I shall deal with them in Italian. They will give us the details of the address. Don't worry, it is all arranged." She seemed to be confident that there would not be any problems. "I know what I'm doing. Leave it to me, Anthony." No more was said until the city drew closer. A tap on the cab window from the courier driver was the signal for them to be ready. Coming to a halt, the van's engine was at last turned off. Sliding back the side door, the grinning driver greeted the pair of them. "Buongiorno!" Seat belts were removed and Mr West waited while Mrs Colarossi stepped out before him. Blinking in the bright sunlight of the morning, and taking in their surroundings, they saw that it was a large hypermarket car park. 'Auchan Cesano' was prominently displayed in massive red plastic lettering on the front of the modern building. Mr West had seen Auchan stores on the outskirts of French cities, and he remembered one in particular had been near to Dunkirk. Giving the driver strict instructions to remain with his vehicle, in view of the contents of the cargo, Mrs Colarossi asked Mr West to accompany her to the ristoranti where they could have breakfast and also make the all important phone call. The driver would have to be patient until they returned to the van, and only then could he have breakfast himself.

Seated at a small table, Mrs Colarossi placed her mobile phone to one side and got on with her first priority, which was food. They proceeded to enjoy a leisurely breakfast, which was cheap and quite filling really. Moving on to espresso coffee and biscottate, which are hard bread cookies, Mr West watched her make the call. Reading the number from a notepad and sipping coffee as she did so, Mrs

Colarossi spoke slowly and quietly to a man whose name was not given. The conversation was conducted entirely in Italian and she noted down a few street names in a particular area of Desenzano, several precise times during the afternoon and also two new mobile numbers to call when they arrived in the designated locations. Ending the call, she finished her coffee and explained to Mr West what they must do. It would be necessary to drive their van into a warehouse building just outside the town of Desenzano, where Mrs Colarossi had been instructed to call the first mobile number and they must wait for a similar white Mercedes van to enter the building, so that the cargo could be transferred to the second van. "You and I are to travel with the cargo in the replacement vehicle, which will be driven by our courier driver, to a property in Sirmione where I have to call this second number. We are to wait there for a yellow DHL Express Italia van to arrive. All these times that I have written down are very precise, and I was told that we must not be early or late, we must be exactly on time at each of these locations." Mr West was intrigued. "What happens when the DHL van turns up?" Closing her notebook and putting away her silver pen, Mrs Colarossi chose her words carefully. "The contents of the casket will be transferred to the vehicle that is making the collection and we shall be exchanging our cargo for a passenger." Mr West wanted to know more of this exchange. "As I understand it, the cargo is a large quantity of cash, is it not?" She smiled at the lawyer. "Not cash." He looked puzzled. "You told me it was a large amount of money?" "It is, but not in banknotes. We are carrying gold bars." He asked why these people wanted the money in gold. "If I tell you that we shall be meeting Mafia Veneta, does that answer your question?" Now he was more worried. "Mafia?" Once more the lady smiled. "Yes, Cosa Nostra." Mrs Colarossi was almost whispering, although there was no-one close to them and there was a lot of noise in the ristoranti. "You say we are taking a passenger in exchange for this cargo? Who is this passenger, may I ask?" She declined to answer his question and arose to leave. He followed her outside and back to the parked van. They stood beside the vehicle, as the driver walked off to get his breakfast. "You will be introduced to our passenger at the appropriate time. It is not necessary for you to know of him in advance." She was using a colder, more menacing tone of voice which Mr West had not been aware of previously. He realised that he didn't really understand her fully, and it was this realisation that unnerved him considerably. "Don't look so worried Anthony darling, all will be revealed in due course, I promise you."

Sitting in their pale blue Alfa Romeo that morning, the two officers were keeping a watchful eye on the target vehicle which was at the far end of a line of parked cars. Rather than enter the parking areas that were intended for vans, motorhomes and caravans, or the area reserved for heavy goods vehicles, the white Mercedes van was in amongst hundreds of vehicles that were mostly cars. Presumably they had done this for a reason, possibly to make it easier to get a clear unobstructed view all around them. Two of the occupants had got out of the van and walked over to the ristoranti area of the hypermarket store. From their discreet vantage point the officers were able to see that the van driver was still at the wheel. This was the situation for the next hour, during which time the officers were in close contact with other units around Milan by radio. Seeing the return of the two occupants who had left the vehicle earlier, they observed the driver getting out and he also crossed to the ristoranti. After a further half hour the driver was seen to be walking back to his vehicle, carrying packages of food and a paper cup of hot coffee. All this time, the officers were using a long range lens to photograph the movements of the suspects in view. It was some time later before the van showed signs of moving away from it's parking bay.

Following the van through the very busy exit zone of the car parks, the Alfa Romeo had difficulty in avoiding vehicles of all types that were queuing to take on fuel, or looking for somewhere to park and others were checking tyres or seeking the car wash. Threading their way through this traffic, were the vehicles that joined the exit road and drove up to get back onto the autoroute. Somehow the pursuit vehicle was able to remain close enough to keep the van in sight, maintaining a safe distance of half a dozen or so cars in between the two related vehicles. By this time it had become a sort of relationship, the white van and the blue car locked into their common destination with a common purpose. Most important at this stage of course, was that the suspects were completely unaware of their pursuers. These officers were highly trained in surveillance and pursuit operations and they had years of experience in such work of this nature. From the Auchan hypermarket near Milan the A4 autoroute continued through Monza, Bergamo and Brescia, making it's way to Desenzano and Verona to the east. Passing by Monza, the famous motor racing circuit could be seen from the road and further on there was Brescia where there was a small airport and other travel interchanges feeding the lakes. It was not long before they were passing road signs that indicated the close proximity of the town of Desenzano del Garda.

At the wheel of the Mercedes van, the driver was referring to the directions given to him by Mrs Colarossi before they had left the hypermarket. Once they came off the A4 it would be a matter of negotiating narrow ancient roads that would inevitably lead through the old traditional style buildings that lined both sides of the roadway with only narrow cobbled pavements. It was the driver's job to find the address of the warehouse in the town as directly as he could. In such circumstances the satellite navigation device would not be a lot of help. When they got closer, the driver would lower his door window and shout to local people for more accurate directions. The driver knew that they were about to get involved in some complicated changes of arrangements that would entail switching vans at some point. As far as he was concerned, the driver was there to do his job that he was being paid to do and he would simply get on with it, no questions to be asked. He wasn't aware of all the details for this job but it was fairly obvious that the casket was going to be transported back to England, minus its present contents, also he would be driving a vehicle on the return trip that appeared to be identical to the one he was driving now, only with different registration plates, probably Italian plates. The driver also knew that as well as himself, Mrs Colarossi, Mr West and the courier driver they would be picking up from Chamonix, there was apparently going to be an additional passenger whose identity was as yet unknown to him. This mysterious passenger would be joining the party somewhere in Desenzano, although the precise location had not been disclosed.

The anxious Mr West stared glumly at the wooden coffin in front of them, and glanced to one side at Mrs Colarossi who was fiddling with the damn iPad again. "Don't you get tired of playing with that thing?" She didn't even look up. "What are you doing with it anyway?" She continued to ignore him. He wasn't that interested in what she might be doing with the irritating device so he picked up his book and forgot about what was going on around him. Then Mrs

Colarossi chose to begin talking in a monotonous tone about the weight of gold, and the value of gold. She reeled off the numbers as though she was some sort of computerised artificial intelligence, without any apparent human feeling. Reading aloud from her illuminated screen, she seemed to be announcing the details of the cargo that was inside the box in front of him. It wasn't as though she was talking to him, or indeed to anyone in particular, the woman was merely dictating from the information on the screen of the iPad in a robotic voice that reminded Mr West of some railway station announcer, or perhaps the announcements that you would hear at an airport departure lounge. "One gold bar, which is usually known as a Good Delivery bar, weighs exactly twelve point four kilos and is twenty-four karat gold. There are eight of these bars in our casket, which comes to ninety-nine point two kilos. This would be the same weight as a fifteen and a half stone human body." Mr West thought she had ended her mathematical sermon, but Mrs Colarossi went on to announce the value of the gold, as opposed to the value of a dead body. "The current price of gold is twenty-four thousand, three hundred and twenty-five pounds and six pence per kilo, which amounts to three hundred and one thousand, six hundred and thirty pounds and seventy-four pence for one such twelve point four kilo bar. Would you like to know how much eight gold bars are worth, Anthony?" He was hoping this would be the final figure of the equation. "I have a feeling that you are going to tell me in any case, so what is your iPod telling you?" Mrs Colarossi corrected him before delivering the actual amount in money terms. "You know full well it's an IPAD and not an IPOD, Anthony darling, and I can tell you that we have just short of two and a half million pounds in our Pandora's Box right there." Mr West thought for a moment about the colossal sum of money that was sitting in the casket, and then he thought about her referring to the coffin as a 'Pandora's Box'. What did she mean by that remark? "Why might you think of it as a Pandora's Box?" She tapped the screen a few times and then held it up in front of Mr West's face for him to read for himself. 'To open Pandora's Box means to perform an action that may seem small or innocent, but that turns out to have severely detrimental and far-reaching consequences.' Mrs Colarossi went on to emphasise the meaning of her statement. "From the moment that we open the box and hand over the contents to our friends in Sirmione, our lives will change forever." Mr West assumed that if the contents of the casket were to be exchanged for a person, then this person must be very important to her, obviously. "Let me get this right, we have sailed across the English Channel, driven across most of Northern France, and driven across more than half of Northern Italy, so that you can hand over two and a half million pounds in gold bars to the Mafia, in exchange for a man?" She answered immediately, which he wasn't expecting. "That is correct, yes."

"Can you tell me if this man is dead or alive?" He wasn't sure why that mattered, but he asked anyway. "Oh he is most certainly alive. Even I would not pay that amount of money for a corpse.... Do you think I'm crazy?" Mr West knew the answer, but he didn't voice the answer. Perhaps Mrs Colarossi was ready to reveal the name of this person who was worth so much? "Would I be right in thinking that you are purchasing a member of the Mafia to bring back to England in order to allow this person to become part of your business management team, is that it?" She didn't alter her expression as she responded to his searching questions. "You are almost right Anthony darling, except that you may be interested to discover he is already one of my company directors, and he has been for some years." Mr West, as her lawyer, was familiar with the list of directors that were involved with her business interests around the world but he could not yet work out which one might have had close ties with the Italian Mafia. "Are you saying that this man has been kidnapped by the Mafia in recent years?" Mrs Colarossi decided to end the conversation at this point. "Don't talk to me Anthony, I have nothing more to say. You will have to wait until I can introduce him to you directly." With that, she put down her iPad and closed her eyes, effectively shutting him out for the time being.

Up ahead, the white van slowed to descend a narrow slip road that led off to the right from the main autoroute and the pale blue pursuit vehicle held back as far as they could without losing sight of the target. From here onwards, the Polizia had deployed several special units, not in cars but on motorcycles. These were not big bikes with officers in leathers, but instead they were using inconspicuous Piaggio Vespa scooters which had small engines that propelled the machines at quite a speed. The Polizia riders wore normal street clothes and this type of scooter was to be seen all over the place in Italian towns and cities, sporting chrome fittings and bright colours, buzzing around the streets and squares like demented wasps. Each of three riders in the specialist unit was equipped with a concealed helmet radio and also a compact helmet camera. They would be able to track the movements of the Mercedes van without arousing any unnecessary attention.

Leaving the van to continue on its way, the officers in the Alfa Romeo responded to an order to pass control over to the officers on two wheels. Already one of the scooter riders was close behind the target van, while a second rider was moving along a parallel road and another unit was further ahead but stationary. Between them, the riders could relay radio messages which would enable them to stay in touch with their target vehicle in whichever direction it chose to go. By alternating between riders constantly on the move, this meant that only one scooter would be in direct view of the van driver at any one time. In this way they could ride as close to the van as they liked, without it being at all obvious that any surveillance was taking place. They could pass either side of the Mercedes, move up close behind it and even slow it down from in front. All three scooters were of a different colour so the van driver would not keep seeing a red scooter hovering too close, for example. The riders had tinted visors fitted to their helmets, which made it more difficult to notice that they were observing the van.

Checking his door mirrors on both sides, the courier driver saw a yellow scooter close behind, but after several hundred metres the rider turned off down a side street as the van continued straight on. The driver was trying to follow his satnav for as long as possible and looking out for a Piazza Garibaldi square. On his satnav screen there was quite a maze of small streets and lots of right and left turns were coming up in quick succession. He saw a blue scooter pull out in front of him, which then proceeded to weave about slowly as though the rider was inexperienced. This turned off shortly, taking a street on the right. Seeing a small square ahead, the driver slowed down to read the sign on the wall of a building. It was not the square he wanted. Yet another motor scooter came out of the square and crossed his path, this time a red Vespa, which forced the van driver to brake hard. He had time to read the name 'Vespa' in chrome letters on the side of the gleaming red paintwork. After a few more left and right turns, and also numerous mini roundabouts, the driver resorted to attracting the attention of passing pedestrians for more precise directions. One particularly narrow street which left very little space to each side of the bulky Mercedes van, resulted in a short conversation with an elderly lady who seemed to know where the Piazza Garibaldi was, but she was somewhat slow in explaining to the driver which way he needed to go. Immediately behind the van a blue scooter rider was sounding his horn because he wanted to get past. The driver thanked the elderly lady and swore in Italian at the impatient rider before moving off. Surprisingly, he found the entrance to the square and drove carefully into the tarmac covered Piazza, which had mature trees in the centre and reserved parking areas marked in blue in some parts of the square. He stopped the van for a moment to get his bearings. A yellow motor scooter approached from the opposite corner of the square and swerved into a parking bay for motorcycles. The rider jumped off his machine to wait outside a public phone box which was occupied, keeping his helmet on. Pulling over to the edge of the square, the van driver got out to consult his passengers in the back, sliding open the door and speaking to those inside for several minutes. Mrs Colarossi pointed out some dark wooden double doors that belonged to the warehouse mentioned in her instructions and the driver walked over to these doors to gain access. He didn't notice that the person inside the public phone box had finished their call and walked away, while the scooter rider remained outside the phone box and made no attempt to enter. By now, the driver had his back to the scooter rider.

On the wall next to the door frame there was a stainless steel intercom panel. The driver glanced over his shoulder momentarily and then pressed the button number four, as had been given to him by Mrs Colarossi earlier. A short pause was followed by the sound of a rough, dry voice. "Chi è?" Following his instructions exactly, the driver repeated the pre-arranged phrase. "Colarossi, oro. Colarossi, oro." Literally this was 'Colarossi, gold.' He stepped back a couple of paces as he heard the doors being opened from the inside. The man who had spoken on the intercom examined the driver's face and took one look at the van outside. Satisfied that it was the expected delivery, the man opened both big doors fully. He backed away into the shadows and motioned with his hand for the vehicle to enter the building. Walking over to his van, the driver selected first gear, looked around this part of the square and turned into the entrance of the old warehouse. He could see the public phone box, but what he could not see was the rider who had arrived on the yellow Vespa scooter. The man in the helmet was standing on the other side of the phone box, obscured by the advertising panels on the windows. Stopping the van inside the spacious warehouse, the double doors were closed behind them. Turning off the engine and stepping out from the cab, the driver opened the side door for Mrs Colarossi and Mr West to get out. Parked a few metres away, near to one wall there was an identical Mercedes van, which was also white. They noticed the rear doors were already opened wide and a group of men in dark overalls were standing by the waiting van. Escorting the three visitors to a cramped office, the man who had opened the doors asked them politely to wait. From the dusty window of the office they saw the men in overalls and black woolly hats unload the casket from their van, and then carefully load it onto the waiting van. The rear doors of the van were closed. Mrs Colarossi, Mr West and the courier driver were led to their new vehicle and they were told to sit in the van and wait for the signal to leave. Watching their original van drive out through the open doors into the bright sunlight, the courier driver was tapping in the location for their next delivery while he waited for the Mafioso to move out of the way. The stocky man in dark clothing was standing with his arms folded across his chest, immediately in front of the van with his back to them, as the double doors were closed again.

  Unseen by Colarossi and West, two of the Mafioso went out onto the street by way of an exit door that was further towards the corner of the square. These two men quickly approached the motor scooter rider, who was still standing next to the phone box, and they grabbed him by his arms before he was even aware of what was happening. The poor unsuspecting rider had been talking on his concealed helmet radio when the two men bodily frog-marched him to his parked scooter. After ripping out the radio cable from his helmet, they let go his arms and both men took out automatic pistols. He was warned in strong threatening terms to leave the Piazza and it was enough to press the cold steel against his neck to force the rider into scrambling onto his Vespa and accelerating away as fast as the little engine would carry him. The rider had seen the white Mercedes van come out of the old warehouse and drive off to the west, which was from where it had entered the square in the first place. He rode off in the same direction as the van, but he was unable to communicate with his fellow motor scooter riders and in any case the white van was by now completely empty, apart from the two drivers in overalls.

As soon as the Polizia officer had been dealt with out in the square, the man who was blocking the exit of the second van stepped aside and waved frantically for the driver to go. The doors were opened for them to leave and the new van turned to the left, taking the exit from the square that would lead to Sirmione, and east of Desenzano.

Sitting in the rear cargo area of the replacement Mercedes van, Mrs Colarossi was busy calling the second mobile phone number. She was advised by a man who did not give his name, to drive to the appointed place at Sirmione and call the same number again at the agreed time. Mrs Colarossi was very pleased with the way things had gone so far, and now that this vehicle was displaying different registration plates, not only the Polizia but also the French Police would not be able to track them across Europe, and as far as she was aware the Police had not picked up their movements between the coast of north-west France and the lakes of north-east Italy. It didn't really matter that in actual fact the whole of the journey had been closely monitored, up until the point where the Italian Polizia had taken over. As long as the exchange that was to take place shortly was also successful, then the return trip for Colarossi and West would be almost impossible to detect by the authorities.

While the motor scooter riders were distracted by the renewed chase involving the bogus vehicle to the west side of Desenzano, what should have become the new target vehicle was now taking the road that ran along the southern shore of Lake Garda, heading eastwards. The Mafioso in their dark overalls were doing an excellent job of misleading the Polizia by driving at speed through many of the narrow streets, doubling back from a series of roundabouts and generally leading their pursuers on a wild goose chase. During the enthusiastic pursuit of the decoy van, all three scooter riders had reunited. The rider astride the yellow scooter was surprised to be confronted with the sight of the white Mercedes van driving at quite a pace towards him, closely followed by a fellow officer on a red motor scooter who believed that he was once more on the trail of the suspect van. Both of the riders came to a halt and the one who had been threatened so forcibly earlier in the Piazza Garibaldi explained to his fellow officer that he no longer had radio communication, and also the fact that this vehicle may not necessarily be the one they wanted. It was decided that the van must be brought to a stop as soon as possible, in order to determine who or what was being transported. They were able to radio the rider on the blue scooter, who by then had visual contact with the fleeing van.

Sirmione del Garda was a narrow spur of land that extended out from the foreshore, and it represents a picturesque peninsula that attracts thousands of visitors, fascinated by the history of the place and its stunning views of the lake and mountain scenery. It was clearly an ideal location for the clandestine exchange. At the northern most tip of this fine peninsula there is a Roman villa that dates from 150AD, and there is a 12th century castle at the centre of Sirmione which is surrounded by water. There are two thermal baths at the southern end with a backdrop of imposing mountains beyond as you travel inland. It was this beautiful scenario that welcomed the Colarossi entourage as it approached the appointed meeting place. Turning onto the single road that runs the length of the historic peninsula, the white van proceeded more slowly and tucked in behind a bus that was bringing tourists to Scaliger Castle, or Castello Scaligero as it is known to the Italians. The van was only going as far as the PalaCreberg Sirmione which would be reached before the castle. At the wheel was the courier driver, and he had visited this place once before during his life, accompanied by his wife and two children. He had taken his family there as part of a holiday and he remembered the trip as being one of the best holidays they had enjoyed as a family. Later, the driver had become divorced from his wife, each of the couple had been granted custody of one child and although both parents had regular access to the other child, life was never the same again. It was with these thoughts in mind that the driver found himself in rather different circumstances this time. It was no family holiday, that's for sure. The bus continued on its way as the van driver turned into the entrance that was the convention centre, PalaCreberg, where conferences and grand performances were held. He drove through the car park, which had a road either side of a tree-lined grassy central reservation, and the road nearest to the lake had rows of parking spaces that faced out towards the waterfront. Heading for the middle of the car parking area, he saw short stumpy Lombardy poplars, standing close together like military guards and they looked like they might begin marching forward at any moment. There was one tree on its own that resembled a giant mushroom. Segregated from the cars, the driver noticed there was a parking area for larger vehicles and he could see vans of various sizes and types, motorhomes and minibuses assembled there. He chose a space that occupied a corner plot, with vacant spaces on both sides. Parking his vehicle, but leaving the engine running, the driver got out to consult Mrs Colarossi and Mr West. It was agreed that this was a good spot so the engine was stopped.

Speaking to the two men when the three of them were inside the back of the van, Mrs Colarossi was making preparations for the handover that was finally about to take place. Seated on the edge of the casket, the driver was listening intently. Mr West was slumped nonchalantly in the seat by her side and he waited to hear the details of the forthcoming meeting with the members of the criminal clan. "We have to be ready for this. I do not want anything to go wrong now that we have come this far. This operation has taken many years to organise and a great deal of negotiation to secure the deal. I will not tolerate even the slightest chance of this exchange failing. Do you both understand me?" Her determination was not lost on either of them. The driver nodded positively from his seat on top of the cargo itself. Mr West had but one question at this stage. "What could possibly go wrong?" Mrs Colarossi fixed him with her firm gaze. "You do know who we are dealing with here, don't you Anthony? Do not for one second underestimate these people. They are capable of anything." He got the point. "Yes, we have to be careful, I do understand." She seemed to accept his compliance and picked up her phone.

Chapter Eight – Exchanging

Redialling the number that she had been given previously, Mrs Colarossi engaged the contact in conversation. Her voice was confident and optimistic. Mr West and the driver fell silent throughout the duration of her call. She was talking Italian the whole time, so the courier driver understood every word, whereas Mr West was not able to understand much of what was said. This call was lengthy and Mrs Colarossi was making frequent notes as she listened to the precise instructions. She put down the phone as she ended the call. "This is what we have to do." Glancing down at her notes, she ran through the list of requirements that had just been relayed to her. "We must take out the emergency warning triangle from under the floor at the rear of this van, and place it in the centre of the next parking space to stop anyone from parking alongside us. Then, leaving the sliding door open on the side of the van nearest to the empty parking space, all three of us have to sit in the front seats of the cab. We then wait for ten minutes, and a yellow DHL Express Italia van will approach us. They are aware of the registration plates on this van, and all we need to do is switch on our hazard warning lights to confirm that we are ready. We are not allowed to get out of this van until they have transferred the goods and we must then wait for them to leave the car park completely before we can examine what they have loaded into our van." Mr West assumed this was a person. "The passenger, presumably?" She nodded. "Within a further ten minutes we should also take the exit and get away from Sirmione and Desenzano. They said we must take the autoroute to Milan as quickly as possible.

While the driver extracted the warning triangle from its compartment under the rear floor, Mr West challenged her trust in these people. "What's to stop your Cosa Nostra friends from dumping a sack of potatoes in the back, taking the gold and we just sit here waiting like lemons? What if your passenger is a dead body? How do you know they will honour their side of the deal?" Mrs Colarossi laughed this off. "They are not my friends Anthony, and don't you think that I have taken precautions to make sure that our passenger is alive and well, and that he is not a sack of potatoes as you put it?" He wanted to hear how she could be so certain of their integrity. "I have insisted that we see the passenger's face on the other side of this window, and furthermore I want to see his eyes opening and hear him speak." She pointed to the small window between the cab and the cargo area of the van. "You believe that's going to happen, do you?" He remained unconvinced. Mrs Colarossi dismissed his concerns and stepped out to join the driver, who had positioned the warning triangle as instructed. "Get in the front with us Anthony, and leave this door open."

Sitting in the centre seat, with the driver to his left and Mrs Colarossi to his right, Mr West stared out of the windscreen in front of him, at the solid trunk of a Cypress tree, and he wasn't feeling at all comfortable with this impending situation. He turned round at ninety degrees and looking through the cab window he could also see out of the open doorway to the side of the van. Mrs Colarossi told him to stop worrying. The driver was keeping a close watch in his door mirror, and Mrs Colarossi was doing the same on her side. Mr West checked his watch for the fourth time in less than ten minutes. "Here we go!" Mrs Colarossi had spotted the DHL van in her mirror. "Don't move!" They watched as the yellow van with its red lettering drove right up to the warning triangle and a man wearing DHL uniform calmly got out and moved the sign out of the way. Barely had the van manoeuvred into the parking space, when a second yellow DHL van suddenly appeared unexpectedly. This second van placed itself squarely across the rear of the white van at right angles and stopped also. "What is going on?" Mr West looked increasingly concerned. The three of them watched and waited. Several minutes passed without anything happening. Close by, on the side where Mrs Colarossi's courier driver was sitting, a door was sliding open. The first DHL van to arrive had sliding doors on both sides, and it was the one facing their open door that was now fully open. Two short stocky men in the familiar dark overalls stepped out and proceeded to climb into the white van. Removing the lid of the casket, one of the men lifted out the first of eight gold bars. Each bar was wrapped in blue plastic that resembled bubble wrap. Such was the weight of the bars that it needed both men to lift each one into their van, where they were placed inside a box that was not a coffin.

It had taken them not much more than twenty minutes to move two and a half million pounds worth of gold from one vehicle to the other. From inside the DHL van the sliding door was closed and again there was no sign of any movement for five minutes, which felt much longer than five minutes to those who were waiting in the cab of the Mercedes van. When something did happen, it was done so rapidly that there was little time in which to react. They were suddenly aware of two dark figures from the second DHL van bringing a struggling man to their open side door. He was bundled into the back of the van, his hands tied behind his back with a length of rope, he was blindfolded and gagged. There was a great deal of scuffling, kicking of feet and muffled grunting but the two dark figures never spoke. Pressing the captive's face against the cab window pane from the cargo side of the vehicle, they ripped off the gag, which appeared to be black duct tape and tore off the blindfold to reveal the man's closed eyes. His head was banged against the window and he opened his eyes. One of his captors struck him in the lower back which made him cry out in pain. Satisfied that they had demonstrated proof of the man's state of well being, they let him fall to the floor and stepped out of the van, their job done.

Mrs Colarossi wanted to rush round to the back of their van immediately, but stopped herself, remembering that she must wait for the Mafioso to depart before they could take any action. Both DHL vans drove out of the parking area slowly and menacingly. She then realised how they must be using a decoy van that was empty, while the other one was carrying the gold, in much the same way as they had done with the two identical white Mercedes vans. Once they were out of sight, the driver got out and Mr West was close behind Mrs Colarossi as she dashed to the open side door. The man was still lying on the metal floor in a crumpled heap, hardly moving at all. Between them, they untied the rope that was binding his wrists and helped him into one of the side seats where the distraught Mrs Colarossi addressed the man by name for the first time. "Alberto, can you hear me? Speak to me amore mio…. Please?" Never before had Mr West seen her show such emotion. She was crying and her tears were falling onto the man's face as she pleaded with him to respond. He seemed to be drugged and he was having difficulty keeping his eyes open. "Anthony, could you get him some water?" Mr West went off to find some drinking water while the driver walked over to a wall near the waterfront so that he could have a cigarette.

Near to the reception desk in the convention centre, Mr West noticed a chilled water dispenser and he filled a couple of plastic cups. He was thinking about this man, Alberto. Sometime during the past few years, Mrs Colarossi had mentioned her late husband to him, but she had merely referred to him by his surname and the odd thing was that the surname was not Colarossi. She had talked about a Mr Bandini and only briefly at that. He remembered her saying that this Bandini chap had suffered a sudden heart attack, very soon after he had taken ownership of the yacht 'Moutine'. Shortly afterwards, Mrs Colarossi as the wife of the deceased Italian gentleman had inherited the yacht. Later, she decided upon a part-ownership agreement that introduced two shareholders besides herself, namely Edward Bilbi and Anthony West, himself. He stood there for a moment, holding the cups of water and pondering the notion that this man Alberto might actually be Alberto Bandini. Could this passenger, for whom she had just exchanged two and a half million pounds worth of gold, be Mrs Colarossi's supposedly deceased husband? Mystified, Mr West wondered why this man in the van, if he did turn out to be Bandini, had not died in England and somehow ended up in Italy? What was the connection with the Mafia, and why would she hand over such a large amount of money to get him back to England? Possibly her husband, if that is who he was, had been kidnapped or in some way abducted, maybe for a ransom? Mr West was vaguely aware that her series of ex-husbands were wealthy men, and they did have one thing in common interestingly, they were all of Italian extraction. One thing was certain they would have plenty of time to discuss the matter during the long drive back across Europe. There was obviously a great deal more to all of this than he had originally thought and he was extremely curious to discover the truth behind this unusual relationship. Mr West, as her business associate and lawyer, felt that Mrs Colarossi owed him a full explanation at the very least.

He went out through the glass doors of the convention centre and he paused to survey the surrounding area before him. Mr West watched cars coming and going, a few people passed by and a fresh breeze caused the trees to sway gently. The white Mercedes van stood motionless. He watched the seagulls landing and taking off from the low wall, beyond which he could see the lake, blue-green and gloriously beautiful. Mountains rose majestically in the middle distance, bathed in brilliant sunshine and the cloudless azure sky showed traces of aircraft trails. Some of the grass verges in the centre of the roadways were covered in bright red poppies. He saw the courier driver walk towards the van and he climbed into the driving seat after throwing his cigarette stub on the ground and treading it into the grey tarmac. Mr West approached the side door of the van where he could see Mrs Colarossi comforting the man, who was now sitting up and he looked less distressed. Handing him a cup of water, Mr West greeted him for the first time. "Buongiorno." The man smiled and accepted the water, which he sipped cautiously. "You can speak English, its fine. Thank you." He put down the cup and held out his right hand. "I am Alberto Bandini, pleased to meet you." Mr West gave the other plastic cup to Mrs Colarossi and shook the man's hand. "Anthony West." Taking a seat on the empty casket, Mr West waited to see if they wanted to talk. Mrs Colarossi sipped her water, put her arm round the man's shoulders and spoke calmly. "Alberto is my husband. We are lucky to have him back alive. Please, we must leave this place now. Let us talk later, when we reach Milan." Mr West understood. He stepped out into the bright sunshine and slid the door shut. Joining the driver in the front, he said it was time to go.

Woken from a deep sleep, Edward didn't quite know where he was. "Twenty minutes Bilbi, get yourself out of bed!" He squinted at the bright light coming in through a small round window and remembered that he was aboard a Coastguard vessel. Dragging his blankets aside, he practically fell out of the bunk which wasn't as close to the floor as he thought it was. Peering out of his cabin porthole, Edward could make out a castle on a headland, probably a mile or two away. He recognised this as Pendennis Castle. They must be close to Falmouth Harbour. Finding his shoes and pulling on a woollen jumper, he splashed some cold water over his face and covered his eyes with a towel. How many hours had passed while he was sleeping? Standing there with the towel held to his face, Edward wasn't really thinking about how to escape, or how he might avoid having to spend the coming night in Police custody his thoughts were much more basic. What he really needed was a proper English breakfast and funnily enough, a cup of tea. The next few days would be no picnic, and Edward was not optimistic that his position would improve significantly. Quite frankly, his immediate prospects looked rather bleak. He sat down to consider how best to deal with the inevitable questioning that would follow his arrival in Falmouth. The most natural reaction from a man like Edward, in a hopeless situation like this, would be to deny everything and simply refuse to provide them with any information that could lead to his own personal circumstances being compromised even further, if that were possible. His biggest problem of course, was that he had above all else escaped from Police custody while in England and that he had been assisted in evading recapture by a third party, who was presumably unknown to the Police at this stage. At the time of his absconding from the vehicle that was taking him to court in Truro, Edward had been facing relatively minor charges, however the more recent offences were stacking up against him and he was actually digging himself a deeper hole. No change there, then. True to type, Edward Bilbi was constantly making his situation worse with every move he made. Would he never learn? These were the thoughts and aspirations that were running through his mind as the moment grew nearer when his personal freedom would once more be severely restricted.

Getting to his feet, Edward arose from the chair and had another look out of the porthole. The entrance to the harbour was ever closer, and the familiar landmark of Pendennis Point was clearly visible by then. He noticed the crisp white sails of yachts that were criss-crossing ahead of the larger vessel. If only Edward could have been out there on the water, sailing free in one of those boats. The door of his cabin was thrown open and two officers of the Coastguard entered unannounced. He was ordered to go with them so he picked up his jacket and left the cabin quietly. One officer was in front of him and the other followed behind, as they climbed some metal steps that led to the upper decks. Edward was greeted by a senior officer, who handed him some papers in a plain brown envelope. "You can hand in this envelope at the Falmouth Police station when you get there Mr Bilbi, if you would be good enough to do so. The man was well spoken and polite towards Edward. "Thank you. May I ask, what is the name of this ship?" Somehow this was important to Edward at the time. "She is Her Majesty's Coastguard vessel, 'Atlantic Princess' and we shall be docking in Falmouth Harbour shortly. It won't be necessary for us to place you in handcuffs Mr Bilbi….. I trust you are not planning to jump ship?" Edward half smiled and he assured the officer that he had no intention of jumping anyway at present.

   Alberto pointed to the casket that was taking up most of the load compartment of the van and spoke to his wife. "That is not for me is it?" Mrs Colarossi expressed her distaste at his remark. "Don't be silly darling it was only a container for the gold, nothing more." He was in a way flattered that his wife was prepared to pay two and a half million pounds to save his life. "Why do we still have it with us for the journey home?" Alberto regarded England as his home, now that it was not safe for him to live in Italy, which was his birth place. "We may need to use the casket to get you into England because you have no passport. You wouldn't have to stay inside the box for long, only while we satisfied the customs authorities that we were carrying my deceased husband from Italy, where you have sadly passed away, to your final resting place at my home in Cornwall." The Mafia had taken Alberto's passport away from him and they had refused to return it to him even when a deal was agreed. Regarding the casket with some trepidation he decided that he would rather not go into that box at all. "Can we do it some other way?" Mrs Colarossi explained to him that provided they were able to sail into the Helford River aboard the yacht 'Moutine' they would not have to go through any customs checks. She un-wrapped some bread and cheese that she had saved for this moment and gave it to him. "We can eat more when we reach Milan, but this will give you some strength until we can enjoy a meal in the city." Alberto thanked her and ate the food eagerly, as he had not eaten for many hours that day.

   Driving at quite a brisk turn of speed, the courier driver was listening to Mr West going over the itinerary. The plan was to stop in Milan for food and drink supplies, refuel the van and then take the autoroute across Northern Italy to the west, where they would be using the Mont Blanc tunnel to cross the border into France. Later, when they got back to Chamonix the second courier driver would hopefully be joining them for the last leg of the road trip. The present driver could then have a well deserved rest from his long stint of driving, and the driver who had stayed in Chamonix would take over to drive to the south of Paris, all the way to L'Aber Wrac'h. That is where they hoped to regain contact with Bilbi and their yacht, while the two drivers would part company with them, so that Mrs Colarossi, Mr Bandini and himself could sail across the English Channel aboard 'Moutine' with two experienced sailors onboard this time. Both Bilbi and Bandini had sailed the classic yacht with Jack Berry originally, which meant that the return crossing should be safer with a crew of four.

Sitting side by side in the back of the van, Mrs Colarossi and her long lost husband were savouring every wonderful moment and making up for lost time. They had been apart for too long. Alberto wanted to hear about the entire sequence of events from his wife's point of view, which was slightly different from his own experience because he had spent most of that time in the hands of the Mafia. "You know I never wanted to get involved with Cosa Nostra, don't you?" She understood how her husband had been tricked into joining the clan as a result of some complex business deals with men who turned out to be extremely dangerous. "I know darling, and you did try to leave their organisation, but they don't allow anyone to leave, once you know too much about their illegal network." Alberto was remembering how it all happened. Those bad memories ran deep, and still they hurt. "When they took me away from you, I thought that I would never see you again. They took me to Verona and I was put in a room with no windows, no daylight. I was told that my execution would not be long. My passport was taken, also my wallet, all my cards and money, my Rolex gold watch, my mobile phone and my shoes. One of the Mafioso came into the room once a day with some water for me to drink and some cheap bread. If I was lucky, he sometimes brought me a piece of fruit or a bowl of soup, but if I complained or asked questions he beat me and kicked me. I gave up hope of ever getting out of that room. I believed that my life was over." Mrs Colarossi picked up the story from there. "After those men took you away, I was writing letters to them in Verona, I was talking on the phone to them many times and I tried everything to persuade them to let you go. In the end I offered them money for your release. At the beginning I was offering thousands of pounds in sterling, but they wanted more, much more. My offer was increased to one million pounds and they were not interested. For me, it was not about the money. All I wanted was to have you back home, and I did not care how much money that was going to take, as long as they released you without taking your life. I offered them two million pounds and they still would not say yes. Finally, I talked to my lawyer in Cornwall and we contacted someone in London who was an expert on the ways of the Mafia, how they work and what they want most. This man advised me to offer them gold. I sat down with my lawyer at his office in Falmouth and we calculated how much gold might satisfy them. We decided to make them an offer of eight standard size gold bars, which would be worth almost two and a half million pounds if they arranged to transfer the gold to a Swiss bank account." Alberto was listening in silence. "Well, to my surprise, and much to my relief, the offer was accepted. We were told to put the offer in writing, which delayed your stay of execution and your release, and we were given strict instructions not to use a means of transport that would involve passing through the customs checks of any European countries. Also, we were warned that we must not allow our transaction with Cosa Nostra or the details of our route through Europe to be detected by the authorities. It was made very clear to us, that if the slightest thing went wrong, you would be killed." Much of what his wife had said was new to him. "What gave you the idea to travel by sea?" She held his hand and continued. "My first thought was to fly from Exeter airport to Brescia, which is so close to Verona, but then I decided that we could not be certain of getting the casket through the customs checks without them being suspicious. We had taken the precaution of lining the coffin with lead, so it was not zinc-lined. That prevents the scanner machines from seeing what is inside the box. I was still worried about using a flight, and I wasn't sure what to do. At the same time as Mr West, my lawyer, and I were trying to find a solution to the problem, something happened which gave me the idea."

It would not be long before they arrived in Milan, as Mrs Colarossi carefully explained to her husband how the yacht 'Moutine' was to play a major part in his rescue, and also how many changes of ownership were brought into play. Alberto was tired and he would soon need to eat, but he listened to the woman who had brought him back to life. Holding her hand, he assured her that he was fine. "Tell me about our lovely ship." She began by reminding Alberto of the time when the yacht was owned by Jack Berry and it was on that fateful day when Mr Berry had lost his life at sea, that the yacht's crew of three had included Edward Bilbi and Mrs Colarossi's husband. Not wanting to dwell on that tragic event, she went on to mention how Mrs Berry had reluctantly, and with some sadness, then sold 'Moutine' to Mr Bandini. "When those men from Verona took you away to Italy the vessel was still registered in your name and so in order to conceal the fact that you had been kidnapped by the Mafioso, I was forced to change the registered owner's name on the documents to allow us to convince everyone that you had passed away. It was important for me to become the registered owner of the vessel if they were to believe that you were no longer alive." Mrs Colarossi talked about the decision to divide the ownership of 'Moutine' between three shareholders. Alberto was curious as to why she had felt it was necessary to change the sole ownership in her name to one of shared ownership in three names. "The plan to sail her across to France was conceived and it was at that point I realised a crew of at least three people would be needed to make the passage possible. Mr West kindly offered to purchase a thirty per cent share in our yacht and my seventy per cent share was reduced to fifty per cent when we later succeeded in tempting Mr Bilbi to join us. We required an experienced sailor for the position of skipper and so it was that Mr Bilbi was persuaded to purchase a twenty per cent share in the vessel." Alberto thought about all of this and he had but one question. "Why Bilbi?" She appreciated that this was an absolutely valid question. "Three reasons really, my love. Mr Bilbi had sailed the yacht some time ago, and also he had met you as part of her crew. This will be important when we bring you back to England. My other reason is that Mr Bilbi was hiding from the Police after being arrested. We were lucky because he asked Mr West for help, and later we both offered him a chance to make some serious money. Mr Bilbi will not get paid if he does not take us all to Cornwall and he must rely on our help in avoiding arrest." Satisfied that she had explained the whole process of the change of ownership to her husband, Mrs Colarossi sat back in her seat. He too was pleased, now that he was aware of all the details.

Slowing down as he approached the Balsamo district, the courier driver was following his directions to the hotel where they would stay for one night. The Cosmo Hotel Palace was to the south-west of Monza and lay just to the north of Milan city centre alongside the autoroute. Parking outside the front entrance of the grand stone building, the driver slid open the side door for his two passengers while Mr West accompanied them into the hotel reception.

Arrangements were made for them to have two rooms, with breakfast included and a table was booked in the restaurant for an evening meal. The four of them met up at their reserved table after everyone had showered and changed their clothes for the meal. Mrs Colarossi was standing behind Alberto, who was already seated at the table, and she gestured to Mr West and the driver for them to take a seat. Once they were all seated and menus had been scrutinised, a bottle of champagne in an ice bucket was brought to the table. Mrs Colarossi proposed a toast to the successful rescue of her long lost husband, with all the theatrical style that she could muster. Everyone around the table was laughing as they ate and drank for the next couple of hours. Tired but grateful, it was such a tremendous relief for Alberto Bandini to realise that he was now enjoying the freedom that he never expected to see. Mr West had noticed a change in Mrs Colarossi's whole demeanour and she appeared to be happy and much less serious than she had been in recent days. Most of the conversation throughout the evening was in English and at other times there were brief exchanges in Italian between the pair across the table and the driver, who was making the most of a lifestyle that he would not usually be able to afford on his modest salary. It was agreed that an early night was in order, and they would also get off to an early start the following morning after breakfast at seven o'clock. The driver excused himself from their company and retired to bed, leaving the others to discuss matters concerning their return to England. "How confident are you that Mr Bilbi will be able to bring our yacht to the port of departure in France?" Alberto directed the question towards both his wife and Mr West. "Well Mr Bandini, it is well known that our friend Mr Bilbi is a bit of a loose cannon, so in my opinion he cannot be trusted one hundred per cent to keep his word but considering the fact that he will want to get paid for completing this task, surely he will at least try to deliver." This was Mr West's view of Edward's position. Mrs Colarossi was more philosophical about Bilbi's role in the operation and she did not see him as a reliable member of the group. "You say that Anthony, but I would not be surprised if the man took it into his head to leave without us and seize the boat for himself. It would also not surprise me if he got himself arrested as he seems to have no sense of self preservation." Alberto was concerned that the last leg of their journey might present them with an unexpected problem.

"What is this 'loose cannon'?" Mrs Colarossi and Mr West laughed and it was explained to him what this phrase meant, especially where Bilbi was involved. "I see, but what can we do if there is no boat waiting for us, how do we get to Cornwall?" His wife said that if such a problem did arise they would have to deal with it when they got there. "There is a good chance that we could find a vessel with a captain who has no crew and wanting to cross the Channel, as this happens all the time. We would be exactly what they are looking for, which is three people who can sail." Mr West corrected her use of the word 'captain'. "I should say that a man with a boat and no crew is not a captain, he is a skipper. It is true what you say about this being quite common to find a vessel that needs a crew to get across to England, but usually the skipper would be heading for Falmouth or possibly the Solent, he would not necessarily be happy about helping people without passports to enter the country via the Helford river." Mrs Colarossi pointed out that only one member of their party did not have a passport, and that was Alberto. "My husband will hide inside the casket if there are any passport checks, and it is unlikely that we will be asked to show our passports by using the route that we have chosen." Before they left the table to retire to their respective rooms, Mr West did have one further question for Mrs Colarossi. "Have you thought about making any changes to the partnership that holds shares in the yacht, now that your husband is back onboard, as it were?" She had indeed already given some thought to this very issue. "Well Anthony, now that you ask, yes I have a suggestion that might be of interest to all of us….. all of us except Mr Bilbi that is." Mr West anticipated what she might be thinking, by the tone of her remark. "You intend to buy him out?" She smiled her business smile. "Let's put it this way, Mr Bilbi's share in the vessel will most likely become available to purchase at some point when we have returned to England, and now that Alberto is coming back onboard, as you say, we may have an attractive offer for you Anthony." He was all ears. "Tell me more?"

"We can discuss this more fully at a later stage of course, but what I would like to suggest is that my husband and I would offer you fifty per cent of the value of 'Moutine' for your thirty per cent share. This figure represents twenty per cent that is currently held by Mr Bilbi, who would no longer be a shareholder in the partnership, plus the thirty per cent share held by yourself." Mr West realised what this would mean in real terms. "You seem to be suggesting that I also would no longer be a shareholder?" She nodded slowly and continued to smile falsely. "Under this new arrangement Alberto and myself would each own fifty per cent of the yacht, and from your perspective you would be receiving more than half as much again on top of the value of your share, which is a generous offer on our part, don't you think?" Mr West appreciated her generosity but at the same time he wasn't entirely comfortable with the notion of relinquishing his share in the yacht and walking away with the money. Mrs Colarossi rose from the table and assured him that he need not worry unduly at the moment. "As I said, we can talk about this proposal at some later stage, so you have more than enough time to think it over." Leaving the restaurant, they went upstairs and parted company at the door to her room. "Goodnight Anthony, see you at breakfast, seven o'clock sharp!" She and Alberto closed the door behind them and Mr West continued along the corridor to the door of his room. The driver was fast asleep in one of the twin beds, and Mr West lay awake in the other for awhile to consider the implications of Mrs Colarossi's bold move to sweep aside Edward and himself, and he was not entirely sure how he felt about the proposed offer.

Chapter Nine – Crossing

She was ploughing through the waves into Falmouth Harbour, the 'Atlantic Princess' returned to her berth at Port Pendennis at high water that morning. Almost in the middle of the harbour entrance there was the Black Rock east cardinal buoy, and further ahead into the channel approach there was The Governor, also marked by a cardinal buoy. Both of these hazards were left to port as the Coastguard vessel rounded the Eastern breakwater, followed by the Western breakwater and then forward into the docks and Port Pendennis. Slowly the vessel was brought onto the jetty, where lines were secured around posts and the crew prepared to disembark. Edward was led ashore by two officers and a waiting Police car was ready to escort him to the Falmouth Police station. This had been arranged in advance by radio communication with the harbour authorities. Sitting alone in the back of the car, Edward watched through the side window as they passed familiar sights in the town. He was feeling defeated and he was at a loss as to what he must do. Perhaps there was nothing to be gained from withholding information from the Police under the circumstances. He was inclined to admit everything and simply to plead guilty to whatever they threw at him. Would that help to reduce his sentence? Edward did not have detailed knowledge of what was going on across the Channel and although he had seen the cargo offloaded in Northern France, he hadn't the faintest idea what they had planned from there on. He guessed that Colarossi and West were presumably going to Italy but apart from the label he had seen on the coffin that indicated an address in the Lake Garda region, he didn't even know what was inside the box. Shortly, Edward would be facing questions to which he had no answers. Naturally the Police would assume that he was withholding information from them, but ironically this was not actually the case. On the whole this was a hopeless situation for him.

They were setting up an interview room, ready to confront Bilbi when he was brought in. D.I. Cook had asked for the elusive Edward Bilbi to be taken to the interview room as soon as he arrived at the station. He didn't want to give Bilbi any time in which to prepare his defence. Switching on the recording device, he sat facing the door. "Good morning Mr Bilbi, would you like a cup of tea?" Edward had barely come through the door when one of D.I. Cook's officers showed him to a chair at the table where the detective was waiting to speak to him. "Please, sit down Mr Bilbi, it's nice to see you again." The two men exchanged a look of mutual disregard. "Milk and two sugars will do nicely thanks." So far that morning Edward had not been offered any breakfast while at sea, and he wasn't happy about being interrogated on an empty stomach either. Opening a bulky grey folder, the detective did not wait for Edward's tea to arrive. "Well my friend, you have been busy recently haven't you? Holiday in France is it?" Edward stared blankly at the detective and said nothing. D.I. Cook tried a different approach. "I wouldn't have thought a man in your position could afford to go sailing. How did you come by such a fine yacht? They don't come cheap, do they Bilbi?" The door opened and tea was brought in. Edward stirred his tea noisily and raised his cup before acknowledging the detective's frivolous questions. He set down the cup and reached into the inside pocket of his jacket. D.I. Cook immediately ordered the officer who was standing behind Bilbi to prevent him from taking out whatever he was intending to produce from his pocket. The officer took hold of Edward's arm and thrust his own hand into the pocket. Pulling out a plain brown envelope, the officer released his grip on Edward's arm. "I'm hardly likely to have a gun on me, am I Cookie?" The detective did not appreciate being called 'Cookie', and he remembered Bilbi using the stupid nickname on a previous occasion. "It's Mr Cook to you Bilbi, if you don't mind!" Opening the envelope and taking out some papers, the detective glanced at the report before resuming his questioning. He was reading from his open folder in front of him. "Suspect Edward D. Bilbi to be escorted to Truro Magistrates Court for preliminary registration of name, address and date of birth only. Date of a further appearance in court shall be set down at this first hearing." D.I. Cook looked up from his folder and confronted the man across the table. "I seem to recall that you failed to turn up at Truro Magistrates Court on the appointed day, Mr Bilbi, so tell me why you chose to make other arrangements?" Edward thought for a moment. "I seem to recall that I needed to go to the toilet, Mr Cook." Saying nothing, the detective turned over a page in his folder. "Trouble is, Mr Bilbi, you somehow managed to use the wrong door when you came out of the petrol station in Carnon Downs. Did you forget which way you went in, or perhaps you didn't fancy going to Truro?" There was no change in Edward's smug expression. "I don't mind Truro, Mr Cook, but the Magistrates Court is not for me, if you don't mind." Smiling politely, the detective moved on undeterred. He had encountered Bilbi's behaviour during interviews before and he was prepared to take his time in order to wear him down gradually over a long period that would inevitably extend to a series of interview sessions. "Have you eaten breakfast Mr Bilbi?" Edward ears pricked up and he was visibly attentive all at once. "What's on the menu?" D.I. Cook stood up, stopped the recording device and moved away towards the door. "Get Mr Bilbi another cup of tea, and see if you can find a biscuit or two. I'll pop back later Mr Bilbi, when I've had my eggs and bacon in the canteen. They do a nice fried breakfast here, you should try it sometime."

It was while he was taking his leisurely breakfast that D.I. Cook thought about Mrs Berry and how well she had performed during the video link with Bilbi, when he was being held in Brest. This might be the right time to bring her in and exert some pressure on Bilbi from the outset. He finished eating and sat thinking about the best approach to the next session of the interview. Picking up his mug of tea, the detective went upstairs to his office. From his desk he called Judith and he scribbled notes on a pad as they talked. "Hello Mrs Berry, it's D.I. Cook here, I'm not interrupting anything I hope?" Judith had been reading and resting so she wasn't really busy at that moment. "No it's quite alright Mr Cook, James has taken Pluto out for a walk, what can I do for you?" The detective wanted to get her involved in the process of wearing Bilbi down. "Well Mrs Berry, I have a proposition for you. We have your old friend Edward Bilbi in custody and I was wondering if you would like to assist me with his forthcoming interrogation?"

"Edward is here in Falmouth?" Judith had presumed that Edward was still in France, and she wasn't expecting to see or hear from him just yet. D.I. Cook appreciated her surprised reaction and he was careful to give Judith some time to compose herself before putting her into the lion's den, as it were. "There is no rush to bring you in on this Mrs Berry, but I could not help noticing how effective your conversation was with Bilbi when we set up the video link previously. You see, I want to unsettle him and throw him off balance and we need to do this early on during the questioning.

Quite apart from his offences and our efforts to get him to court at some stage, Bilbi is a useful witness to provide evidence against the other crew members who were aboard the vessel that was believed to be transporting an unknown cargo to somewhere in Europe." Judith understood how she might play an important role in all of this and she was prepared to help the Police with their inquiries. "How would you like me to help, Mr Cook?" He briefly went over the basic facts as they were, and suggested that she and James would be welcome to join the detective at his office shortly before lunch that day, so that they could implement a plan of action.

At the wheel of her Porsche and clearly enjoying the drive, Judith chatted to James along the way. He picked up on the nervous tone in her voice, as she was talking faster than she would do usually. The prospect of talking directly to Edward across a table at the Police station was obviously weighing on her mind as she drove. James tried to reassure her and he attempted to encourage her from a positive aspect. "Don't worry Judith, all you need to do is be firm with Edward and don't let him try to lie his way out of this. The detective must believe that you are the best placed person to persuade Edward that he needs to be honest and admit as much as he knows." She accepted what James was saying but it wasn't going to be that easy. "Yes, I can see that, and I did feel more confident when Edward was a face on the video screen. This will be different James the man will be in the same room for goodness' sake."

Soon they arrived at Falmouth Police station and James opened the entrance door for Judith to walk in ahead of him. She wasn't sure quite what to expect. Within minutes of their arrival, D.I. Cook came down to reception and greeted them warmly, as he always did. "Please, Mrs Berry do come upstairs to my office, we can talk better there. Nice to see you again Mr David and I'll try not to take up too much of your time." Once they were seated around the detective's large desk he began to outline the details of the proposed interview session. James and Judith listened carefully as the detective spoke of his intended strategy. "There are many different techniques that we use to conduct these interviews, as you can imagine, and the interrogation of a suspect is always complex and very often unpredictable. Someone like Bilbi does not necessarily respond well to conventional methods of questioning, so we shall need to utilise more sophisticated ways of extracting information from a subject like him. I want to place him in a situation where he is not entirely comfortable and with your help Mrs Berry I am hoping that we might be able to unsettle him to a greater degree. Of course, we shall be using the typical method of wearing him down over a long period of time, like you see in TV dramas by depriving him of food, sleep and contact with anyone outside the room, but that can be done after we have tried this unconventional approach to begin with." Judith sympathised with the detective's line of thought, but she was still very concerned about her own ability to say the right thing and at the right time too. "I can understand what you are hoping to achieve Mr Cook but are you sure there's any point in me appealing to Edward's softer side?" D.I. Cook was fully aware of the close relationship between Mrs Berry and Edward in the past and he wanted to push the boundaries in order to force Bilbi into opening up sooner rather than later. "I saw very clearly how Bilbi reacted to the way you treated him over the video link, and I was most impressed. Actually, I was surprised how well you were able to manipulate his behaviour, which is something that my officers and even myself cannot do anywhere near as effectively." Although Judith accepted the detective's well meaning comments as a compliment, she could not help feeling that her involvement in this way would not bring the results that D.I. Cook was anticipating. He went on to talk about the timing of the interview. "What we intend to do, is to confine Bilbi to the room where he has already undergone some preliminary questioning and meanwhile we shall have lunch in the station canteen if you would care to join me, Afterwards, there will be a second interview room set up for us, and I would like Mrs Berry to take a seat in the room before Bilbi is escorted to that room. By the time we lead him out of the first interview room Bilbi will have gone without breakfast and lunch, and crucially he will not be prepared for the sight of Mrs Berry sitting there at the table. With your permission Mrs Berry, I propose that Mr David along with my officers and myself remain in an adjoining room that has a camera, so that we may observe and listen to your 'private' conversation with Bilbi." Judith looked at James and he nodded with approval. She agreed to talk to Edward in this staged one-to-one meeting. The detective stressed that she was going to be in a safe, secure environment and that Bilbi on the other hand would be at an extreme disadvantage and he would be totally out of his comfort zone for as long as the Police wished to prolong the interview. The whole of the session would be recorded of course, in both audio and video formats. D.I. Cook impressed upon Judith that at any time during the interview if she decided that she wanted to halt the session they would stop everything immediately.

Walking past the door to the interview room where Bilbi was waiting, the detective led Judith and James to a room further along the corridor and off to the other side. An officer came out of the first room to speak to D.I. Cook. "Bilbi is asking to see his lawyer Sir." The detective ushered James and Judith into their room, directing the officer to look after them. He then entered Bilbi's room and closed the door behind him. Immediately it was obvious to him that Bilbi was in an agitated state. "What seems to be the problem Bilbi?" Edward leaned forward and he placed both hands on the surface of the table. "When do I get something to eat, how long do I have to wait and I demand to see my lawyer, what are you going to do about it?" He was glaring at the detective and sweating slightly as he continued to lean across the table. D.I. Cook paused deliberately, examining his wrist watch for a moment. Leaning forward he reduced the space between their faces. He made a point of establishing intense eye contact with Bilbi and paused again. "Where exactly is your lawyer Mr Bilbi, can you tell me?" Edward hesitated, confused. "I can see that you haven't thought this through, have you Bilbi? You are referring to Mr Anthony West are you not?" Then followed a few minutes during which Edward was clearly struggling to form meaningful sentences. "Let me help you Mr Bilbi…. We both know that Mr West is not in Cornwall, don't we? Perhaps you would like to explain where your favoured legal representative is residing at this moment in time?" Without allowing Edward to answer the last question he quickly moved on to the subject of food, which was likely to be of greater importance to him than him having a lawyer present. "How about we fix you up with a sandwich, eh Bilbi? What do you say?" Edward leaned back defeated in posture and his stomach dictated to his mind in a way that rendered all other side issues irrelevant in the face of sheer hunger. The detective stood up and walked him to the door, where an officer placed one hand on Edward's shoulder. "Let's find you a quiet place to eat, and then you can tell us what you know about your friend Mr West."

At this point, the detective was executing his clever move. They took Edward along the corridor to the room where his next interview session was about to commence, and the poor man had no idea what was coming. Opening the door, they allowed him to enter the room and then immediately closed the door after him. D.I. Cook dashed into the adjoining room, leaving the officer to stand guard outside the interview room where Edward was about to meet a familiar face. "Judith!"

Sitting at a smaller table than the one in the previous room, Judith Berry calmly invited Edward to sit down and she gently pushed a plate of sandwiches wrapped in cling film over to him. He lowered himself into the chair and looked at the food. It was as though he was waiting for Judith to grant him permission to unwrap the sandwiches. She almost felt sorry for him. Despite everything, he was the mischievous school boy once more. Gone was the desperate, hard faced look of a man on the run. Edward seemed all at once resigned to his fate, and he appeared to be ready to accept any reasonable offer. Judith saw all of that in the first five minutes. She refrained from speaking while Edward began to eat his lunch. He didn't want to rush the first food he had seen in something like fifteen hours, but at the same time he longed to speak to Judith. The pair of them sat at the table in silence, Edward making the most of his sandwiches and Judith waiting patiently as she studied his manner. Also noting every move of Edward's, from the privacy of the room next door, the detective and James watched the interaction between the two subjects at the table. An officer was sitting at the large screen and the three of them listened to a very intimate conversation that was beginning to unfold slowly.

"Sorry Judith, I really needed that. Why are you here?" She pretended to be offended but smiled as she replied. "Don't you want me here Edward?"

"You know I do. Is it alright to talk now?" Judith assured him that she had asked to speak to him in private. "They said they would bring us some tea, but otherwise we can talk as freely as we wish. I was worried that you had gone off to France and stolen a yacht or even something worse." Their conversation was interrupted briefly as a female officer knocked on the door before entering. She set down a tray of tea and cakes before leaving quietly. "Why did you have to go to France, Edward?" With her soft voice and searching grey eyes Judith appealed to his honesty, if he had any left in him. "It's complicated."

"Well it's bound to be complicated if I know you Edward Bilbi, but you must have had a reason to go?" He fell silent and those in the adjoining room held their breath. She tried a different approach. "Who was with you on that boat Edward? Did they force you to take them across the Channel?" She was thinking about the cargo, which D.I. Cook had said was an important question, but she was reluctant to put too much pressure upon Edward too soon. His gaze was wandering around the room as though as he was deciding how much to reveal. Judith waited and held back from posing a further question until he was prepared to deal with those already unanswered. The moment arrived when neither of them could be certain who might resume the conversation. D.I Cook was thinking to himself, "Come on Bilbi, let's have it…. What are you waiting for?"

"There was going to be a lot of money in it for me, and now I realise that I should never have got involved in the first place. I do feel rather stupid actually. The truth is that I owe them nothing, and they were probably just using me to get what they want." Edward put his head in his hands and Judith felt obliged to intervene. "Who are they Edward, who has made you do this?"

"I haven't stolen the vessel Judith and you probably have more memories of her than I do." Sitting up straight at last, Edward was very slowly beginning to have more trust in her. There was a hint of some cracks appearing in his self imposed wall of defences. She detected a noticeable change in his body language. Across the small table this was the closest the two of them had been for some time. The absence of an electronic recording device helped to create the illusion that only Edward and Judith were in this room, and it was within this enclosed bubble that both of them began to feel more relaxed in each other's company. "You already know she is 'Moutine' don't you?" Judith fought back the emotion that was welling up inside her and she remained committed to the task in hand.

"Yes, I am aware of that. May I ask who does she belong to now? Who is the owner?"

Edward managed to smile slightly. He saw himself reaching out with his hand to touch her hand, but he stopped short of doing so. "You remember Mr Bandini, the rich Italian gentleman who acquired the yacht from you after...... Jack lost his life? Well, it was the wife of Mr Bandini who became the new owner when he too passed away suddenly." Judith wanted him to clarify the true ownership of the yacht that had once been her own husband's pride and joy. "So a Mrs Bandini owns 'Moutine', is that what you're saying?" "Not exactly, no. This woman is Mrs Colarossi, not Bandini by name. She was the sole owner of the yacht to begin with but for some reason she decided to set up a three-way partnership. There are three shareholders, all of whom have a different share in the boat." Judith was waiting for Edward to name the three shareholders. "Perhaps you would like to tell me who these shareholders are, and who owns how much?"

"Mrs Colarossi is the majority shareholder in 'Moutine' and she owns fifty per cent of the shares, Anthony West owns thirty per cent as a secondary shareholder and there is one other shareholder who has only twenty per cent of the shares." Edward let her work out for herself who owns the twenty per cent. "The other shareholder would be you?" He just nodded. "Are you the third shareholder Edward?" She knew that it was necessary for him to acknowledge the question verbally, for the benefit of those recording the interview. He didn't appear to suspect anything as far as she could see. "I am indeed, for what it's worth. The shares in the yacht haven't done me much good so far." If at that point Judith had been fitted with a microphone in her ear, which she hadn't, the detective would have been prompting her to probe deeper about Mr West. He needn't have worried she was doing a great job. "You mentioned Anthony West who I understand is your lawyer?"

Edward nodded annoyingly, but this time he did explain further. "Mr West is my lawyer yes, and he is also Mrs Colarossi's lawyer, something that I was not aware of until very recently." She could tell that this was something that was bothering Edward in some way. "Do you have a problem with that Edward?"

"I won't bore you with the details Judith, only to say that Anthony introduced me to Angelina Colarossi when I was at a disadvantage, and it became very clear to me, while at the lady's home that there was something going on between them. I got the impression that it was a great deal more than a business relationship." Edward had polished off the cake and he was hoping for another round of tea soon. Judith was ready to uncover more information about the occupants of the vessel that was crossing the English Channel, now that she had established the structure of her ownership. "Given that you would not be able to sail 'Moutine' single-handed to France, who sailed with you as crew?" Shifting his position in the chair, Edward was becoming restless and he began to fidget with the teaspoon in the saucer, which caused a tinkling sound that was distracting and pointless. He didn't make any attempt to answer her. "Could you stop rattling the spoon please Edward and tell me who you enlisted as your crew for the passage?"

"It is true that I was appointed as the skipper for the trip, however I did not select the crew. In fact I would never have chosen those two clowns as shipmates if it was up to me. It was Mrs Colarossi who foolishly decided that she and Anthony were going to sail a forty foot classic yacht across the English Channel, and until they press ganged me into joining their motley crew they did not have the faintest idea how they were going to carry out their plan."

"So as I understand what you are saying Edward, you agreed to help them take 'Moutine' over to France and you would be the skipper. What I don't understand, is why did this lady and her lawyer want to go to so much trouble to move the yacht from where she was berthed on the Helford River to a port on the coast of Brittany? Was it just a pleasure cruise?" Sinking back in his chair, Edward had a look of despair on his face as he went on to explain how this trip had been anything but a pleasure cruise. "There is no berth on the Helford for 'Moutine', and all I know is that the yacht was at Gweek Quay for her extensive restoration, before she was brought downriver to prepare for the Channel crossing." Judith had already seen the yacht leaving the river that morning and D.I. Cook had discussed the details from his investigation into the boatyard's encounter with the three people who had boarded 'Moutine at Gweek. She knew about the mysterious cargo, and the fact that it was a wooden coffin. "How many people went onboard your yacht at Gweek?" This was really a loaded question because she was implying that the answer is actually four, if you include the body of a deceased person inside the casket. Edward was momentarily unsure as to what Judith was getting at. He didn't have any reservations when it came to talking about the cargo, mainly because he had no idea what was in the box. "There were three of us; myself, Mr West and Mrs Colarossi, that's all." She gave him a quizzical look, to which he responded. "What? You believe there was someone else?" She waited for him to elaborate, but he didn't. "Well if not someone else, could there have been something else?" Edward realised that she was asking him about the cargo, but at the same time he was curious as to how Judith could possibly know about it. He chose to divulge more about the cargo, but he became wary of her questioning and he would have some questions of his own at some point. "The men in the boatyard were ready to load a box onto the boat before she was craned in. I saw two men who were courier drivers carrying the box downstairs at Mrs Colarossi's house. They put the box in the van I assume."

"What sort of box, Edward?"

"It was a large wooden coffin, with brass fittings."

"Were you surprised to see this 'box' being loaded aboard the yacht?"

"It did surprise me yes, but my job was to get the boat to France, along with the crew and cargo. I was to be paid well at the end of it, and I didn't ask questions about the cargo or either of the crew, such as it was." Judith then asked him to describe what happened once they had crossed the Channel. By then, Edward was giving up hope of being offered any more tea.

"Midway across the Channel there was a helicopter overhead and I'm pretty sure that it was tracking our progress although I couldn't work out why a Police helicopter might be interested in our vessel."

"How did you know it was a Police helicopter?"

"I wasn't absolutely certain that it was, but I did have a gut feeling about the way it was keeping pace with our course. Anyway, as we neared the French coast we were intercepted by an English Coastguard vessel which demanded that we heave to."

"Did you do as they asked?" Edward had to admit that he did not comply with their request and that he had chosen instead to increase speed and attempt to reach French territorial waters by doing so. He explained to her how the Coastguard vessel was unable to follow them beyond the limit of French territorial waters by law, and they held their course for a small harbour on the Britanny coast. Judith asked which harbour they were making for and whose decision it had been to refuse the boarding request.

"Mrs Colarossi and Mr West had instructed me to enter the harbour of L'Aber Wrac'h and it was my decision not to allow the Coastguard to board us. This decision was based upon the fact that darkness was falling and we were almost into French waters anyway. We turned off our navigation lights and also lowered our radar reflector dome so as to be less visible."

"So you were able to land at L'Aber Wrac'h, then what happened?"

"Yes, there was a van waiting at the jetty. I stayed onboard 'Moutine' while two men who had brought the van unloaded our cargo and transferred the casket to the waiting vehicle. Shortly afterwards, Mrs Colarossi and Mr West disembarked and joined the men in the van, which drove off with the casket inside." She asked Edward about what he did after they had gone. He told her how the French Police had stormed aboard the yacht while he was having his breakfast and arrested him before he was even aware what was going on. "I didn't have time to resist, I never heard them coming. They took me to Brest and that's where we talked on the video link. You must have thought of me as an idiot for thinking you were in the same Police station, in France?"

"No not really. You were tired and confused, so you weren't to know that I was in Cornwall. Now Edward, you can tell me what was in that casket and why it was so important for them to take it to Italy?"

Edward was running out of answers and also he had an uncomfortable feeling about Judith's motive for asking so many questions. Was this an informal chat between old friends, or was it more of an interview, or could this be interrogation even?

"I told you Judith, I have no idea what is in that box. I did see a label which suggested that the box is destined for Desenzano in Italy, but they never told me why they must get it there. I am as much in the dark about all of this as you and your friend the detective."

"Mr Cook is not my friend, what are you suggesting Edward?"

She saw him smile.

"What time is it Judith?"

She glanced at her wristwatch and told him it was just coming up to three o'clock.

"Interview terminated at fifteen hundred hours!"

Judith realised this was an odd thing for him to say.

"Are we done?" Edward stood up and raised both of his arms, as though someone was pointing a gun at him or as though he was about to be searched. His smile had faded away. It was pretty obvious to both of them that Edward had decided this was game over.

"You have let me down Judith."
In the adjoining room, D.I. Cook looked at James who turned towards the detective, and no words were needed.

Chapter Ten – Infiltrating

Early that morning, at the Cosmo Hotel Palace the courier driver and Mr West were helping themselves to everything they could see in the breakfast bar, when they were joined by Mrs Colarossi and her husband, just before seven o'clock. "Buongiorno amici miei. Good morning my friends." Mrs Colarossi gathered her group together at a nearby table, once they had all selected their choice of food and drink. Seated around the glass topped table, they were absorbed in the business of enjoying a splendid breakfast and to begin with there was little in the way of conversation. Mr West sipped his orange juice, as he mulled over the proposition that Mrs Colarossi had put to him the previous night. This was still troubling him, even after a good night's sleep, despite the loud snoring of the driver coming from the bed next to his. Would he rather have a thirty per cent share in the yacht or perhaps the generous sum of money was of greater interest to him. After all, Mr West did not have a particular desire to go sailing, either as a passenger or as a crew member. Alberto seemed to be more talkative at breakfast as he too had slept well. The driver was engrossed totally in putting away as much food as he possibly could in the time available, which he washed down with copious amounts of hot coffee. Meanwhile, Mrs Colarossi was more refined in the way she ate and drank. She was giving instructions to both the driver and to Mr West, mostly in English for Anthony's benefit. In between mouthfuls the driver did appear to be listening to her as she explained how they would be taking exactly the same route across northern Italy as they had before, only this time it was with a different vehicle and an empty casket as the cargo. Mrs Colarossi was going to look after Alberto in the back of the van, where she could also make any arrangements using her precious iPad. In the front of the van, Mr West could assist the driver with any directions and probably help to keep him awake by providing him with someone to talk to. "When we are approaching the Mont Blanc tunnel, we shall make a short stop at a convenient service area and Alberto will climb into the casket. He will remain concealed until we have passed through customs on both sides of the border. There are discreet air vents along the edges of the casket's cover that will allow my husband to breathe during the short time that it will take to negotiate the tunnel from end to end. Alberto does not have a passport or any identification papers so he must not be visible at any time. We do have the necessary papers to cover a deceased person who is being brought back to my home in England. The next stop will be a hotel in Chamonix, where we shall pick up the backup driver who asked not to travel through the tunnel for personal reasons. From the hotel the backup driver will take over and there will be three of you in the front seats for the journey across northern France, returning to L'Aber Wrac'h as arranged." She went on to mention that there would be a rest halt somewhere south of Paris, but there would be no change of driver this time. On arrival at the small harbour on the coast of Britanny they would be making contact with the yacht 'Moutine' and their hired skipper, Mr Bilbi. The plan was to load the empty casket aboard the vessel, allowing both courier drivers to return to Italy with the vehicle. Mrs Colarossi, Alberto and Mr West would then be able to continue their journey across the English Channel in order to enter the country by way of the Helford estuary, just south of Falmouth Bay.

As there didn't seem to be any questions from anyone in the group Mrs Colarossi arose from the table and with a dab of a napkin to the corner of her mouth, she ended the short meeting. Alberto Bandini did consider complaining about the part where he would be expected to climb into the casket, however he realised that such a complaint was futile. The decision had already been made and his tempestuous wife was not likely to change her plan, not even for him. He also understood that if he refused to get into the box, there was no other way of crossing border controls without him being detained. Alberto had tried to think of an alternative method of hiding himself within the van, but he had failed to come up with anything sensible so he was resigned to accepting her decision as it was.

Leaving their respective rooms, the four of them carried their bags out to the van. Soon they were back on the autoroute and heading west. The early morning sun was behind them, there was only light traffic and each of them was steadfastly following the agreed plan. This fast road would be taking them towards Turin and they would be turning off to go more to the north-west, beginning the long climb into the mountains. Alberto began to gain strength as the day passed. His wife was pleased to see him smiling and they were both relieved to be leaving Italy behind in a way, which was an odd feeling. Eating up the miles at a good rate, they were making progress towards the border with France. She was watching him dozing off and she thought of how close she came to losing him. The day that the Mafioso had abducted Alberto from their peaceful home in Cornwall was still very painful for Mrs Colarossi to think about. Several men had arrived at the entrance gates in a black van just as Alberto was going into the garage to polish his beloved Ferrari one quiet Sunday afternoon. Without thinking properly he had let them enter the courtyard. The men were wearing overalls and he assumed they were workmen because his wife had mentioned that she had recently arranged to have some repairs done. Poor Alberto was easily overwhelmed and he was bundled into the van before he was aware of what was happening. Mrs Colarossi heard him shout once, but by the time she had ran out to see what was going on it was too late to stop them.

"Have you thought about your Ferrari, Alberto?" He had woken from a light sleep only minutes earlier. Mrs Colarossi wanted to talk to him about anything and everything now that she could. "Every day I think about her, you know I do. Angelina you are my first love and my Ferrari, she is my second love. I cannot wait to be back in England to see the most beautiful car ever to be designed." His wife did not share his love of the car to that extent, although she did regard it as being a pretty thing, and she also liked the red colour. "If that is how you feel about the second love of your life you can drive me to London so that I can go shopping in Harrods."
"I will be happy to drive you around the world my darling. Why stop at London?"
"While you have been away Alberto, it is me who is driving that car and it is me who is taking it to the garage every week to have something fixed that has fallen off. It is me who has to spend thousands of pounds to keep the red car going. You must think about changing this car for a different one, maybe an English car like Jaguar or Aston Martin."
"Don't be silly, darling, I will never be parted from my Ferrari, never." This was where the conversation moved on to a change of subject. The pair of them discussed the matter of applying for a new passport for Alberto, and they intended to report the current one as being lost. His passport had been confiscated by the Mafia along with all his personal valuables, including his watch, credit cards,

mobile phone, driving licence and his cash. Mrs Colarossi explained to her husband that it would be necessary to create a completely new identity for him, which entailed giving him a new name, especially in view of the fact that there was still a passport in Italy for a person named Alberto Bandini. She was concerned that such a process might prove difficult and also time consuming.

"I would like to use the family name of Colarossi, is that possible?" This made perfect sense to Alberto and if his wife could not assume the name of Bandini, then surely he must be known by the same surname as his married partner. Mrs Colarossi was unsure of this suggestion, but it remained a possibility. He then pointed out that if they did report the passport as being lost, the authorities would simply provide him with a replacement new passport in the name of Bandini, based upon a document such as his birth certificate. "In that case Alberto, we need to arrange for you to have a birth certificate that relates to your new identity. This can be done. Anthony has contacts who can provide this kind of service." He regarded Mr West as a useful lawyer and generally Alberto did not have a problem with the man. However, he was sometimes troubled with slight suspicions about Anthony West. Their lawyer seemed to be rather too familiar with his wife at times. He could not quite put his finger on what it was that unsettled him, but there was something. Mrs Colarossi always dismissed her husband's concerns regarding Mr West as being akin to jealousy. She would tell him how silly it was for him to have such notions and that he need not worry at all. Alberto remained unconvinced.

At the wheel of the new van and refreshed from his all day breakfast, the courier driver was familiarising himself with the layout of the controls which was different to those of the previous vehicle. Keeping one eye on the road ahead he was making a metal note of all the switches and gauges. He noticed the radio and CD player, the digital clock, temp gauges for outside temperature and engine coolant temperature, the speedometer and rev counter. The mileage for this van was considerably lower than the last one and it was a newer vehicle, which explained the revamped instrument panel. In the centre of the main cluster of warning lights and brightly coloured symbols there was a small bulbous dome-like glass protuberance. The driver briefly touched this object and then forgot about it.

Mr West found the driver easy to talk to, much to his relief, and also the driver spoke good English which was just as well because Mr West knew very little Italian. It was to be a long drive so lack of conversation might have been uncomfortable after awhile. The lawyer did not have a device like Mrs Colarossi's iPad to play with so the journey would have been rather boring without the opportunity to talk some of the time. They discussed world affairs, cars, women, families and sport. While the driver admitted to having a passion for an Italian football team that Mr West had not heard of, the lawyer declared a preference for classical music over football. It turned out that both the driver and Mr West liked Italian opera, and in particular the works of Giacomo Puccini. "Do you know La Tosca, Mr West?"

"You can call me Anthony, and yes I do know Tosca. Also I like Madama Butterfly, do you know that one?"

"I am Pietro or Peter if you prefer. I saw Madama Butterfly at the teatro in Milan some years ago, and it was wonderful. The costumes, the music, the voices and the whole atmosphere of the production was magnifico."

The two of them continued in this way and the miles rolled by. Pietro was born in Lucca, not far from Florence and it was with some pride that he mentioned Puccini's birthplace was also the ancient city of Lucca. "The great man Puccini is from my city!" Mr West was impressed and he could not help laughing when Pietro began to sing an extract from La Tosca at the top of his voice. His singing voice was not particularly good, it has to be said, but Mr West did find his rendition quite amusing nonetheless. Fortunately, the driver's operatic performance could not be heard inside the back of the van.

Several hours later, the white van was entering a service area just outside Courmayeur. Finding a discreet parking space that was close to other vehicles so as not to appear conspicuous the side door slid open. Daylight greeted Mrs Colarossi and Alberto as they climbed out. "Anthony, could you get us all some refreshments please and the driver can stay with his vehicle. Alberto and I need to walk around while we can." Mrs Colarossi was issuing orders as usual, but someone had to take charge if things were to be properly organised. Mr West obediently trotted off to the services building and Pietro the driver stood by his van smoking a cigarette. Alberto and his wife had been confined to the cramped seating area of the cargo compartment for many miles and there would be many more miles to cover yet. Once they had rested for a short period, it was time for Alberto to hide inside the casket for them to pass through the Mont Blanc tunnel. Coffee and hot croissants were brought to the van, along with some fruit and bottled water. Alberto was helped into the casket as the driver and Mr West held the heavy wooden lid, with Mrs Colarossi holding onto her husband's arm. Alberto steadied himself with his other arm and lowered himself down into the lead-lined ornate box. The inner surfaces of the casket were covered in cream silk, which was padded for comfort. "Mio Dio.... I don't like this" The sight of Alberto lying in the casket was almost too much for his wife, who began to wonder if this was such a good idea after all. She was having second thoughts and she could see that Alberto would rather not be in this position for long. He lay on his back, staring upwards at the roof of the van, his feet together and his hands clasped tightly to his chest. Muttering Hail Marys under his breath, Alberto naturally closed his eyes as the casket lid was replaced. Mrs Colarossi had refrained from saying goodbye as it seemed highly inappropriate and she did not want to scare her poor husband even further. Instead, she handed him a small bunch of grapes.

The casket was closed, Mrs Colarossi took her seat beside it and Mr West joined the driver in the front. All was ready for the approach to the tunnel entrance and they would first have to undergo the customs checks. There was a customs checkpoint on both the Italian side of the International border and again on the French side of the tunnel. As far as the customs officials were concerned, Mrs Colarossi had transported an empty casket from England via France to Desenzano in Italy, to allow her to collect her deceased husband's body from the shores of Lake Garda and bring him back to her home in Cornwall, which was to be his final resting place.

Pietro pulled up slowly at the checkpoint barrier and stepped out holding their papers. He chatted with the customs officials by way of maintaining a relaxed, friendly exchange of routine procedures, showing them the three valid passports that related to the three known occupants of the vehicle. Following the men outside the checkpoint building, the driver waited patiently for them to examine the interior of the van. Generally, these were leisurely checks and the contents of each vehicle were not usually scrutinised closely. Only if there appeared to be an attempt to conceal or disguise the goods being moved would they take a much closer look. Unless they became suspicious about some aspect of their vehicle or the three occupants themselves, and provided their papers were in order it should not take long to clear customs. The two uniformed officials climbed inside the van through the rear doors, not the sliding side door and admired the ornate casket which was taking up most of the load space. One of the men spoke to Mrs Colarossi, offering their condolences to her for her sad loss. Probably out of respect, more than anything, they did not wish to interfere with the casket itself and apart from waving a hand-held scanner over it they were not unduly concerned about it. Mrs Colarossi explained to the men how she had brought the empty casket from Cornwall with the help of her lawyer and friend Mr West, and now they were taking her deceased husband from his birthplace in Italy to her home in England where he could be laid to rest within the grounds of her property there. She was of course most convincing in her manner of speaking, as she conveyed her feelings without appearing to be over emotional but with a restrained and serious tone to her voice that commanded the appropriate respect. Mrs Colarossi conducted the whole of the conversation in Italian and Mr West did not need to intervene at any stage. Satisfied that all was in order, the customs officials handed back their passports and the carefully prepared documents that claimed to represent permission to transport human remains as issued by the relevant authority. The driver thanked them and closed the rear doors, while Mrs Colarossi returned to her seat beside the casket, where her husband lay quietly and anxiously inside. Pietro closed the side door and joined Mr West in the front of the van. They pulled away slowly and there were no obvious signs that they wanted to get through the tunnel as quickly as possible. Pietro was talking to Mr West as they drove along the autoroute from Courmayeur to the Mont Blanc tunnel entrance on the Italian side. He had used this route many times before on regular delivery runs. "You see how the Italian customs do the checking? This is not a problem for us, but you will find things different on the French side."

"How is it different?"

"They will ask more questions and maybe they will want to know why the scanner cannot see what is inside the box. We will have to be careful. I think we will be O.K."

Mr West assured the driver that he and Mrs Colarossi would talk nicely to the French customs officials when the time came. "They didn't see the gold with the scanner when we passed through before, so perhaps we do not need to worry." Entering the tunnel they ceased talking and concentrated on what lay ahead.

Touching the lid of the casket, Mrs Colarossi wanted to remove the lid and comfort her husband but she managed to resist the urge. Both she and Alberto understood that it was essential to keep to the plan. Like the driver, she was aware of the difference between the Italian customs mentality and the more thorough approach that could be expected on the French side of the border. It would only take quarter of an hour to drive through the tunnel. The driver was maintaining a speed that was above the regulation fifty kilometres per hour minimum speed, and below the maximum allowed which was seventy kilometres per hour. Pietro was averaging sixty kilometres per hour so as to make the best possible progress. Mrs Colarossi was already thinking ahead and she was prepared to resort to drastic measures if any of the customs officials suggested opening the casket for detailed examination, which was actually unlikely.

The van slowed down behind several heavy goods vehicles as they neared the exit of the tunnel. From the artificial lighting of the tunnel interior they came out into daylight as the trucks channelled off to one side and into a separate lane. While the trucks were going through the heat detectors, the white van paused at the barrier that was flanked by the customs checkpoint building. A tall officer in uniform tapped on Pietro's door window and waited for the glass to lower. He asked the driver for the passports of all passengers, taking a step back, while at the same time asking Pietro to step out of the vehicle for a moment. This time the conversation was entirely spoken in French. Walking around to the rear of the van, the officer wanted to know what cargo they were carrying. Following the officer, the driver was asked to open the rear doors. Pietro opened both doors fully and stepped aside. Looking at the casket solemnly and studying the documents that the driver had produced from a plastic folder, the customs officer was taking some time to arrive at a decision. He was joined by a second officer who proceeded to scan the entire length of the casket with his device. They exchanged a few words of unease, finding that there was no image of the contents on the small screen. Clearly the officers were puzzled by this and they questioned the driver about the construction of the casket. Pietro pointed out the section of one of the documents that showed the casket lining as being made of zinc, and he boldly suggested that perhaps their scanner was slightly faulty. Because of this delay, Mrs Colarossi felt obliged to intervene from her seat towards the front end of the load area. She directed the driver to let her out of the side door and she then walked up to the two men in uniform. Speaking fluent French, Mrs Colarossi impressed upon the officers how important it was to respect her deceased husband's body, and she demanded to speak to their superior. Such was the imposing nature of her forceful demand that when faced with this direct show of strength from a woman of considerable stature, these officers quickly adopted a more lenient approach. Mrs Colarossi was fully aware that the casket was actually lead-lined as opposed to zinc-lined, and the purpose of this mode of construction was to prevent the customs scanners from detecting the gold bars that were being carried on the outward journey. This requirement wasn't absolutely necessary during the return journey because there was a body inside the casket, albeit Alberto's very much alive body. Assuming that the scanner devices were unable to distinguish a dead body from a living body, in theory they could have used a zinc-lined coffin but that would have posed problems with having to carry two coffins in the van. She later realised that the second van made available for the switch in Milan could have contained an empty zinc-lined casket which would have allowed them to pass through the checkpoints without arousing any suspicion.

 One of the officials went off to call his superior on the phone, leaving his colleague to pacify Mrs Colarossi who had resorted to pacing up and down behind the van. She made a point of asking Pietro to close the doors of the van because she was most concerned that her husband would get cold. It was with great restraint that the customs official stopped himself from laughing. He was thinking, they don't get much colder than being dead. Had he known that Alberto was far from being dead in that casket he would have seen things in a very different light. Mrs Colarossi was talking quickly in French and she never ceased to pace up and down as though she was highly agitated. She asked the official how he would feel if some policeman was suggesting that he open a similar casket that contained his wife, simply to prove that his deceased wife's body was really inside. The poor man became extremely uncomfortable with that analogy. Fortunately for him the other official returned and announced that his superior had authorised the casket's entry into France on condition of the wife of the deceased signing a document to declare that the casket was for the purpose of transporting human remains to a country of origin, and that it did not contain drugs, currency, alcohol or jewellery. Mrs Colarossi agreed to sign the document, but she stressed that her deceased husband was not being returned to his country of origin as that was Italy, but rather he was being brought back to her home in England following the recent funeral in Milan. Both customs officials looked at one another and they decided to process the entry of this vehicle's contents with the least amount of hassle as they could possibly manage. For all they knew, the box might have contained machine guns and explosives, however by this time it was accepted that this woman was genuine and in the interests of their own state of mind, she would be allowed to pass through France with the casket to her destination in England. After a few further questions regarding her intended port of departure and the registered name of the vessel that would be conveying the casket across the Channel, and once the all important document had been signed, they were cleared to proceed. Mrs Colarossi put on her best polite smile and thanked the men for their patience. She even complimented them on the way they had carried out their job with such professionalism. Mr West escorted her to the seat in the van before the Frenchmen could change their minds. With Mrs Colarossi safely strapped into her seat, he jumped into the front of the van and urged the driver to be on his way. "Let's go Pietro, take us to Chamonix!"

From the back of the van Mrs Colarossi was making contact with the courier driver who had remained in Chamonix and as she ended the call there was a tapping sound from inside the casket in front of her. She alerted the driver by banging on the window of the cab. Pietro pulled into a layby and slid open the door to listen to her. "Help me lift the cover off Alberto's box I think he wants to come out." They lifted the heavy lid away from the casket and the driver went back to his driving. Mrs Colarossi could not face the sight of her husband lying in the casket so she waited for him to emerge. Alberto blinked, staring at the metal roof and he was thinking how this was like coming back from the dead, which was not a pleasant thought. For a few moments he stared upwards and he did not move. What was that small domed glass object on the roof? It reminded Alberto of an eyeball. He continued to stare at the object and it was when a tiny red light came on near to the glass part in the centre that he realised what it must be. This was a camera? Placing his hands on either side of the casket, Alberto sat up carefully. He was bit stiff from being in the same position for too long. Turning to look at his wife, he asked her curiously, "Why is this vehicle fitted with cameras?"

"Don't be silly darling, it is not."

"Tell me, what is that?" Mrs Colarossi followed the line of his pointing finger with her eyes and immediately she became alarmed. Her husband had not noticed the object before, probably because he had closed his eyes almost as soon as he lay down in the casket. She banged on the window and with more force this time. Pietro could not stop at once as there was no layby for the next couple of kilometres. "What now?" He parked his van as soon as he was able and went round to the side door. "Is there a problem?" Both Mrs Colarossi and Alberto looked at the driver. "I was not aware that this van is fitted with cameras Pietro?" She pointed up at the object set into the centre of the roof.

"There is no camera...." He saw the domed glass of the object and quickly realised that it was the same as the one he had seen on the instrument panel in the front. Pietro arrived at the shock revelation before Mrs Colarossi did. He asked her to look at the object in the cab, where he voiced what they were all thinking. "You know what this means? This van is bugged!" Mr West looked on in disbelief. "There is a camera here in the cab?" Pietro confirmed that not only was there a camera on the instrument panel of the vehicle but there was also a second camera fitted to the underside of the roof in the back. He ran his fingers around the white metal surround of the lens and he could feel there was a tiny hole, which presumably was the microphone. "I am sure they are both cameras, and also they have a microphone." Mrs Colarossi gestured for the driver and Mr West to move away from the cab and she pulled Alberto from where he had taken a seat in the back of the van. The four of them walked a short distance onto the grass verge of the layby to hear what she had to say.

"We have been using this van which has been bugged by the Mafioso all this time. They will have seen and heard everything we have done, from leaving the warehouse in Desenzano, to the conference centre in Sirmione, to the hotel near Milan and through the Mont Blanc tunnel to here. We must destroy the cameras but already they know where we are."

"Yes, but they do not know where our route is taking us from Chamonix, so we cannot be followed to the boat." The driver's remark was perfectly justifiable. Mrs Colarossi was thinking back along the route that they had taken so far, and she was pretty sure that when they had spoken of their intended destination this had been discussed at the hotel and therefore not inside the van. She asked Pietro to disable the cameras before they set off again. He produced some tools from a compartment in one of the rear doors and got into the cab, where he unscrewed the metal surround of the first camera, lifted out the internals of the thing and severed the wires with cable cutters. He repeated this operation with the second camera that was mounted on the underside of the roof in the cargo area. Satisfied that these two devices were no longer a threat, they conducted a search of the van to make sure that no more cameras were hidden. Only then did they resume the short drive to Chamonix. Stepping into the van, Mrs Colarossi gave the driver a piece of paper on which she had written the address of the hotel where they would meet up with the other driver. "We keep this information about the cameras to ourselves, you understand. Do not speak to anyone about this, not even the driver in Chamonix."

Chapter Eleven – Joining

Pietro found the hotel and parked up. The van was taking up two parking spaces but the parking area was quite empty anyway. Everyone stayed in the van apart from Pietro who went into the hotel lobby and enquired about the driver. Checking the name on his piece of paper, the hotel receptionist called the driver's room. Pietro waited for ten minutes and the driver appeared at the foot of the stairway. The two men greeted one another, before going outside. Approaching the van, they were met by Mr West who stowed the courier driver's bag behind the front seats. Sitting nearest to the passenger side door, Mr West was joined by the two drivers, Pietro taking the centre seat and the other driver sat behind the wheel for the next leg of the trip. Mrs Colarossi and Alberto stayed out of sight while the men sorted themselves out in the front. Moving off slowly, the van rejoined the main autoroute and settled into a steady pace. Pietro introduced his colleague to Mr West as Fabio. "Pleased to meet you Signor West, I am from Verona."

"You can call me Anthony I am from Cornwall in England." The driver Fabio said that he had heard Cornwall was a beautiful part of England. He was concentrating on driving the vehicle, which was new to him so they stopped talking for awhile. Fabio glanced down at the hole in the instrument panel where the concealed camera had been. He said nothing.

Now that they were on the move again, Alberto was talking to his wife, safe in the knowledge that no-one was listening in to their conversation. "We cannot underestimate the Mafioso, they don't like me walking away from the clan and even if we have given them all this gold they still want more." He was concerned about the way that the van had been bugged and he feared there was more to come. "They will not stop until they have what they want." Mrs Colarossi understood how her husband must be feeling and she too was anxious about what might lay ahead of them.

"We are quite close to Chartres, you can see the top of the cathedral over there." Fabio was pointing out the landmark as he drove towards the Loire valley. Consulting his map that was opened out in front of him, Pietro remarked that Chartres was about ninety-five kilometres south-west of Paris. "This would be a good place to stop for a rest, I think." Next to him, Mr West agreed as he too looked at the position of the city relative to their destination. "From there we go to Le Mans and further west to Rennes, and then to north-west Britanny. That is four hundred kilometres I would say." Across the wheat fields the two spires of the famous cathedral were clearly visible even at such a distance. On the outskirts of the city they were approaching an Aire de Service that seemed to be an ideal location. All five of them were able to leave the van and make use of the facilities as there was no cargo to stand guard over, and it was not necessary for Alberto to be hidden from view during this part of the journey. After wandering around visiting the different areas of the site they all sat down to eat in the restaurant and plenty of strong coffee was ordered. Mrs Colarossi kept looking this way and that, imagining that someone might be watching them. Her husband was also very sensitive to his surroundings. Fabio the driver wanted to know more of the arrangements that had been made for when they arrived at L'Aber Wrac'h. "Have you decided to return to England with the same boat that was used to bring the casket to France?" Anticipating a problem at the destination port, Mrs Colarossi could not be absolutely sure that the notoriously unreliable Mr Bilbi was going to bring the yacht to the harbour on time, or even at all. "Providing the boat is available, we should be able to make the crossing, but if not we can easily find an English skipper who is in need of a crew to get back to his home port. This is quite a common situation along the French coast so I am not too concerned." Pietro pointed out that not all skippers would be happy about taking the casket onboard. Mr West smiled and assured him that if offered money for their trouble, most would take it with no questions asked. "As long as our friend Mr Bilbi turns up with our yacht in one piece, we don't have a problem. He is well aware that if he doesn't complete the return passage then he will not get paid. That should be all the motivation he needs if I know Bilbi." Alberto was more concerned about having to climb into the casket if there was an encounter with the Coastguard or customs vessels possibly. Mrs Colarossi was still thinking about the cameras.

When they gathered outside the van after finishing their lunch break, Fabio took the opportunity to have a quick look inside the load area of the vehicle. He did so while the others were grouped around the iPad that Mrs Colarossi was showing them. She was keen to demonstrate how versatile this wonderful device was, and how incredibly accurate it was when it came to navigation and fact finding, not to mention the range of 'apps' that she had installed. Fabio noticed there was a hole in the centre of the roof panel with some exposed wires protruding from the small hole. He tapped the other driver on his shoulder to let him know that he was just going off to the toilet before they continued with the trip. Fabio had previously noted that there was something missing from the instrument panel and he had wanted to check inside the rear compartment of the van to see if anything had also been tampered with. He sprinted over to the services building and sent a lengthy text message from his mobile phone while keeping a watchful eye on the glass doors between him and the exit.

Once they were on the road again, everyone settled down for the last leg of the road trip that would bring them to the place where they were hoping to rendezvous with the yacht 'Moutine'. This would take approximately five hours, or possibly less if they made good progress. Mr West was feeling much better, now that he was sitting up front and he could watch the passing scenery. Previously, when he had been confined to the back of the van with Mrs Colarossi there were no windows to look out of and the time had passed slowly. He preferred to see the place names of the towns and villages as they drove through them and even the vehicles that were travelling in the opposite direction had some interest for him. As they drove through Le Mans, it occurred to Mr West that he had seen the famous Monza motor racing circuit near to Milan, and now he was close to the legend that was Le Mans, which was well known to most people for the twenty four hour race that had been held there every year for many years. Mr West usually made a point of following the Formula One motor racing season, if only through the television coverage and the newspapers. He didn't have the time or the money to follow the races around the world from circuit to circuit, as some dedicated fans of the sport were prepared to do. "Do you follow motor racing Pietro?" Seated next to him Pietro had also noticed the road sign that welcomed drivers to the famous circuit. "No I do not follow the racing, but sometimes I like to watch it on the TV." He said that he was more of a football fan. Fabio voiced his approval of the sport and he had a different view. "I used to travel with my Papa to see the racing at Monza, and when he passed away some years ago now I still like to go there with my son. We support the Ferrari team of course. You can see us wearing the red caps with the yellow badge." Mr West admitted that he was more of an armchair fan really. "You should go to the track Signor West, it is so exciting. For me it is the sound of the engines and the smell of the oil and the tyres... you don't get that on the TV." It was true to say that to be there at the race track, or equally at the football ground was much more of an exciting experience than simply watching the spectacle on television. "You are right Fabio, it is so much better to go there yourself."

Mrs Colarossi was fascinated by a film on her iPad, while Alberto was taking a nap as best he could. It was one of the old classics in black and white. She loved the romance, the clothes and the music. It was too early to be attempting to make contact with their man in L'Aber Wrac'h, if indeed that was where he was. She had Bilbi's mobile number and when the time came she would need to establish where the yacht was located, and of less importance to her, where Mr Bilbi might be. Hopefully he would be aboard the boat.

From his bunk in the cell Edward half opened one eye as the door lock rattled noisily. A uniformed officer came into the cell and roused Edward from his slumber. "Fifteen minutes Bilbi! D.I. Cook wants to see you. Get yourself tidied up!" The heavy door was slammed harder than necessary. Edward was of the opinion that the officer must find it amusing to make so much noise first thing in the morning. He splashed some cold water on his face and cleaned his teeth with a face cloth, still feeling rough after a poor night's sleep. Putting on a ragged jumper and dragging his shoes on, Edward stood as close to the door as was possible, while leaving only just enough space for it to open. The same officer swung open the cell door and he intended to stride in. He practically collided with the grinning Edward who was barring his way forward. "Get out of the way Bilbi, you idiot! Pretending to be almost knocked over, he staggered backwards. Grabbing Edward by his arm the officer bundled him out of the cell and into the corridor. "Come on Bilbi, look lively and stop messing about!"

Facing his most elusive offender across the familiar interview room table, the detective was not in the mood for games. "Good morning Mr Bilbi, how are you today?" Edward chose not to answer that one. "Interview commencing at eight hundred hours." D.I. Cook switched on the recording machine, sat back in his chair and regarded the man opposite him for a moment. "You have been arrested for the second time Bilbi, and you are already charged with escaping from custody while you were being escorted to the magistrate's court in the city of Truro. Thanks to my colleagues in France we are also charging you with aiding and abetting two missing persons, by the names of Mr Anthony West and a Mrs Angelina Colarossi who are wanted in connection with the illegal transportation of a cargo, as yet unknown, to a destination in Italy, also unknown. What have you got to say for yourself?" Edward shrugged with disinterest. "Sounds like you have missing persons who are moving unknown cargo to unknown destinations. You don't have much to go on, do you Cookie?" That was enough to antagonise the detective at this early hour of the morning. "Don't get smart with me Bilbi and I've warned you before, don't call me 'Cookie', it's 'D.I. Cook' or 'Sir' to you! Do you understand me?" Edward nodded and he assumed a straight face. "I won't warn you again Bilbi, do not shake your head at the machine. Speak up man! Do you understand me?"

"Yes…. Sir…. I understand."

The detective picked up a plastic bag from the floor next to his chair and rummaged among some items inside the bag. He took out a mobile phone and handed it to Edward. "These are your personal belongings that were confiscated in Brest, and we have kindly brought them back to Falmouth for you. See how we look after you Bilbi?" Edward said nothing. He picked up the phone from where it lay in the centre of the table and asked about the other items in the bag. "What about my watch and my wallet, Sir?"

"Just the phone for now Bilbi. You are hardly in a position to negotiate. Now, for the record Mr Bilbi is switching on his mobile phone. Would you do that for me now please, Mr Bilbi?"

D.I. Cook waited for Edward to comply with his request. The phone was activated and Edward held it up so that the detective could see the small screen. "It would appear that I don't seem to have any missed calls, and I don't have any unread text messages either, Sir, but then you would already know that because your officers are quite capable of switching on my phone for themselves." He put the phone down and leaned back.

"How would you like to do me a little favour Mr Bilbi? Say I fix you up with a bit of breakfast, and perhaps we might consider dropping one of those charges against you if you do me this small favour?"

"What sort of favour? How is anything I do for you going to make the slightest difference?"

"Well it's like this you see Bilbi, at some stage I am willing to bet that your friends who are on their way to a funeral in sunny Italy will be wanting to return home to Cornwall. In order to cross the English Channel, their most obvious choice of travel arrangements would surely be to use the boat that got them over there in the first place, don't you think?"

"How would I know?"

"Of course you know Mr Bilbi, and I can see to it that you get a damn good breakfast as long as you agree to help us with our enquiries. Neither of us want to drag this out any longer than is necessary, do we?" He could see that Edward was weighing up the chance of an all day breakfast against helping the Police with their enquiries, and it didn't take him long to arrive at the obvious decision. Both Edward and the detective were well aware that as far as Colarossi and West were concerned, Edward did not owe them anything. "What do you want to know?"

"It's not so much what we want to know, it's more about what we want you to do."

"You want me to go somewhere?" Edward was hopeful.

"No Mr Bilbi, I would rather you stay here now that we have you where I can keep an eye on you. Just bear with me for a moment and then we'll get you some breakfast. Would I be right in thinking, that when you were picked up by the French Police, you were onboard the yacht 'Moutine'?" D.I. Cook needed to be more certain of the events that had unfolded on the other side of the Channel. His investigation could not be based upon vague assumptions and pure guesswork. Bilbi was in possession of the facts.

"That's right, I was onboard the boat when they jumped me."

"Why did you remain onboard after the others had left? What were you expected to do?"

"Ha! They were expecting me to swan around the coast of Britanny for a couple of weeks and by some miracle I was to avoid the French Coastguard, the English Coastguard and whatever else they threw at me. I wasn't safe at sea and I couldn't go ashore, so they would have found me eventually, I'm sure of that."

"You could have brought her back across to the Helford single handed, a sailor of your experience?"

131

"Believe me it did cross my mind to make a run for it. Didn't have much choice though did I really? They said I must be in L'Aber Wrac'h harbour with the yacht ready for the return trip and I wasn't going to be paid a penny until they were safely back in Cornwall."

"How were they going to contact you?"

"As soon as their business in Italy was finished, and when they had crossed France to where I was supposed to be waiting, they would call me on this mobile. No chance of that now is there?" Edward saw the look on the detective's face as he said this. "Don't tell me, you want me to take that call, when it comes?"

"There you go Bilbi, that wasn't difficult was it? Mrs Colarossi and Mr West will call you as arranged, and you are going to speak to them on that phone, except you won't be waiting in L'Aber Wrac'h, you will be here in Falmouth. I'm sure you can convince them that all is well and everything is going according to plan." D.I. Cook was smiling now.

"Actually there is a problem with that." Edward was quick to realise something that had not occurred to the detective. He pointed out that if they made the call from within France to his mobile phone in the U.K., the call would register as being an International call and this would show up as connecting through the U.K. network. D.I. Cook was impressed with Edward's quick thinking, but he was confident that this slight problem could be overcome quite easily.

"Yes, that would be a problem as you say, but I have a colleague on the French side who can redirect the incoming call through a French network and the caller will be unaware of what is happening. Don't you worry Bilbi, we have the technology!"

"So you want me to say that I am at the jetty and ready to leave for England. How is that going to make any sense when they arrive at the jetty to find there is no boat, and there is no skipper?"

"Like I said, don't you worry yourself we can take it from there. You will have done your bit, and we can drop the charge against you of aiding and abetting Colarossi and West, who will be taken into custody and questioned." Hearing this, Edward was mistakenly assuming that the Police were planning to arrest Colarossi and West as they arrived at the jetty, whereas the actual plan was to allow them to sail the yacht 'Moutine' across to the Helford or even Falmouth, where they would be arrested on English shores. D.I. Cook was not going to reveal to Edward how the vessel was to remain on the jetty with no-one onboard and when Colarossi and West failed to rendezvous with Bilbi, they would simply assume that their rogue skipper had either gone absent without leave or maybe he had got himself arrested by the French Gendarmerie.

Tapping on the window behind him, Pietro signalled to Mrs Colarossi and her husband that it was only ten minutes to their destination. She saw him holding up ten fingers to the glass. Alberto was waking from his lengthy nap as his wife fiddled with her phone. It was a bumpy road that led down to the harbour and she was trying to press the right buttons on the phone, while the van rocked about noisily. "What are you doing?" Alberto rubbed his eyes, not knowing where they were or what time of day it was. He had slept longer than he had intended. Mrs Colarossi managed to key in the correct number. "I am calling Mr Bilbi to let him know that we are here." Alberto had not realised how far they had travelled since leaving the services at Chartres. "Hello, is that you Mr Bilbi, can you speak up please?"

"Hello, yes, I'm here. This is not a very good line, sorry."
"Where are you now?"
"I am in L'Aber Wrac'h at the jetty, waiting for you. How long will you be?"
"Ten minutes, so get the engine started and be ready to cast off."
Edward confirmed that he was ready and the call ended there. Fabio the relief driver was being directed to the marina which was off to the right at the next roundabout. He was partly following his satellite navigation device on the dashboard and also listening to Pietro and Mr West, who were offering helpful directions in both English and Italian. Coming up on the right hand side there was a large sign, 'L'Aber Wrac'h Marina – Landeda, Bretagne' and shortly after they could see the lines of boats tied up at the pontoon jetties. Both drivers had been present when the cargo was collected from the yacht 'Moutine', so finding the berth was straightforward for them. "There she is! Over to the left."

Fabio stopped the van close to the vessel's mooring lines and they all got out to stretch their legs after the long drive. Mrs Colarossi was giving orders as she always did, making sure that everyone had something to do. "Go and find Mr Bilbi and bring him out here!" Mr West boarded the yacht and disappeared inside the cabin below deck. The group were approached by a man wearing a Breton cap who proceeded to wave a piece of paper under the nose of Mrs Colarossi and then began demanding that someone must pay the overdue fees for the berth. She took the list of charges from the man and examined the amounts. The first thing that was immediately obvious to her was that 'Moutine' had not moved from this jetty during the period of time from when they had set off for Italy, up to the present day. Mrs Colarossi was just beginning to appreciate that this was odd, when Mr West strolled back across the wooden ramp. He wasn't in any hurry to declare his findings. "Well….where is Mr Bilbi?" Shaking his head slowly, Mr West held up both hands. "He's not on the boat. There is no-one onboard." Looking around, Mrs Colarossi was thinking that Edward might have wandered off to a bar or some local café. The man in the cap was getting impatient and he continued to make his demands for payment in a stream of French expletives that were becoming ever stronger. Mrs Colarossi needed to be able to think properly about the ensuing passage to England so she dismissed the man in the cap swiftly. Using her best French, she asked him to wait a moment and that she would accompany him to his office to make the payment. Taking Mr West to one side, and out of earshot of the Frenchman, she suggested that the empty casket could be taken out of the van and transferred to the yacht while she was distracting the manager of the marina. "Don't let anyone see Alberto go aboard, and talk to the drivers for me." Saying this she ushered the manager away from the jetty, following him to the administration building further along the harbour.

Using her credit card to settle the outstanding bill, Mrs Colarossi satisfied the manager of the marina that there were no unusual circumstances surrounding the vessel and she also assured him that they would be leaving almost immediately to cross the Channel. Thanking him for the use of his facilities, she made a hasty retreat from his office and returned to the jetty. No sooner had she stepped onto the ramp in order to go onboard the yacht than one of the drivers came over to talk to her. It was Pietro and he had been asked to make a request on behalf of the other driver. "Excuse me Mrs Colarossi, but Fabio has something he wishes to discuss with you please." She had no idea what the driver might want, but she didn't mind delaying their departure for a few minutes if the man wanted to talk to her. "Where is Fabio?" Pietro led her over to where the van was parked. He was sitting at the wheel waiting. Mrs Colarossi got in at the passenger side and asked Fabio what he wanted. "I am sorry to put this to you at the last minute because I understand that you have made your arrangements. I would like to travel to England with your crew if it is possible? I have some sailing experience and I can help Mr Bandini with the difficult part of the passage. What do you say?" He seemed to be genuine and she could see the advantage of having an experienced sailor to give Alberto some support. Mrs Colarossi was on the point of making a decision when Fabio went on to mention a further skill of his that was potentially very useful to her. "Signor West has told me that you and your husband have a Ferrari in England." He produced a card from his wallet and handed it to her. "I am qualified Ferrari engineer and I can fix your car if it has any problems. I can do this service for some small payment, only to cover my hotel room in England, please?" Fabio looked at her with puppy dog eyes and waited for her answer. How could she refuse? She thought about her Ferrari mechanic in Cornwall, Giuseppe. She knew he was getting near to retirement age and that he wasn't always well. Perhaps this man Fabio could be of some use to her? Handing him back his card, she held out her hand. They shook hands and Fabio thanked her. "Grazie mille, Signora Colarossi."

"Prego, Fabio."

The slight change of arrangements was explained to Pietro, and he would have to drive the empty van back to Milan, which he could do at his leisure as there would be no need to keep to a deadline. Mrs Colarossi brought the other driver onboard the yacht with her, after bidding farewell to Pietro and thanking him for all his good work. As the van left the marina, Fabio was sitting with the others around the cabin table below deck. Alberto and Mr West listened as Mrs Colarossi introduced Fabio as the fourth member of the crew. "We seem to have lost Mr Bilbi and as we all know, he was the experienced crew member and skipper. However, we do now have my husband Alberto who also has much experience in sailing this yacht, and Fabio tells me that he has sailed before. My friend Anthony can do everything that a sailor needs to do, and he only needs a little instruction, that is all." She did not talk about Fabio's claim to be a Ferrari mechanic, that could wait until later. It was too early for Mr West or Alberto to decide if they could trust this man Fabio, he would have to prove himself during the passage.

The four of them sat at the table with coffee and biscotti, discussing the timing of their forthcoming Channel crossing. It was by then mid-afternoon and Alberto announced that it would be advisable to go to sea on the next low tide, when all the more dangerous rocks were visible and also this would allow them to leave the harbour before darkness falls. Mrs Colarossi felt that Alberto was the most suitable crew member to assume the role of skipper, taking into account his familiarity with the vessel and his knowledge of navigation. This proposal was approved by Mr West and Fabio and everyone agreed that Alberto was indeed the obvious choice for this position of great responsibility. All that remained to be done was to plot the course to Cornwall and establish a rota for sleeping. Mrs Colarossi volunteered to act as ship's cook and there would always be three of the crew on deck, with one sleeping. They would be making for the Helford River and seeking an anchorage there. Alberto went up on deck to check on things. He hadn't been aboard 'Moutine' for what seemed quite a long time, so it was important for him to make sure that everything was as he remembered it. The twin fuel dials were showing more than half full for both of the diesel tanks, the battery voltages were all reading normal and the water tanks were also well up to capacity. Alberto walked along the side deck and stood on the foredeck, looking out over the bow, crouching down to examine ropes and cleats. He continued his tour of inspection along the other side deck, returning to the cockpit where he looked up at the forward masthead and also the mizzen masthead. All sails were furled and tied, there were large fenders hanging over the sides of the hull, the red ensign fluttered from the flagstaff at the stern and the tiller gently swayed from side to side as she bobbed on the water. He went below to check the navigation area of the cabin, sitting at the chart table and familiarising himself with the switches and screens. Alberto asserted himself as skipper of his vessel by sending his wife and Fabio off to get provisions, while he and Mr West were staying onboard to make ready to set sail. His wife would know what to buy from the grocery store at the marina and she had the all important credit card to settle the bill. Meanwhile, Alberto was more comfortable with Mr West to assist him with preparing 'Moutine' for her next voyage, as the driver Fabio was as yet of unknown character.

After helping Mrs Colarossi to gather provisions at the grocery store, Fabio made a visit to the conveniences while she was talking to the store assistant. The text message that he was sending this time was even longer and more detailed than the previous one. He went back into the store and carried some of the boxes of food and drink as they returned to the yacht. Fabio was asked to join Alberto and Mr West on deck, where he was given basic instructions in handling the sails and rigging of 'Moutine' and Mrs Colarossi was busy in the cabin, stowing away provisions. She fixed up a simple meal around teatime that was to give them a head start because later it would be mainly hot soup and bread rolls, with biscuits and coffee or tea as they sailed through the night. Whereas most of the outward passage had been covered in daylight, this return trip was to be mostly overnight sailing and they hoped to arrive off the coast of Cornwall by ten o'clock the following morning if all went well. The three men came down to eat the meal that Mrs Colarossi had set out on the table for them. "What type of boats have you sailed Fabio?" Alberto wanted to get to know more about their new crew member. "I started with small sailing dinghies when I was young, and later I moved up to catamarans. A friend of mine was a member of a club on Lake Garda, which is not far from where I live in Verona. He invited me to join the same club and I bought a catamaran for myself. We did some racing at weekends which was single handed sailing in eighteen foot cats, so nearly five and a half metres." Fabio was being watched by Mrs Colarossi and also Mr West was taking an interest in him as a fellow crew member. Then it was Fabio's turn to ask the questions, and he did ask a lot of questions within a short space of time. He wanted to know where they were making for and how long the passage was expected to take them, who would take over the navigation when the skipper was sleeping, which members of the crew were better at steering the vessel and who was better at setting the sails. He asked about keeping watch at night and what precautions did they have in place if they were to encounter fog or heavy weather. All of these were reasonable questions of course but Mrs Colarossi in particular noticed the way Fabio was a little over inquisitive somehow. It was just a feeling she had, as she observed his manner. As the meal was finished, Fabio asked Alberto if he could see the charts. Standing next to her husband at the chart table, Fabio was asking more questions about the various instruments and screens, some of which were oddly precise questions in a technical way, she thought. Perhaps she was just being over sensitive and it was not at all unreasonable for the man to ask about these matters, given that one of the crew would have to stand in for Alberto during some stages of the channel crossing. Neither Mr West nor Mrs Colarossi were sufficiently competent to manage some of the aspects of sailing the yacht, which had been Edward Bilbi's responsibility and were now Alberto Bandini's.

Chapter Twelve – Compromising

Switching off his mobile phone, Edward looked up at the detective with anticipation. "That's it, I've carried out my part of the bargain, so where's this breakfast that you were talking about?" True to his word, D.I. Cook was feeling much more confident about the situation over in France and the chances of enticing the yacht 'Moutine' back to her home waters were much improved by that one phone call. "Alright Mr Bilbi, follow me and we can sample the delights of our canteen breakfast menu. This might be a good opportunity for you and I to have a man to man talk." Edward wasn't sure that he liked the sound of the detective's last comment.

James and Judith drove into Falmouth to pick up a few things before returning to Helford Passage. Having seen and heard what went on in the interview room at the Police station, James was interested to hear from Judith herself how exactly the experience had affected her. At first she hadn't spoken much about the interview with Edward, but later she came back to it. "You know James, the real problem that I have with Edward is that he has two very different sides to his character. If you catch him in the wrong situation at the wrong time he appears to be hard, devious and sometimes quite ruthless but at some other time and in a better place he can be friendly, warm and really quite charming in his own way." Judith was driving and James was listening as she went on to confide in him "That interview was D.I. Cook's idea, and I understand why he believed it was the most effective way to get Edward to open up, but for me it was so difficult. I assured Edward that it was a private conversation between the two of us, but all the time I was thinking it was actually an interview and the detective was recording all of it. Then at the end when Edward realised what was happening, I felt awful. He said that I had let him down. Did I James?"

"No, you didn't let him down, despite what he said. You have to remind yourself what the detective is trying to achieve. He has to find out to what extent Edward is involved in whatever is going on, and also he needs to extract more information about this Colarossi woman and her lawyer, Mr West."

"I know how difficult it must be for Mr Cook to get to the bottom of this investigation, and I do realise that this case is particularly important to him. Edward Bilbi has been a thorn in his side for too long and from what I hear this may turn out to be the detective's last big case before he is due for retirement. You see, I know Edward better than most people, and he gets caught up in dealings that are the wrong side of the law. He becomes involved with the wrong people and it seems to happen to him almost by accident. I am not making excuses for him because much of what he has done is clearly unlawful; it's just that he could be a good person if only he put his mind to it and if he ignored these distractions when they intrude into his normal life. There is always a stronger character who leads Edward astray and unfortunately it keeps happening." Judith became pensive.

"When the interview was over, did you feel that it was worthwhile, Judith?"

"Yes, I think I got through to Edward and he did divulge a lot of information that was useful to the investigation. I believed Edward when he said that he didn't know what was in the box and why they were taking it to Italy. Now that it has all fallen through, as far as Edward is concerned, he feels very foolish and rather stupid. He won't get paid for what he had to do and to rub salt into the wound he has been rearrested by the Police here in England."

James was wondering what was going to happen when the yacht returns to Cornwall and what will become of Edward?

'Moutine' was ready to go to sea. She looked every inch the classic yacht, tied up at the jetty. Alberto was supervising his crew, standing at the helm as Mr West moved forward to be ready at the mast and Fabio was amidships to deal with hoisting the mizzen sail. From where he was positioned, Fabio could also assist Mr West with the hoisting of the mainsail. Mrs Colarossi sat in the cockpit waiting to take over the helm from her husband when he needed to go below and check the navigation screens. Alberto let go the ropes that led back onboard from the post on the jetty. He increased the speed of the engine a little and selected the gear to go astern. The yacht moved away from the jetty slowly and once clear of other vessels, Alberto pushed the tiller away from him, steering gently in a wide arc. He then selected forward gear and brought her round to a course that was midway between two rock formations. There was a concrete post on the rocks to the port side of 'Moutine' and this was painted green at the top. When they had entered the harbour previously the green marker had been kept to starboard, with the red marker on the port side so it was now the opposite way round to leave the harbour. Holding a course of west-north-west, Alberto set the speed at four knots and asked his wife to take the helm. "Keep her on a straight course, which you can see on the compass there, WNW and stay away from all those rocks on the starboard side. There are lots of them, but we are at low tide so they are more visible." He watched her holding the tiller firmly and when he was satisfied that she was keeping a good lookout he went below to the chart table. This only took him around ten minutes to plot a course that would put them on a bearing of north-west for most of the channel crossing. As before, they would need to approach the shipping lanes at right angles in order to pass through them safely. Alberto picked up an accurate weather forecast to establish the wind strength and the wind direction, which he scribbled down on a sheet of paper and with this information to hand he went up on deck to organise the sail plan. Mrs Colarossi was relieved of her duties at the helm and Alberto issued orders from a standing position, with tiller in hand. In his role as skipper of the vessel it was his responsibility to ensure that both crew members who were on deck had a clear understanding of what was expected of them. Alberto directed Mr West to release the mainsail on the boom and prepare to hoist the sail. Fabio was instructed to go through the same procedure with the mizzen sail on the boom. Alberto lashed the tiller so that he could attend to the mainsheet and both sails were hoisted to the mastheads. Mr West was able to feel his way along the side deck to the relative safety of the foredeck, holding onto the shrouds which were the thick steel wires that supported the mast. He had been shown how to attach the foresail to its forestay and also how he must hoist the foresail which had to be secured once it was set correctly. By the time Mr West had made his way back along to the cockpit all sails were properly set. Fabio was heaving on the halyard for the small sail at the very top of the main mast, known as the gaff sail. Basically, 'Moutine' was of a gaff-rigged ketch configuration, as opposed to a Bermuda rigged sloop which would only have one mast, whereas a vessel like 'Moutine' had two masts.

The engine stopped and the only sounds were the wind passing over the surface of the sails, and the rushing of the water against the hull of the boat. For the first time since he had fled from Italy inside a van with no windows, Alberto could experience true freedom and it was a feeling like no other. He stood facing into the wind, his head held back defiantly. The sun felt warm on his face. This was going to be the start of his new life.

Fabio was watching the skipper. He saw the man at the helm. So this was Alberto Bandini, the proud owner of his yacht. Fabio thought to himself how this man appeared to be in a world of his own. For him this was a special moment. Mr West the lawyer was speaking to Fabio and he could not fail to notice how closely the Italian was observing his compatriot. "How about some hot coffee, eh Fabio?" He turned and saw Mr West.

"Yes, I would like some coffee, thank you."

"Oh hello Anthony, is everything alright up there?" Mrs Colarossi was washing dishes at the galley sink. She certainly preferred the comfort afforded by the luxuriously fitted out cabin quarters to braving the elements up on deck, even if that meant assuming the role of cook, pot washer and tea maker. Mr West moved her wet weather clothes to one side and sat down. "Don't you get seasick down here?" She smiled as she dried the dishes.

"No not usually. I must be quite lucky in that respect. Did you want some hot drinks, or are you just taking a rest?" He said that three coffees would be much appreciated if she was offering. While the water was heating up they talked about their new crew member who had volunteered so enthusiastically. "What do you make of this man Fabio, is he all that he appears to be Anthony?"

"Well, now you ask, I did wonder about him actually. He was asking lots of questions earlier. That's fair enough, when you think he has joined a crew not knowing anyone and he doesn't know the boat either, but I got the impression that he was trying to gather more information than he really needed. Did you get that impression?"

"Yes, I did. Something that he told me before we came aboard also bothered me. He says that he is a qualified Ferrari engineer, and he talked about servicing our car if we needed his help." Mrs Colarossi turned off the gas and poured hot water into the coffee mugs, as she stirred each one. Mr West asked if she had seen any proof of the man's claims.

"He showed me a business card that looked convincing, but anyone could print that sort of card I suppose. He said that if we wished to pay him for his services this would help him with his accommodation costs while he was in England." Mr West thought about this for a moment.

"I think we should keep a close eye on Fabio during this passage and perhaps we should also try to test him somehow?" Mrs Colarossi agreed with him and she was thinking that if this man Fabio could sail a yacht, he could also fix Ferraris and he was an experienced long distance van driver, was there anything else that he was capable of doing that they were not aware of?

Carrying the coffees up the steps, using a tray that had holes in it for the mugs, Mr West was in the cockpit handing out the hot drinks. He passed one to Alberto and one to Fabio who sat down opposite Mr West. They watched the bow wave breaking up ahead and quietly drank their coffee. Alberto lashed the tiller while he took up a seated position also. "She is sailing nicely now. We must keep a good lookout for other vessels nearby, especially the bigger ships. This will be more important later when we cross the shipping lanes." Fabio mentioned the French fishing boats that could be a hazard. Alberto was well aware of such risks. "You are right it is the nets that are not always clearly marked with buoys. We do not want to go near them because it can be a serious problem if we get the fishing lines fouling the propellers or even worse, wrapped around the rudder." Although the fishing vessels would show up on the radar screen, the huge nets and the associated tackle that they use do not appear on the screen. Sometimes large expanses of netting can be drifting near the surface, when a trawler has had to cut a net that has become tangled and then left the net to float away.

Once he had finished his coffee, Alberto was ready to go below so that he could organise the watch rota, which meant the skipper would decide who was on watch and who was resting at any given time of day or night. He would make sure to spend some time at the chart table, recording weather forecasts and navigation details. Mr West was on forward lookout and Fabio was at the helm as their skipper went below deck. It was Fabio who was best able to react if there was a change in the wind direction, but both of them understood what must be done to alter the set of the sails if it became necessary. For most of the trip there would be three crew members up on deck, while the fourth crew member would be resting in their bunk below deck. Fabio could see that Mr West was further forward and he was keeping watch, so he wasn't paying any attention to what Fabio was doing. With one hand firmly on the tiller and maintaining a straight course, the Italian was using his mobile phone with his free hand. Fabio knew very well that the range of his phone would only extend to twenty miles off the coast of Britanny so he was taking this opportunity to send a text message via the French network while it was still within working range. Under normal circumstances he would have used two hands for typing the text, using one finger on each hand but in order to keep a firm grip on the tiller Fabio was forced to do his typing with one finger only. He was sure that no-one could see him and it only took him less than ten minutes to complete the message, which he sent off discreetly before the skipper returned. By the time Alberto came back on deck to speak to Fabio at the helm, the mobile phone was hidden away in Fabio's pocket.

Shouting forward to where Mr West was standing, Alberto brought him aft to the cockpit and Mrs Colarossi joined them a few minutes afterwards. The crew listened to their skipper as he went over his passage plan. Alberto issued the three of them with hand held VHF radios and it was agreed that channel twelve was to be used for all onboard communication between them, whenever direct conversation was not possible, such as in an emergency situation. He went on to outline the watch rota, the most interesting part of which was how much sleep each crew member would get, and how often!

"I have divided the four man crew into 'Red Watch' and 'Blue Watch', with each watch of two crew having four hours on watch and four hours off watch. 'Blue Watch' is Fabio and Mr West, so 'Red Watch' is my wife and myself. This is the rota for normal weather conditions and if we have bad weather conditions we need to have three crew on deck."

Fabio had a question, which came as no surprise to Mrs Colarossi and Mr West.

"When, and if, we have three of the crew on watch, do we stay on deck four hours?"

"No Fabio, we change to three hours on and three hours off, because we get more tired." Alberto had already anticipated that question, and he was pretty sure that the question would come from Fabio. Before Alberto was able to continue with his crew briefing his wife also had a query about sleeping arrangements. "Do you want both of the crew who are off watch to be taking sleep?"

"No, it is better if one is sleeping and the other one is on galley duty and navigation."

Alberto explained that he had written out a chart on a sheet of paper and this was pinned on the wall board above the navigation area down below. He assured his crew members that as skipper he would try to be on watch for as many hours as possible during night time sailing and also if they ran into bad weather. Alberto and Fabio were more experienced in the use of the electronic instruments, but all four members of the crew would need to have a basic understanding of the AIS screen during the hours of the passage where they were crossing the shipping lanes. Alberto would take over this task if they encountered fog conditions as this was a highly dangerous situation in which to navigate safely.

The crossing from the north-west coast of Britanny to the Helford Estuary was expected to take nineteen hours if all went well and according to plan. Alberto's weather forecast indicated that there was to be a south-westerly wind of fifteen knots for the first five hours or so, and from then onwards the wind was likely to drop in strength considerably towards the middle of the Channel, with some rain also likely. After passing the midway point, there was some uncertainty as to what the wind might do. The forecast suggested that the early morning period could see strengthening winds from more of a north-westerly direction. They were expecting the wind to veer north-west by dawn.

"I don't want to see any of the crew on deck with no lifejacket, and you must clip on your lifeline when you go forward or when we have bad weather. Don't forget to attach the VHF radio to your lifejacket belt. Is that understood?" His crew immediately responded with a collective 'Yes'. As there were no further questions, and Alberto had covered all the most important points Mr West and Fabio went off watch, leaving Mrs Colarossi and the skipper to take the first four hours on watch.

Carrying the empty coffee mugs to the galley, Mr West said he was going to sit at the chart table and observe the ships that appeared on the AIS screen. Fabio was happy to get into a bunk and grab some sleep after the long drive across France and half the day up on deck. Within one hour of brisk sailing the French coastline was no longer visible. France was dipping below the horizon and that would be the last sight of land until they came upon the coast of England. Seated at the small table in the navigation area of the cabin, Mr West found the movements of shipping quite fascinating. He was reading off the names of the vessels and where they were bound for. Making notes on paper he wrote down the origin of each vessel and noted the direction in which they were heading, along with their speed in knots. The dark blue shapes were passenger vessels, the green ones were cargo ships, the red ones were tankers and the purple shapes were pleasure craft, which include yachts. Fishing boats showed up in pink and the light blue ones were tugs. Further up the screen, near the top edge Mr West could see the west to east procession of vessels that were following the Traffic Separation Scheme nearest to the French side of the Channel. It would be later, when 'Moutine' was positioned further towards the north-west that the east to west procession of vessels would appear on the screen, as they were following the TSS nearest to the English side. Viewing this array of tiny boats crawling across the illuminated panel in front of him, Mr West was absorbed in the precise detail of it all, as he would be if he had his lawyer's hat on while compiling evidence for a legal case that he was preparing to go to court. It was easy to forget that these tiny coloured shapes were actually huge oil tankers, chemical tankers, container ships and cruise liners, all moving through the murky waters of the busiest shipping lanes in the world. Some would be steaming ahead at a rate of more than thirteen knots, all through the night and in all weathers.

Having set off from L'Aber Wrac'h around mid afternoon 'Moutine ' was making good progress, and the first four hour watch for Mrs Colarossi and Alberto was easy sailing, all in daylight and hardly any shipping to worry about. The following four hours would take them into the convoys of vessels that would be crossing in front of them, passing from left to right. These ships would be heading for the French waters around Calais, Belgium, the Netherlands, Scandinavia and the northern coast of Germany. Towards the end of the second watch it would be dark and 'Moutine' might be motor sailing or even motoring by then.

Getting up from the chart table Mr West went over to the galley to heat up some canned soup, which he poured into two metal flasks ready for going on watch. He nudged Fabio who was lying in his bunk. "Come on Fabio, we have to go on watch." The heap under the sleeping bag stirred and Fabio's head appeared. His blank expression was a picture.

"What time is it, where are we?"

"Seven o'clock and we are wanted up on deck. Here, I've made us some hot soup. Wake up and let's go." Mr West was already climbing the few steps up to the companionway. Fabio followed more slowly, clutching his flask. They met up with Alberto and his wife who pointed out several ships that were close by and Alberto said that as the skipper he would only grab two hours sleep, so that he could give his full attention to the AIS screen while they were negotiating the shipping lanes. Mrs Colarossi went below and retired to a bunk for the next four hours. Mr West suggested that Fabio should man the helm, as he had slept the longest.

Going forward to his favourite place on the yacht, Mr West settled into a corner of the bow where he was sheltered from the wind by one of the foresails. He liked to sit here for his watch, flask of hot soup in his hands, looking out ahead and enjoying the droplets of spray that were thrown up from the bow wave now and then. Far out towards the horizon he could make out the shapes of some ships that were some distance away at present so there was no imminent danger. Mr West was used to sitting in a warm dry office on land, which was why this experience for him was especially gratifying. Far removed from the everyday clutter of paperwork, computers, phones and time schedules, he rather liked the freedom of the open sea. The wind on his face, huge expanses of water and sky, moved him in a way that he could not explain. It was at times like these when his thoughts were at their most clear and bright. Not just his head was cleared, but even more exhilarating was that his very soul was cleared of the meaningless trivia that accumulated during his working week. Mr West had remembered to clip on his lifeline to the guard wire that ran along the outer deck and he had also remembered to switch on his handheld VHF radio that was attached to the waist strap of his lifejacket. Fabio called him on the VHF and he asked him if all was O.K.

"Yes thanks Fabio, no problems here, over." The radios were for emergency use really but there was no harm in exchanging a few words from one end of the vessel to the other.

"Make sure your radio is fully charged and keep your lifeline clipped on at all times."

Mr West confirmed that he had taken these standard precautions and they signed off.

"Thank you Mr West, this is Fabio standing by."

For the next couple of hours Alberto and his wife were sleeping in separate bunks and the skipper had set his mobile phone alarm to vibrate silently. The phone was in the top pocket of his dungarees to wake him when he needed to move to the navigation table. Just as Alberto was rising from his short sleep and climbing out of his bunk without the need to disturb Mrs Colarossi, the wind strength was reducing considerably. He sat down at the table and studied the colourful screens. The west to east convoy of boat-shaped icons had dropped down from the upper edge of the AIS screen nearer to the centre and it became apparent to Alberto that within the next hour or so 'Moutine' was about to cross the first of the two shipping lanes at right angles. He fixed himself a sandwich and a mug of tea, preparing to monitor the AIS display for the second two hours of his off watch duty. Barely into his first sandwich Alberto was aware of footsteps descending from the companionway. Fabio had lashed the tiller while he came below to bring something to the attention of the skipper.

"Non abbiamo vento! We have no wind!"

Alberto put aside his tea and sandwiches to accompany Fabio up on deck. All sails were luffing, which indicated that the wind had indeed ceased to blow. This was not entirely unexpected at this time of day. Mr West was notified on the radio that he should take down the two foresails, Alberto attended to the mainsail himself while Fabio dealt with the mizzen sail before returning to the helm. The engines were started up once all sails were furled and tied. Mr West was making his way along the side deck and back to the cockpit to hear what the skipper had to say. Alberto checked the fuel gauges routinely.

"We shall proceed under motor power only and I am watching the AIS to get us through the shipping lane. Fabio, you can keep her on course and I will radio instructions when you need to change course or slow down. Mrs Colarossi will provide us with food when she finishes her sleep and she can relieve Mr West as soon as possible. I think it is time for Mr West to get some sleep. I can assist Fabio if it is necessary." Alberto went below, leaving Mr West and Fabio in conversation. They could see the larger vessels passing ahead of them, looming ever closer.

Staring at the screen and sipping his tea, the skipper refreshed the display to give him an accurate position in real time. Two of the cargo ships in particular were already giving him cause for concern. Many of the vessels in the shipping lane were showing speeds of seven to ten knots, some were showing twelve to fifteen knots but these two were now moving at a speed in excess of twenty knots. One he checked was named as 'Ever Logic' originating from Taiwan and this vessel was on a course of sixty degrees which was east north east, travelling at twenty point six knots. The second vessel that Alberto checked was named 'Maersk Idaho' originating from the United States and this one was showing a bearing of thirty-three degrees which was north north east, and travelling at twenty point seven knots. What was worrying Alberto slightly in relation to their present position, was that the second of these cargo vessels had not left sufficient distance between herself and the vessel further ahead. He could see that the 'Maersk Idaho' would most likely change her course and also head north north east and this would put 'Moutine in a potentially difficult situation. Alberto could direct Fabio to steer north north west on a bearing of three hundred and thirty degrees, which meant that if 'Moutine' maintained a speed of five knots they would pass astern of the leading cargo vessel. The immediate problem, following this manoeuvre would be the close proximity of the approaching cargo vessel that was advancing at more than twenty knots. Alberto had to exercise his knowledge and experience as skipper to make the right decision in terms of safety, based upon the information in front of him. He decided that it would be foolish and maybe even irresponsible to attempt such a manoeuvre, taking into account the uncertainty of this margin of error. The sun was very low on the horizon to the west and within the next hour it would be nightfall. Alberto saw this image in his mind of a container ship of three hundred metres in length and fifty thousand tons, bearing down on their sailing yacht of only a mere twelve metres in length and nineteen tons, coming out of the blazing sunset. This was not something he wished to see. He picked up his handheld radio receiver and alerted his helmsman. Fabio was instructed in no uncertain terms not to take 'Moutine' astern of the leading cargo vessel under any circumstances. Alberto made it clear to Fabio that both of these vessels directly ahead of them were steaming at a rate in excess of twenty knots and they could not expect to pass between the two ships at less than a quarter of their speed. Fabio understood that he must reduce speed and be prepared to heave to if necessary. The skipper would provide him with a safer course later.

Arising from her bunk aboard the yacht, Mrs Colarossi conducted herself in much the same manner as she would have at her mews house in Gyllyngvase. Taking her time, she changed her clothes, washed her hands and face, cleaned her teeth and slowly made her way to the main cabin area. Her husband greeted her from his seat at the chart table.

"Buonasera amore mio." Mrs Colarossi chose not to speak. Alberto was not surprised.

"Would you like to prepare some of your wonderful food for the crew?" His wife ignored his attempt at flattery and proceeded to the galley. She busied herself with the cooking of cheese and bacon crostini slices, arranged in four individual bowls with tomato sauce, pepper and mushrooms. Alberto had put on his wet weather gear and his lifejacket ready to go up on deck. He sent Fabio and Mr West below for their off watch rest period. The skipper made sure that all the crew were handed their hot food, before Mrs Colarossi made her way up the steps to join her husband on watch. She too was now kitted out in her bulky sailing clothes, much to her discomfort. Alberto checked with Fabio that he was happy with navigation duties at the chart table and Mr West climbed into his bunk at last, exhausted.

Since the change of watch, 'Moutine' had been on course to go astern of the two cargo vessels that had passed by so quickly. Alberto checked the distance and time ahead of the next group of vessels approaching from the west before he left the screens. He increased the speed of the engines and lashed the helm centrally while he ate his hot crostini. His wife was standing under cover, also eating but keeping watch at the same time. It was getting dark and most of the nearby vessels were now showing lights. The skipper took the empty bowls to the galley, pausing to flick on a panel of switches that activated the yacht's navigation lights. He exchanged a few words with Fabio, who seemed to be at ease with his new duty and then he returned to the helm. Mrs Colarossi was advised to clip on her lifeline and move a little further forward, so as to get a better view of the water that lay ahead of them. The next four hours would see them through the first of the two shipping lanes and out into the separation zone that runs between the shipping lanes. Alberto had organised his watch rota so that blue watch could take over at three o'clock in the morning, and this crew change would be carried out while 'Moutine' was in safer waters. That was the plan, at least.

Chapter Thirteen – Struggling

It was now Red Watch on duty, so Mrs Colarossi and Alberto were out on deck taking in the night sky. Distant lights of cargo ships, oil tankers and container ships making their way across the dark sea showed brightly against the surrounding gloom. There was barely any breeze at all. The skipper noticed that due to the extent of cloud cover he could not see any stars. Fabio was seated comfortably at the navigation screens and Mr West was sleeping deeply in one of the bunks. Making a few notes on paper, Fabio put together a synopsis of the weather forecast and their actual position in terms of latitude and longitude, along with distance travelled and distance to shore. He gave some thought to what might lay ahead and he decided that he must speak with the skipper. Up on deck Alberto was sitting by himself at the helm watching for any signs of change around them.

"Capitano, we have some big wind coming!"

"You mean strong wind, not big wind. It is better English my friend."

"The wind is getting bigger. Big numbers! Forecast is saying twenty-five knots and later is thirty-five knots. I think this is strong capitano, yes?" Alberto appreciated Fabio's play on words and realised that there was some preparation to consider. Reading the sheet of paper that Fabio handed him, Alberto saw that not only would the wind increase in strength by some degree but it would change direction quite significantly also. It was going to be a rough night indeed. If there was ever a time when a skipper must stand up to the plate and take full responsibility for the safety of his ship and his crew, this was it. Alberto knew he had to get them through the next shipping lane and overcome adverse weather conditions if they were going to reach their home port in England. He owed it to 'Moutine', he owed it to his wife and most of all he felt as though he owed it to his old friend, Jack Berry. The tragic loss of one of his crew all those years ago had not affected Alberto in the same way as it had affected Edward Bilbi, but he wasn't a man to forget an experience like that. This time, if the sea state was to become challenging and if they ran into a situation that was potentially life-threatening, Alberto was not going to lose any of his crew.

"Here is what we do Fabio." The skipper handed him back the sheet of notes. "You can cover the AIS screen and be prepared to come up on deck to assist if we need you. Leave Mr West to catch up on his sleep, which should give him one hour more rest. When he is ready to join us on deck you can ask him to go on watch. I want three of us out here if it gets really rough. We shall proceed through the shipping lane under motor power and no sail set."

Alberto had seen in Fabio's notes that the south-westerly wind would later veer round to a south-easterly. What this meant in real terms was that 'Moutine' would need to be on a heading of north north-west once she had cleared the shipping lane which had to be taken at right angles. Alberto realised that not only would the south-easterly wind be on the stern but also the wind would very likely be in excess of twenty-five to thirty knots. When any yacht is forced to sail downwind, this is called on a run, and if the wind then becomes so strong that all sails must be lowered this is known as being under bare poles. Every yacht will behave differently when swept downwind with much reduced control and steerage, due to larger waves than usually encountered, and the most dangerous aspect of such a situation is that the vessel will turn slightly in one direction or the other. This action places the vessel beam on to the wind and the waves, both of which have much greater force than the vessel can withstand. The result is that the boat broaches and suffers a knockdown. Equally dangerous is that if the bow of the vessel ploughs into a wave, usually when the vessel is moving faster than the waves themselves, this stops the boat and a following wave can pick up the stern, which turns the boat end over end. This is known as pitch poling and is not to be recommended! All this was going through Alberto's mind as he walked himself mentally through his intended strategy. Fabio returned to his position at the chart table and as instructed he did not disturb Mr West.

Not wanting to alarm his wife unduly, Alberto would have to make sure that she was aware of the impending change in the weather conditions, preferably before they arrived, while at the same time not scaring her with all the details. If things became extremely difficult he would have both Mr West and Fabio on watch and he might choose to send Mrs Colarossi below, where she could be more useful by monitoring the navigation instruments. Looking ahead towards the lights of the seemingly slow moving ships that were going from east to west this time, it was hard to imagine the bad weather that was predicted in the most recent forecast. The slight breeze was only picking up a little and the waves remained moderate in height. It is often said that there's a calm before the storm. This was the calm and it was inclined to lull the unsuspecting crew into a false sense of security if not taken seriously.

'Moutine's' engines enabled her to maintain a speed of five knots through the water as things were. They were close enough to the shipping lane to be able to choose a slot so the skipper got on the radio to Fabio for information and advice. Alberto listened while Fabio relayed what was showing on the screen in front of him. There was a cluster of cargo ships and two or three tankers moving right to left across their bow then there was an interval that would allow the yacht to pass ahead of the next batch of vessels.

"This group of ships ahead are moving at eight knots and the tankers are thirteen knots. Behind this group the ships following are moving at eleven knots. We can enter the open water in less than one hour capitano." Alberto thanked him and signed off. At the same moment there was a sudden shift in the wind direction. 'Moutine' swayed from side to side briefly as the wind veered across her stern. Turning his head instinctively Alberto noticed the wind pressure rising in his ears, which coincided with the change of direction. He had experienced this sort of phenomena before. Consequently the sea state was about to change also and the wave height increased proportionally. Alberto called his wife on the radio and asked her to make her way back to the cockpit. He alerted her to the fact that some rough weather was approaching but it was nothing to worry about. There were no sails to manage so the skipper and his wife remained close to the helm. Anticipating a spell of more demanding sailing, Mrs Colarossi held her husband's hand for a few brief moments as they both sensed an increased level of anxiety.

Aware that the boat was moving about much more than she had been earlier, Mr West awoke to find several objects falling to the floor in the galley area. Mrs Colarossi had not stowed away everything after the recent meal and she had overlooked a couple of plastic bowls which were now rolling around at floor level. Mr West practically fell out of his bunk, pulling on his yachting suit. He saw Fabio hunched over the chart table, writing on a pad as he periodically glanced at the AIS screen.

"It's getting a bit rough Fabio; I must get up on deck." Thrusting a sheet of paper into the hand of Mr West, having torn it from his pad, Fabio urged him to go carefully.

"We have big wind coming signor West and the capitano needs more crew!"

He wasted no time in clambering up the steps and Alberto was just about to organise the deployment of a storm sail. The skipper asked Mr West to take over the helm for him so that he could go forward. It was important to rig up a storm jib while the conditions were not too difficult. Mr West had strapped on his lifejacket before taking hold of the tiller as Alberto clipped on a safety line and edged his way along the side deck. They were about to cross the area of open water that was between the groups of advancing cargo vessels. Reaching the foredeck, the skipper was once more in control of his ship. Alberto had a head torch in place over his hat and he remembered where the second forestay was ready to move further forward into the stem of the bow. It was all coming back to him now in the hour of need. He located the storm sail inside the foredeck locker, attached the steel wire to its mounting bracket and hanked on the storm jib. Using the head torch allowed him to keep both hands free to hoist the canvas, having attached the shackle of the halyard and pulling on the rope until this small sail was correctly set. The function of the storm jib was to provide them with a certain amount of control in terms of steerage when sailing downwind, particularly if the wind was to strengthen substantially later. Alberto made his way back along the heaving side deck, taking the jib sheet with him. This was a line that fed through the specially designed deck fittings and back along the coach roof so that the sail could be managed from the forward end of the cockpit.

   Rather than direct Mr West to deploy the storm jib, the skipper had dealt with this task himself mainly because it was something that he had done before on this vessel, and also because it had to be done quickly in conditions of poor lighting. Total darkness was all around them now, with only the white, green and red navigation lights visible. At times the lights of the distant cargo ships would momentarily dip below the rolling waves and then reappear minutes after. Mrs Colarossi volunteered to go below and fetch them some flasks of hot soup and her husband manned the helm. Finding a sturdy bulkhead to lean against, Mr West was glad of something

solid to support himself while he kept a constant lookout. It began to rain lightly at first and by the time Mrs Colarossi had returned with the hot soup it was raining more heavily. She took a seat beside Alberto and steadied the tiller with one hand which helped him to grasp the flask without losing control of the helm. Mr West had been handed his flask at the companionway and he was enjoying the beef broth as he surveyed the seas ahead. The rain was coming down heavily, reducing visibility even further. Mrs Colarossi was beginning to feel scared as the wind gathered force. Alberto was the more confident of the three of them and for him it was the rush of adrenalin that would sharpen his senses for the rough ride that was to come. Before this night was out, 'Moutine' would be tested throughout the struggle against the storm and her crew would have to face whatever the elements threw at them. This was all about the battle to overcome adverse conditions. It had always been this way for sailors going to sea. The skipper was hoping to be able to keep his wife with him until they were clear of the shipping lane. Once they were out into open sea he would send her below to take over from Fabio at the chart table so that he could bring a more experienced member of the crew up on deck where he was needed if the weather deteriorated as it was expected to do. For now they were holding their own, creeping along steadily at slightly less than five knots. There was a device at the head of the main mast that was connected to a gauge on the panel that was just under the covered part of the cockpit, and this was showing over twenty knots wind speed at present. Mr West eyed the approaching navigation lights of the leading vessel as it loomed ever closer to them. He gestured to the skipper to draw his attention to the alarmingly short distance between the yacht and this much larger vessel that was bearing down on them. Alberto acknowledged Mr West's concern and picked up his VHF radio. He asked Fabio to double check the nearest ship that was approaching on their starboard side to establish collision avoidance measures, should they be necessary.
"She is COSCO Belgium, registered in Hong Kong, heading for Port Said in Egypt and her speed is now up from eleven knots to fourteen knots. This ship is three nautical miles away from us and if she keeps to this speed we will crash in twelve minutes capitano." Alberto disliked Fabio's use of the word 'crash' and more to the point a mere

twelve minutes would not see them clear of the COSCO Belgium's bow.

"Why did you not give us this information sooner, Fabio? You can see that we are on a collision course, what are you thinking?" There was no answer. Alberto switched off his handset and immediately proceeded to take evasive action. He put the throttle lever into neutral, leaving the engines running and stood with the tiller firmly grasped in his hand. The wind speed was now increasing to nearly thirty knots. All eyes were on the ship to their right, which appeared as a vast black shape in the night sky. Mrs Colarossi was sent below and Alberto insisted that Fabio came up to see this. Mr West realised how close it was going to be. He was more than a little nervous but he saw that the skipper was fully in control of the developing situation. Instructing Mr West to take over at the helm it was time for Alberto to put the engines into full astern. This brought the boat to a complete halt, with large waves slapping into the stern and the water frothing wildly as the engines fought against the flow of the strong current. Holding their breath and bracing themselves for impact, they watched the COSCO Belgium sweep past. Alberto estimated that it was only a matter of one hundred yards or so between the two vessels, which is extremely close in nautical terms. Fabio came out of the companionway hatch in time to witness this frightening spectacle. Slamming the throttle lever back into neutral, the skipper shouted to Mr West that he must hold her straight ahead. All seemed relatively predictable until the wake of the cargo vessel hit 'Moutine' on her bow. This forced the yacht over to port and into the worst position possible. She was now at the mercy of the wind and waves so the knockdown was inevitable. The crew had no time to react. Heeling right over to her starboard side, both of the masts swung violently through a full ninety degrees and the keel lifted clear of the water on the port side. The tops of the masts dipped into the water on the starboard side before 'Moutine' righted herself suddenly as the heavy ballast of the keel counter balanced the rolling motion of the yacht.

It was highly likely that the lookout aboard the cargo ship didn't see the yacht at all and even if 'Moutine' had shown up on their radar screen the captain would not have had time to alter course or slow down. Once the larger vessel had passed the stricken yacht and after the considerable wake had subsided, only then were the crew able to recover and assess the damage. Alberto was able to brace himself by placing both his feet squarely on the cockpit side lockers as the boat rolled over, which was the tried and tested method of avoiding going overboard in the event of a knockdown. He had relied upon his quick reactions and years of training to save himself from leaving the boat as the knockdown occurred. Mr West was slightly less fortunate, in that he was flung across the width of the cockpit, but luckily for him he still had his lifeline clipped onto his belt hook and as luck would have it the lifeline was clipped onto the port side guardrail. This meant that as the vessel rolled over to starboard Mr West didn't fall overboard, when the line had snapped taught at its fixed length. It was Fabio who came off worst during the whole incident. There was nothing for him to hold onto and he didn't have time to brace his feet so he was thrown forward suddenly, hitting his head on the flailing boom which had then rendered him unconscious. It was nothing short of a miracle that none of the crew ended up in the water.

   The skipper was the first of the crew to recover his senses and he saw that Mr West was safe at the end of his tether, so he went to Fabio's aid straight away. His fellow Italian was out cold and he appeared to have a cut on his forehead which was bleeding but not excessively. Alberto waited for Mr West to detach his lifeline and he left him to attend to Fabio while he went below to check on his wife. Mrs Colarossi had sensibly climbed into a starboard side bunk just prior to the incident and therefore she was wrapped in a soft duvet that had cushioned the impact. Apart from being a little dazed and confused she was uninjured. Her husband asked her to follow him up on deck because he wanted her to tend to Fabio, allowing the skipper to get back to the business of tackling the storm.

   It was not safe to put up any sail as the wind continued to increase in strength and it was still coming from the south east. Alberto eased the throttle lever forward but not too much, and 'Moutine' gathered momentum, almost surfing the foamy white crests of the waves that were sweeping under the stern of the yacht. His next priority as skipper would be to ensure that his vessel was less likely to be pitch poled as a result of her being over-whelmed by the following seas. There were two ways of doing this. One proven method involved trailing warps astern of the yacht, which in layman's language means having anywhere between three and six very long ropes attached securely to the stern of the boat, and these would break up the wave pattern immediately astern of her. The longer and heavier the ropes were the better. Another time honoured method of achieving the same result was to have something like a plastic milk crate or a large strong bucket trailing behind the vessel, which again would be lashed onto the stern rail. The correct nautical term for such a hastily rigged device was a drogue, and this was in fact very similar to the smaller of two parachutes used to slow down a jet aircraft as it is landing on an aircraft carrier at sea. Alberto had a word with Mr West to explain what must be done.

"We have to wait for Fabio to come round, and then I need you to help me rig up some trailing ropes over the stern. If we don't do this soon, there is a risk that she could roll over, end to end. That would be more serious than the knockdown we just had." Mr West understood and he remained with the injured Italian while the skipper manned the helm. It would take two of them to set up the trailing warps, and obviously Fabio was not in a fit state to assist them. By lashing the tiller centrally this would free up two of the crew to handle the ropes. Mrs Colarossi was once more sent below to fix up a bunk for Fabio and both Mr West and Alberto could carry him down into the cabin.

From under the blanket there was movement, and a pitiful moaning sound. Realising he was regaining consciousness; they picked up Fabio and swiftly transferred him to the cabin below decks. It wasn't pretty but with everything going on around them and the worsening weather conditions there was no time to lose. With the semi-conscious Fabio bundled into one of the bunks it was a case of all hands on deck for the next couple of hours. Mrs Colarossi was on lookout duty and the two men set about hauling ropes out of the large locker that was serving as a cargo hold for the empty coffin. Alberto glanced at the box in which he had crossed the border from Italy to France and he hoped that was the only time he would have to go in there. Mr West followed the skipper's instructions as together they tied on each of four heavy ropes which were then uncoiled and dropped into the water below the stern. Instantly these trailing warps extended to their full length, barely visible in the darkness and only inches under the surface of the inky black water. 'Moutine' was clear of the shipping lanes, the storm jib was doing its job of keeping the yacht on a straight course and the lengths of rope trailed astern of her. Alberto was at the helm, tiller in hand while Mrs Colarossi and Mr West clung onto the stainless steel rails of the pushpit that surrounded the aft section of the cockpit. A reading of thirty-five point two knots had registered on the wind speed display at the height of the storm. The rain was drenching the crew from behind them, blown furiously at an angle of over forty-five degrees. After one hour of ploughing through the steep waves Alberto suggested to his wife that she might as well return to the cabin, where she could see to it that Fabio got some hot food and drink. She agreed to bring up some more beef broth and bread for both of the men on watch.

Moving around the cabin interior was not easy in such a sea state. Mrs Colarossi was doing her best to organise coffee, soup and bread and Fabio was by now sitting up and talking. She sorted out flasks and bread for Alberto and Mr West before spending some time with Fabio. He had managed to climb out of the bunk, helped by Mrs Colarossi and he wedged himself into a seat at the table near to the galley, where she joined him for a tasty meal.

"Your cooking is excellent signora. Thank you. Your husband is a lucky man!."

"How is your head Fabio? You will be wanted up on deck as soon as you are fit."

"Give me a short time after this food and I will help the capitano and signor West."

They talked a little about the knockdown and how bad the storm was turning out to be, mostly in Italian. Mrs Colarossi listened to Fabio as he admitted to feeling responsible for causing a near collision with the cargo ship. He realised that Alberto must be angry with him. She advised him to get on with what had to be done and keep out of his way for awhile.

'Moutine' was holding a straight course quite nicely and the wind was gradually reducing in strength. By four o'clock in the morning there could be seen the first hint of light in the predominantly dark sky. Alberto was exhausted but he decided to wait for the calmer conditions that would inevitably follow the storm, probably within the next hour.

"The sun will be coming up when this wind drops. We can all take a rest. I think it is done." Alberto saw Fabio coming up from the companionway as he said this. Letting go of the tiller, the skipper indicated with a motion of his head that Fabio should take over the helm. Alberto walked past him and went below without saying a word. Mr West also headed for the cabin, giving Fabio a pat on the shoulder as he followed the skipper. Alone at the helm, Fabio was left to contemplate his previous actions in solitude.

Falling into his bunk, Alberto was asleep the minute he threw a blanket over himself. He had done his job as skipper and taken his crew safely through some pretty extreme weather. Apart from Fabio's head injury, no-one went overboard and his ship was intact. They had avoided a direct collision with the cargo ship 'COSCO Belgium', which had led to a knockdown and they had endured a thirty-five knots gale for several hours without incident. Now it was the right moment to consolidate and to prepare for the last leg of the passage. Mr West and Mrs Colarossi were sitting at the table having coffee and he was asking her if she was looking forward to going home. She sighed as she seemed to be thinking about that for the first time. Speaking in a hushed voice she answered him.
"It will not be the same Anthony, now that my husband is coming back home with me. You must understand that I have to be the good wife. I hope that it will not be difficult for you. We have to be discreet Anthony." Staring down at his hands, Mr West had given this some thought already.
"Don't worry Angelina, I do understand. Of course you must return to your marriage and your life at home. I will be there for you when you need a lawyer."
"You are more than a lawyer to me Anthony….. You know that."
Neither Alberto nor Fabio heard these whispered words, and they did not see Mrs Colarossi reach out her hand across the table to gently touch the hand of Mr West.

It was nearly two hours later when the skipper awoke from his well earned rest. He cast aside his blanket and immediately went up on deck to speak to Fabio. Alberto looked out at a surprisingly calm sea state, as he gazed in wonder at the sunrise. Taking in a deep breath of fresh air and stretching his aching arms he suggested to Fabio that he should lash the tiller and he could join them down below. The early morning sky was a blaze of colour.
"That is why we go sailing, eh Fabio?"
"Si capitano, it is worth the pain."
He followed Alberto down the steps and the crew gathered around the table for an early breakfast. Mrs Colarossi presented them with a

splendid array of freshly prepared hot food and everyone was relaxed in conversation after the stressful night that had passed. There was no-one on deck, the engines were set at a low speed and 'Moutine' was almost at a standstill. Alberto issued his proposed schedule for the next three to four hours.

"Thanks to my wife we have this beautiful breakfast and before lunchtime we will have sight of land. It will be good to see England again. We should have a fair wind to hoist the sails so let us raise our glasses and drink to our arrival in Cornwall."

"To Cornwall!"

For this breakfast time toast it was glasses of orange juice but later, on the Helford River it would be glasses of champagne to give thanks for a safe return. On the extensive list of provisions that had been loaded aboard the yacht prior to their departure from Gweek at the head of the river, Mrs Colarossi had made sure that there was a bottle of fine champagne in the fridge for just this special occasion.

The skipper declared that he and his wife would stand the last watch so that Fabio and Mr West could rest at their leisure, which could be above or below deck as they wished. It was Mr West who grabbed this opportunity to dive into a soft bunk as he hadn't slept since before the bad weather had started. Fabio chose to sit at the navigation table despite his previous poor record. He poured himself a second glass of orange juice and took some aspirin for a slight headache. Sitting back in the comfortable seat he rested while he waited for Mr West to fall asleep. Almost one hour later Fabio was using his mobile phone, when he discovered that he had picked up a weak signal from the English coast. He began sending text messages in Italian to a number that he had used before. Fabio's covert messages were mostly intended to communicate the position of the yacht and their estimated time of arrival at the Helford Estuary. In front of him were the instruments that provided him with all the information that he could possibly want. He was able to supply very accurate data that revealed exactly where the yacht was at that precise moment and also where she would be located at the end of her cross channel passage. Fabio could see the companionway hatch from where he was sitting, and also Mr West's bunk. Later he was able to send further text messages to provide up to date information as the signal got stronger.

Between them, Alberto and Mrs Colarossi hoisted all three sails and they were enjoying sailing 'Moutine' at her best. It was almost as though she could sense the sights and smells of the river that was her home port. They were simply flying along at a respectable six and a half knots. The bow wave was spectacular and Mrs Colarossi stood with her sunglasses on, savouring every wonderful moment. She held onto a stanchion tightly and glanced back at where Alberto was also on his feet, steering their pride and joy towards the coast of Cornwall. This was the other extreme to motoring through the night storm. Since the wind had picked up earlier it was now blowing briskly from the north-west and 'Moutine' was on a port tack, with all sails out to starboard which was perfect. They were on course for the Helford Estuary and apart from a few ships at anchor in Falmouth Bay there were only a handful of yachts sailing close to the coastline, their crisp white sails set against the ultramarine skies. Alberto and his wife were extremely happy. It doesn't get much better than this.

Chapter Fourteen – Anchoring

From an office at the Gendarmerie in Brest, the French detective Maurice had set up a surveillance unit at the marina in L'Aber Wrac'h. It was to be a lengthy operation and somewhat boring for his team of officers because there wasn't any information to give them even an approximate date when the suspects Colarossi and West might arrive to board their yacht. Maurice had arranged with the manager of the marina for his officers to make use of an old lookout tower which was ideal for this operation. The structure was nothing more than a shed on sticks really. By climbing carefully up an old ladder that was bolted onto one of the four legs, two officers were able to get a good view of the harbour and all of the vessels that were tied up on the jetties. The marina manager was asked to notify the officers who were on lookout duty when a vehicle approached the yacht known as 'Moutine', which he would do by calling them on a mobile phone. Also, by requesting payment for the yacht's pontoon berth fees the manager could obtain a close look at the people who were about to board the vessel, as well as identifying the vehicle in which they had arrived. Dotted around the marina there were CCTV cameras and the officers in the old lookout tower would be using binoculars and a camera with a long range lens to gather evidence. Maurice hoped to intercept the vehicle as it was leaving the marina exit, and after the crew of the yacht had boarded the vessel. Once it was all in place it was just a matter of waiting. Officers in teams of two sat in the surveillance post, high above the forecourt outside the office building and they changed shifts every six hours, so over the twenty-four hour period it was covered by four teams. Maurice was confident that the suspects would return to this harbour, having arranged for Edward Bilbi to be ready and waiting with the vessel that was to take them back across the English Channel.

Thanks to D.I. Cook's detailed investigation that was ongoing, the Police on the French side could organise their observation tactics most effectively. The detective in Falmouth had instructed Maurice to allow the yacht and its crew to leave France, and it was most important for his officers to remain concealed throughout the operation. The crew of the yacht 'Moutine' must not have the slightest suspicion that they were being observed as they prepared to embark on their passage to England.

D.I. Cook had believed all along that this investigation would turn out to be much more than merely a chance meeting between Edward Bilbi and Mrs Colarossi, with some sort of link involving Anthony West who had an interest in both parties as their lawyer. Each piece of evidence, as it emerged during the investigation would reinforce the detective's strongest suspicions that there was a lot more to this case than anyone realised. So many aspects of the case remained unclear and there were so many unanswered questions that were still hanging in the air. The whole significance of the yacht that was shortly to return to Cornwall mystified the detective, the casket and it's unknown contents was also nagging away at his trained detective mind, the purpose of the trip to France by sea and the road trip to Italy was tantalisingly out of reach to him. At this stage of the investigation D.I. Cook was finding it increasingly difficult to justify the use of costly Police resources and his demands to utilise manpower on both sides of the Channel were met with some degree of doubt on the part of his superiors in Truro, who were wanting to see some actual results. D.I. Cook was putting forward a sound and very convincing case for his efforts but he could sense that those in authority did not have the same belief in the successful conclusion of the detective's swansong as he had.

When the day came that heralded the arrival of a plain white van entering the gates of the marina at L'Aber Wrac'h, there was a certain amount of excitement among the team of officers that were working for Maurice the French detective. It was the same type of vehicle as the one that had previously transported the cargo from the waiting yacht, in as much as it was a white Mercedes Sprinter van, except this one had different registration plates. These vans were common enough throughout France and the rest of Europe but it soon became apparent that this particular vehicle was making directly for the jetty where 'Moutine' was tied up at the pontoon. Seeing the van on his CCTV screen, the manager of the marina alerted the officers who were on duty at the top of the lookout tower and he watched as the van drove slowly onto the ramp of the jetty that was under surveillance. It was important for the manager to stay in his office and the officers on lookout told him to wait until the occupants of the van approached him. One of the officers had his camera trained on the suspect vehicle as it parked close to the yacht. They watched as three people got out of the van, followed by two more people. From out of the driver's cab three of the people stepped out and a side door was slid open to allow two more people to get out. One of the two who had been inside the rear compartment was a woman and the rest were all male persons. The officers then observed one of the men stepping onboard the vessel and at this point they suggested that the manager should approach the group with his bill of payment. This had been discussed in advance with the surveillance team and it was intended as a legitimate means of establishing close contact with the members of the group without arousing suspicion. Walking towards the lady of the group, the manager held out his invoice and then proceeded to put on a show of demanding payment for his outstanding services. Several of the men in the group were looking around at nearby boats and generally taking in their surroundings. One of them was seen to look up at the tower, but he had to shield his eyes from the sun which was coming from behind and above the structure at the top of the supporting legs. This was very fortunate for the two masked officers who were crouching behind the wooden panels of their lookout post and taking photographs of the events unfolding beneath them. The man who had gone aboard the yacht shortly before, came back out and spoke to the woman. After asking the manager to wait for a moment, the lady accompanied him to the marina office building. It was while the manager and the lady were inside the administration block that the officers witnessed some activity near to the van. Two of the men opened the rear doors of the van and lifted out a wooden casket that did not appear to be at all heavy because of the way they seemed to be carrying it so effortlessly. Continuing to watch and photograph the swift movement of the cargo, the officers recorded the transfer of the casket from the van to the yacht. This was done by the time the woman walked out of the manager's office. She spoke to one of the men from the van and after they had purchased provisions for their forthcoming trip the man walked away to the toilet block on his own.

Eventually, four of the five people went aboard the yacht and one man reversed the van away from the jetty. From their position at the top of the lookout tower the officers made contact with a second team who were standing by at the exit gate. When both teams of officers were satisfied that the three men and the woman were staying onboard the vessel at the jetty, they boxed in the van that was leaving by placing unmarked Police vehicles in front of it and also immediately behind it. This was essentially the end of Pietro's trip to Italy.... He was going nowhere anytime soon.

Later that same day of course, 'Moutine' was seen leaving the harbour, and bound for England. With her departure confirmed the work of the surveillance team was completed and Maurice was able to pass on the good news to his counterpart in Falmouth. His team had gathered a great deal of evidence, particularly in the form of detailed photographs and one of the drivers of the van used to transport the as yet unidentified cargo was now in custody on the French side. The driver was taken to the Gendarmerie in Brest where he was to be questioned further and the vehicle was driven to a specialist Police workshop to be given a thorough forensic examination.

D.I. Cook was now permitted to ramp up the investigation on the English side and he was very grateful to Maurice for all the excellent Police work that had been carried out so far, which extended to the tracking of the van's movements, not only across France but also into Italy. It was at first thought that the same van had been used to move the cargo across the continent and then used to bring back some other cargo in the same container, only with different registration plates but this would be proven otherwise as the forensics progressed. The detective drove to the Police headquarters in Truro and he attended a meeting with his superior officers in order to determine how the investigation would be co-ordinated from there on.

Driving back to Falmouth from headquarters, the detective was thinking about this one case. The majority of the files that came into his in tray, usually sat there for a few weeks and following a series of routine inquiries each case would be closed. His officers could deal with those sorts of minor investigations. None of them were murders or even serious crimes; they were not usually complicated or particularly challenging for a detective of D.I. Cook's experience. However, this one was different. This one would stay with him long after he had retired from the force. Bilbi was in custody again for the second time and the detective was nearly ready to apprehend the other two suspects in a case that had been full of twists and turns. It wasn't over yet. D.I. Cook wasn't going to let go of the bone until he found out what was inside that box when it left England, where the box was taken, why the box was being brought back to England, what the Colarossi woman was up to, where does West the lawyer fit into all of this and who else might be involved? Where were they going to drop anchor this time? The detective realised, as he pulled into the Police station compound, that there was actually more that he had not yet uncovered than he had already exposed.

On the outskirts of Brest at a workshop where Police technicians were conducting their detailed examination of the white Mercedes van, a number of interesting facts were to be discovered. All the routine checks for any evidence of narcotics had proven negative, and they had not found any weapons or documents. Further examination revealed something slightly odd about the vehicle. The technicians noticed a small hole on the underside of the roof in the cargo area of the van, and just inside this hole there were some coloured wires that appeared to have been cut. Thinking that perhaps an extra interior light had been fitted which may have been removed at some stage, they did not give it too much attention, but afterwards when they found there was an identical hole in the centre of the instrument panel at the front of the vehicle they grew more suspicious. As the forensic examination progressed to the driver's cab they realised what these holes were for. Thrown into the storage bins on the dashboard there were two cameras, also with wires that had been cut through. One of the Police technicians picked up one of these cameras using his latex gloved hand and placed it in a clear plastic bag which was then labelled for reference. It was a camera of the type that would be found inside the rooms of properties to provide security surveillance, and this one included a discreet audio microphone. Outside the vehicle the registration plates were not the same as the ones previously detected during the pursuit of the van across northern France. Either the plates had been changed; and the same van was used to make both the outward journey and the return trip, or they were looking at two different vans entirely. Once the vehicle had been analysed for fingerprints and DNA the forensics were complete. Maurice received the results of the vehicle examination in his office at the Gendarmerie in Brest and he was ready to interview the Italian driver they had arrested leaving the marina at the wheel of the suspect van. Pietro was brought to an interview room where he was shown to a chair opposite the French detective.

"Now, Monsieur Pietro it would seem that you have a lot of questions to answer. This does not have to be a long interview if you give me all the right answers."

"You can call me signor Pietro Di Napoli if you please." The driver disliked being addressed as 'Monsieur Pietro' by the stupid French policeman.

"Pardon monsieur, I will call you signor Napoli if that is what you wish?"

"Di Napoli."

Maurice accepted the correction offered to him and got on with the interview. He began by questioning the driver about the vehicle. Maurice declared that earlier his team of forensic experts had carried out a thorough search of that vehicle and that they had found several items of interest. The detective needed to know what part this man had played in the process of transporting people and cargo from the small harbour in Bretagne to Italy.

"Signor Di Napoli, is it true that you were hired to drive this white Mercedes van? I am showing signor Di Napoli a photograph of the vehicle for the recording machine."

"Yes, I was hired to drive the van in the picture." Pietro recognised that it was not just any white Mercedes van because he could see himself standing beside the vehicle in the picture. He assumed that the French police must have taken the photograph by following them somewhere in northern France. Maurice asked Pietro who had hired him and why.

"The lady who paid me to drive the van is signora Colarossi. I was told to pick up a cargo and two people from L'Aber Wrac'h and take them to Desenzano at Lago di Garda. That is all I know." Pietro had already decided in his own head that he would try to convince the detective that he was just a driver, and he didn't know anything about the people or the cargo. He was quite happy to answer any questions regarding the job that he was paid to do and the names of any people that he was aware of.

"Who are the two people?"

"Signora Colarossi, and signor West."

"I am thinking that you would have a second driver to cover the distance of your trip, or did you have a lot of stops for sleep?" Of course, the detective knew full well that the van made very few stops along the route because his men had tracked it all the way to Chamonix and many photographs had been taken of all four people that were in the van.

"There was a second driver yes. He was called Fabio and he was Italian like me, but I was not told his family name. I have not worked with him before this job."

"Tell me about the cargo."

"One box."

"What kind of box? What was in the box?"

"It was a bara, I think you say cercueil. Coffin in English."

"Do you know who was in the box?"

Pietro explained that he did not ask about the dead person. He did not want to know and he didn't really like the idea of carrying the casket anyway. It was just another collection and delivery job so he did what he was being paid to do without asking any questions.

"They gave you a collection point at the marina which was a numbered jetty, so what was the name of the boat?"

"I think the boat was called 'Moutine', which I remember because it sounds French."

"Were you told where the boat had come from?"

"From England, but they did not say where in England."

"So everybody on this boat got into your van?"

"No, they told me that one man was staying on the boat and I don't know his name."

Maurice wanted to find out more about the route that was taken, especially the part of the route that entered Italy. The detective had received a file from the Italian police, which did contain a lot of information about the vehicle's movements but it had to be said, was not particularly well written. Much of what happened was lost in translation as the saying goes.

"Where did you cross the border from France into Italy?"

"I was told to use the Mont Blanc tunnel so we crossed at Chamonix. The other driver, Fabio was too scared to go through the tunnel and he stayed in Chamonix."

"Why was he scared, did he tell you?"

"Fabio told signora Colarossi that he was in the tunnel fire of 1999 and the fear of the tunnel has stayed with him to this day. He agreed to join us when we crossed back to the hotel in Chamonix."

"I understand that three of you continued to drive through the north of Italy, and your next destination was to be Desenzano, is that correct?"

"Yes, but we did have to stop at the services close to Milan."

"Why did you stop there?"

"We did not have the address for the delivery."

"Wait a minute, you are telling me that you have a cargo with the collection and delivery papers, and you do not have the delivery address? That is not normal procedure is it?"

Pietro was thinking carefully for a moment before answering. He was never told why the address in Desenzano was only to be given to them when they reached the outskirts of the city of Milan, although this became very obvious later on. There was the whole episode of the switching of vans, the transfer of the cargo and ultimately the meeting with the DHL vans at Sirmione. This was the point during the interview where it was absolutely crucial for Pietro to get his story right. If he was going to walk away from this a free man the facts would have to add up as far as the French police were concerned.

"I really have no idea what happened about the address, but I guessed that maybe the man or woman in the box must be important and perhaps that is why they wanted the delivery address to be kept secret up to the last few miles before we got there. I am only guessing. I mean, what if the person in the box was in the Mafia?" Pietro laughed and he pretended that he was only joking. Which he was, actually.

"How were you given the address?"

"It was given to signora Colarossi at the Auchan Cesano hypermarket on her mobile phone and they passed it to me for the satellite navigation. The address was very difficult to find and I could not use the satnav when we got close."

"I want you to give me this address where you delivered the cargo." Maurice had his pen poised for the answer.

"I cannot give you this address, I am sorry. It was a square with many garages, and some workshops, you know like storage places. I did not see any names on the outside of the buildings. I can't remember what the square was called. The streets were very narrow and it was difficult to get our big van through the traffic."

Maurice knew that the driver was telling the truth about the hypermarket car park near to Milan because his men had followed the van there, and they had obtained photographic evidence from that location. So far, everything that this man Pietro Di Napoli had told him during the interview matched their surveillance evidence precisely. The detective was beginning to accept that the driver was telling the truth.

"Alright, what happened when you arrived at the secret address? You do remember that part?"

"Yes, but it was very quick. There was a man in dark clothes and he was wearing a hat and scarf. The scarf was covering his face. He opened some big double doors, I drive the van inside the building and we stop. Some more men open our doors at the back and take out the box and they changed the number plates on our van. That's it."

"What do you mean, that's it? What happened next?"

"They take the box away, then load a different box into our van, close our doors, bang on the side of my van and we go. Finito."

Maurice stared across the table at the Italian driver. The box was delivered, nobody saw what was in the box, nobody got paid and nobody got hurt. Happy ending. What?

"Hold on, you are saying that these men loaded a box into your van. What was in the second box, do you know?"

"The box they put in our van was the same as the one they take out."

"Yes, but what was inside the box that you are shipping to England? Come on, this is important!"

"Empty box."

"What?"

"I am sure the box was empty because Fabio and me lifted the box onto the boat at the jetty in the marina, and it had no weight."

Maurice did not know what to make of Pietro's story, which was beginning to make no sense and the more the Italian talked, the less credible was his account of what happened. Having said that, the officers who were in the lookout tower at the marina had witnessed the loading of the casket onto the yacht, and it was obvious to them that the casket was not at all heavy, because of the way the two drivers had carried it. The detective switched off the recording machine and got to his feet. An officer who had been standing near to the door of the room was told to escort the driver to a secure cell.

172

Maurice went off to get some lunch. He was no nearer to finding out what this was all about, and he did not have sufficient new information that would help his colleague over in England.

Climbing out of his bunk, Mr West spoke briefly to Fabio who was sitting at the chart table in the far corner of the cabin. He bid him good morning and went up the steps to go on deck. What a sight met him there. The green hillside fields of Cornwall were now very close and the entrance to the Helford River was just off the starboard bow. He saw Alberto at the helm and Mrs Colarossi was pointing excitedly at the shoreline.

"We are nearly home now!" Mr West was so relieved to see the coast of Cornwall after being away for so long. Already he was thinking of a pint of beer that was waiting for him at the bar of some local pub; he thought of his home, his car, even his office and how he would appreciate returning to his beloved England.

"Here Mr West, you can take the helm. My wife and I will lower the sails when we enter the river, and we can let you and Fabio finish this passage. Alberto joined his wife further forward as Mr West was handed the tiller. 'Moutine' sailed gracefully into the mouth of the Helford Estuary under full sail, approaching her home port. Mrs Colarossi picked up her iPad and she made a short video recording of their return to home waters. Passing the green marker cone of August Rock on her starboard side, the classic yacht rounded head to wind and her pristine white sails slowly furled in a cascade of rippling canvas. Alberto walked back to start up the engines, feeling much more relaxed and looking forward to setting foot on English soil. His memories of his birthplace in Italy were mostly good, but there were also some darker times mixed in with the fond recollections of his childhood. From the moment when he had foolishly allowed himself to become entangled with the Cosa Nostra his whole life had changed, and not for the better. Alberto thought that he could walk away from the vice like grip of the Mafia, but someone had told him that you can never leave the highly organised crime syndicate that has controlled parts of Italy for many years. They will always come after you, no matter where in the world you might try to hide. Mrs Colarossi had gone to extreme lengths to bring him back to her home in Cornwall and it had taken a great deal of time, money and painstaking negotiation to even get close to the people who had the power to make it happen at all. His wife had made use of some very clever and extremely complex procedures in order to ensure the safety of her husband throughout his dangerous exile to the United Kingdom. Both of them will have to live the rest of their lives constantly in fear of being subjected to the ruthless and systematic revenge of an organisation that knows no limits and respects no boundaries.

Following her husband down below to the cabin, Mrs Colarossi needed to find some time to arrange for a courier to meet them wherever they decided to go ashore, so that all four of them could be taken to her property in Gyllyngvase. Although Falmouth Harbour would have been the obvious choice, it was also the more risky route to her safe house. It was preferable to use the narrow rural lanes which would be much quieter and easier to manage. They had not been able to make arrangements with a courier in advance of their arrival because the dates and times were so uncertain. Had the encounter with the stormy weather resulted in damage to the yacht, which fortunately it hadn't, they may not have arrived at the Helford as planned.

Alberto found that Fabio was still seated at the chart table. The Italian driver put away his mobile phone hastily when he saw the skipper approaching.

"It's alright Fabio; I think we can find our way upriver from here. You can give Mr West some assistance if you are ready."

"O.K., yes I am ready. There is a good anchorage just here on the chart capitano, if you want to take a look?" Alberto moved closer to the chart table and examined the location that Fabio was pointing out. At the same time the skipper was wondering why someone who had no prior knowledge of these waters would care to suggest a suitable anchorage, when Alberto himself had often picked up moorings and anchored on most stretches of this river. The area chosen by Fabio was to the south side of the river, immediately opposite the entrance to Porth Navas Creek on the north shore, and a short distance before the mouth of Frenchman's Creek on the south shore. Alberto questioned this.

"That was not quite what I had in mind, but do tell me how we propose to go ashore, as we have no tender aboard?" For a vessel of her size, it was slightly unusual that she did not carry a rigid tender for rowing ashore, or even an inflatable dinghy and apart from an emergency life raft which complied with regulations of seaworthyness there was no other means of leaving the yacht.

"I have thought about this place, and it seems to me that your ship would be more hidden here. The water has good depth at all states of the tide and I see there is a ferry available at Helford Passage. We cannot go into Frenchman's Creek because at low tide we do not have enough water under the ship. This chart shows many moorings downriver from here and also oyster beds and eel grass which means that we are not allowed to anchor there."

Alberto considered his reasoning, which was basically sound, and as it was now getting towards midday it was the time of low water. This prevented them from motoring up to Gweek at this time of day. Perhaps Fabio had found the ideal Helford anchorage?

"Alright Fabio, we can drop anchor at this place you are suggesting. We can call the ferry on the VHF radio and go ashore at Helford Passage. From there we can meet the courier that my wife is contacting now. What about the casket, have you thought of that?"

"Do you really need the empty box capitano? We can leave it onboard, it is of no use."

Alberto saw a look in Fabio's eyes that disturbed him for a moment. As the skipper of his vessel, Alberto knew that he should not allow his better judgement to be overruled by a man who has much less experience and is of unknown character. However, as there was no better suggestion on the table, he decided to go along with Fabio's idea.

Up on deck Mr West was alone at the helm; he was watching the riverside slipping by on either side; the steady throbbing of 'Moutine's' diesel engines and the call of the seagulls were the only sounds to disturb the peaceful tranquillity of the Helford. This was such a contrast to the raging storm that had prevailed out there in the English Channel. He was just getting used to the feeling of sailing his own yacht, how he wished that was true, when Fabio came up from the companionway to join him.

"I see that you are the master of your own ship!"

"Maybe not this one Fabio, but perhaps one day....." Mr West was brought back to the real world with a bump. He watched the Italian walk all the way along the side deck up to the foredeck. Fabio wasn't wearing a lifejacket and he didn't clip on a lifeline, but then it wasn't really necessary as they were only moving slowly and the water was calm. Fabio stood for awhile looking up ahead and Mr West wondered what he might be thinking.

Seated at the cabin table, Mrs Colarossi was calling a pre-arranged number of a courier firm in Helston to arrange for a vehicle to be ready and waiting for them when they went ashore. Alberto had talked to her about what Fabio was suggesting and he explained how this would involve taking the ferry to Helford Passage from the anchored yacht. Although Mrs Colarossi also considered that particular location an odd choice, she didn't see any reason why it might not be suitable. They had been hoping to make it all the way to the head of the river and dry out against the wall of the quay there, but the timing had turned out to be wrong. Alberto sat at the chart table and stared at the blue, green and yellow of the chart. He was contemplating the possibility of taking 'Moutine' right into Porth Navas Creek, where she would be sheltered from an East wind, should the wind change direction while they were away from the boat. His wife announced that the courier would be on their way from Helston shortly. She asked Alberto if he would like a cup of tea, as it had been mugs of coffee during the channel crossing. He agreed that it was just what he needed as it happened. They shared tea and biscuits at the table and left the crew of Fabio and Mr West to take full responsibility for bringing their yacht to her anchorage. It would be a matter of half an hour before they reached the point at which the skipper would join them on deck to ensure that the anchor was lowered correctly and safely. Once 'Moutine' was properly secured and providing that the skipper was happy with the chosen location, they would all go below for a glass of champagne and toast the successful conclusion of the whole operation. That was going to be quite a moment indeed. It was a pity that one of the crew would be absent from that celebration, namely Mr Edward Bilbi, but the man had presumably deserted ship for reasons known only to himself and consequently he would not be paid for his services as skipper for the first half of the passage.

Mrs Colarossi asked her husband to call the Helford Ferry on the VHF radio but he said that he would rather wait until they were safely at anchor before he made the call, as he might change his mind and decide to head for Porth Navas Creek instead. He preferred to make this decision later. Mr West lashed the tiller centrally and stepped forward to the companionway so that he could attract the skipper's attention.

"Porth Navas coming up on the starboard side, skipper!" Alberto put down his teacup and got up from the table. He ascended to the cockpit as Mr West returned to the helm.

"I see Fabio is in position ready to drop anchor; has he done this before?" Mr West shook his head and replied that he didn't know. Alberto was aware that Fabio had sailed aboard catamarans previously, but the procedure for anchoring that type of vessel was somewhat different to that of a yacht. The next moment Fabio held up one arm and shouted that he was about to drop the hook, which he shouted in Italian. As he was doing so, Alberto was selecting neutral gear and keeping the engines running which would allow him to motor astern in order to get the anchor to bite on the riverbed. 'Moutine' was drifting against the tide and gradually almost coming to a complete stop. He could see that Fabio was using the windlass to wind the heavy anchor chain over the bow roller, as the anchor itself was descending into the green water under its own weight, soon to hit the bottom. It was while Alberto was concentrating upon the delicate manoeuvre to go astern very slowly, and at the same time waiting for the anchor to take hold, that he could hear a motorboat approaching. He felt the anchor chain go taught and stopped the engines. Coming into view immediately ahead was a red and white boat, which Alberto recognised as being a Plymouth Pilot; the same type of vessel as the Helford Ferry.

Alberto naturally assumed that it was quite reasonable for the ferryboat to approach a vessel that was about to pick up a mooring, or as in the case of 'Moutine' about to drop anchor, and ask if anyone aboard needed a lift ashore. He was thinking how this would save them having to radio the ferry when he noticed there was no lettering on the sides of the boat. The ferryboat would have had the words 'Helford Ferry' clearly displayed in large white letters, along with some other lettering in smaller characters. It was too late by the time Alberto realised this was not the ferryboat and he froze at the sight of two men in dark clothes who were boarding his ship. So quick was the confrontation that both Mr West and Alberto were unable to prevent the boarding. A rope was thrown across to Fabio by one of the men on the foredeck of the red and white boat and each of the two men advanced along the yacht's side decks, one on each side. Mr West dropped to the floor of the cockpit when he saw that both of the assailants carried large machine guns and they were aimed at Alberto and himself. The skipper remained standing, raised both arms and defiantly shouted for them not to shoot. Fabio had quickly attached the rope of the other vessel to a cleat on 'Moutine's' foredeck and then he stood on the coachroof of the cabin, in between the other two men. Alberto saw that Fabio had produced a weapon, and he too was aiming a handgun at the skipper and the terrified lawyer. All three of the gunmen moved towards the aft quarters of the besieged yacht and there was nothing that Alberto could do to stop them.

Chapter Fifteen – Abducting

Many thoughts raced through Alberto's mind as events began to unfold in slow motion, expanding the seconds into minutes and confusing the brain's ability to quantify what was happening in real time. He dare not reach for the VHF radio at his belt and the flares that could have signalled an emergency situation were just inside the companionway, clipped into their brackets on a board. Somewhere down at his feet, Mr West was lying prone on the floor of the cockpit, trembling uncontrollably and trying desperately not to scream like a schoolgirl. Alberto knew that his wife was still down below in the relative safety of the cabin and he suspected that she might not be aware of the imminent danger he was facing, barely a couple of feet above her head.

The skipper's hands were as high in the air as he could possibly stretch his arms and the three menacing figures were now so close that Alberto was able to make out what they were wearing, what they were carrying and he saw the awful expression on Fabio's face. The other two men wore hooded black facemasks. They both had backpacks strapped onto their shoulders and the weapons appeared to be automatic sub-machine guns. In the afternoon sunshine and aboard a beautiful sailing yacht, on one of the most idyllic stretches of water that you could imagine, this should have been a most perfect day to finally escape from the evil that was the Mafia, and yet here they were again. How dare these people set foot on his ship? Alberto was overcome by rage, and by fear, and most of all by extreme sadness to see all of their efforts come to nothing. He had never felt more helpless in his whole life.

Unseen by the crew of 'Moutine', the smaller boat had emerged from the mouth of Frenchman's Creek where the Mafioso had lay in wait at an old quay, hidden by large oak trees. As soon as the two Italian mobsters picked up the call from Fabio, they had cast off from the quay and then set upon the unsuspecting yacht before her crew had time to react. The element of surprise was very much in their favour and there was little that Alberto could have done to prevent the overwhelming impact of the boarding. During the past few days the two Italians had taken their time visiting the local pubs, the village stores and even the yacht clubs to gather information about the layout of the area. No-one paid too much attention to these European visitors, who were not so different from all the other tourists that were wandering around taking photographs, eating ice creams, crossing the river back and forth on the ferry and generally doing what tourists do. Visitors of all nationalities were to be found in this part of Cornwall that was steeped in history and rich in natural beauty. It was so easy for the two men to plan their operation and having Fabio onboard the vessel that was bringing Alberto Bandini right into their hands from France was the icing on the cake really.

Defeated and demoralised, the skipper of 'Moutine' could not see a way out, and this was only to going to end badly. His biggest worry at that particular moment was that he didn't know what Mrs Colarossi would do when she realised that something was not quite right. Neither of the masked men spoke, and it was Fabio who broke the silence by addressing Alberto in Italian, while pointing his gun directly at the skipper's head. From his position on the floor, Mr West couldn't see any of the three attackers and he did not understand what Fabio was saying to Alberto.

Raising his head just a little, Mr West was able to see into the companionway and near to the top of the steps he could make out the face of Mrs Colarossi. The terrified lawyer put a finger to his lips to impress upon her that she must not make a sound. Responding to Fabio's demands, Alberto stepped up onto the starboard side deck and made his way along to the foredeck with both hands on top of his head. Fabio escorted him forward at gunpoint as the two dark figures with their deadly weapons slowly retraced their steps, keeping their sights trained on the cockpit area of the yacht towards the stern. Leaving the masked gunmen to step aboard the motorboat with Alberto, it was Fabio who released the rope that was holding the two boats together. The smaller vessel moved away slowly at first, going astern before picking up speed as it headed out towards the centre of the river. Rising and falling on the wake of the speeding motor vessel, 'Moutine' was once more alone at her anchorage.

Down below in the cabin area of the yacht Mrs Colarossi cautioned Mr West to wait until they were absolutely certain that the boarding attack was over. They heard four pairs of footsteps move from the coachroof above them to the forward end of the vessel and this was shortly followed by the sound of the motorboat increasing speed as it sped away across the river. When the only sound was that of the yacht bobbing on the ripples that moved gently under her hull, ebbing away to the riverbank, both of them hesitantly went up on deck to investigate. There was no sign of the small boat, or the gunmen, or the skipper. Now the peaceful tranquillity of the river was restored and above the calls of the seagulls there was something else. It was the hollow empty vacuum that was left behind after someone was taken away so forcefully and without any warning. Mrs Colarossi just stood there with one hand to steady herself at the mast, looking out over the water. They had ruthlessly abducted her husband at the precise moment they had dropped anchor after all those miles of bringing him back to his new life. She wanted to cry, but she did not.

All was quiet at Falmouth police station and D.I. Cook was pacing up and down his office, waiting for news. The detective needed something to happen. He was waiting for the moment when he could take action. Headquarters in Truro had denied him the use of helicopter surveillance, mainly due to the fact that nobody could predict when the suspect yacht would arrive off the coast of Cornwall, let alone which part of the coast. Although D.I. Cook favoured the Helford for obvious reasons, there was nothing to stop the vessel from landing at a multitude of inlets and creeks, or even coming in at Falmouth harbour. The best he could do in difficult circumstances was to set up two units, one of which was covering the pontoon jetty at Helford Passage on the north shore and the other was in position at the Helford River Sailing Club on the south shore of the river. Each of these two units was comprised of one patrol car and two officers only. The detective was working on the assumption that 'Moutine' had set out from the harbour at L'Aber Wrac'h around three o'clock in the afternoon on the previous day, and he knew that it was reasonable to estimate a channel crossing time of approximately nineteen hours. If there were no delays and no unforeseen incidents during the passage, the yacht could expect to make land at about ten o'clock that day. D.I. Cook saw a window of opportunity between ten o'clock and midday, when one of his units on the Helford might catch sight of the suspect vessel. As a precaution, he also had in place a third unit which was covering Falmouth Harbour. However, this was barely any coverage at all in real terms because there were hundreds of moorings in the harbour at

Falmouth and many more moorings along the length of the Helford River. Quite apart from the moorings there were so many areas of water where a vessel of this size could drop anchor, it was impossible to foresee where they might choose to land. The detective's team of officers that had been based at Mrs Colarossi's property was pulled out, and all evidence of the work that had been carried out there was removed. D.I. Cook was just about able to put in place a fourth unit to cover surveillance at the Gyllyngvase mews house complex, having exhausted all his available resources. His superiors were not going to give the detective any further leeway with this case and as far as they were concerned the entire investigation was unlikely to produce any major revelations anytime soon, if indeed at all.

A small boat motored into the entrance of Porth Navas Creek and reduced speed at once. Fabio was crouching low at the foredeck, while the two gunmen were just inside the cuddy, standing over their captive who was seated. Alberto was sitting handcuffed, his hands behind his back, watching the river as it receded into the distance. Both of the men guarding Alberto had slung their weapons over their shoulder so that the black metal merged with the dark clothing and the backpacks, which were also black. Anyone within a few metres would not necessarily notice that these men were armed. Fabio had hidden his handgun beneath his jacket, in a shoulder holster. One of the gunmen stood back and he was holding the long wooden tiller, steering the boat round to port as they approached the jetty that belonged to the Porth Navas Yacht Club. It wasn't until the boat nudged the wooden boards of the jetty that Alberto realised where this was. He had visited this place some time ago with his wife and it seemed odd that his captors should choose to bring him here. Before stepping ashore, each of the Mafioso took out a dark grey heavy duty pvc case, of the type that would be used to carry fishing tackle. They placed their guns inside these cases and assumed the appearance of fishermen. Alberto was lifted onto the jetty by both men, as he was still handcuffed. Fabio tied the boat onto a post and walked with the others, keeping Alberto in the middle of them as they grouped together closely. He noticed that his captors knew exactly where they were going. Unknown to Alberto, the two gunmen had carefully cased the surrounding area adjacent to the yacht club, and by taking a narrow footpath they were able to avoid the main building which was the clubhouse. The footpath had a low gate at its entrance to the woodland, which they closed behind them as they set off through the trees. Only one person met them coming from the opposite direction and this was an elderly man who bid them good afternoon. He moved to one side to allow them to pass, before continuing on his way. It was shortly after that the man turned round and gave the group a second look as they disappeared around a bend in the path. He wondered where these four foreign-looking gentlemen were going to at this time of day. They struck him as being foreign because they had dark tanned skin and almost black hair. One of the men did smile to acknowledge his greeting but none of them spoke. Thinking nothing of it, he assumed they were just fishermen looking for a spot further upriver that was away from the usual fishing places.

Alberto was finding the handcuffs very uncomfortable; his arms and shoulders ached and the metal bands were making the skin of his wrists sore and red. He complained out loud.

"Why don't you take these things off me, I can't walk properly?"

"When we get to the house, and not before!" Fabio spoke quietly but firmly.

"What house? How far is it?" There was no answer. Alberto stopped talking and walked unsteadily between his captors, cursing under his breath at his growing discomfort. Winding through the ancient oak woodland, this walk along the path would have been a joy under different circumstances. Sunlight was streaming through the upper branches of the tall trees and creating dappled patterns on the forest floor. Alberto noticed the distinct aromatic smell of the whole forest, which was intoxicating. He had no idea what was to become of him or where this was leading. Apart from the sound of their footsteps on the soft earth there was only the musical calls of birdsong somewhere aloft.

Aboard the yacht 'Moutine' there was a mood of sadness and frustration. Mr West and Mrs Colarossi descended to the cabin quarters where they sat together at the table with mugs of coffee. They had decided to call the ferry on the radio and they were waiting for the boat to arrive. The lawyer asked Mrs Colarossi if she thought it was worth contacting the Police.

"I don't think we can Anthony; we can hardly tell them that my husband was trying to enter the country with no passport, and we believe that he has been abducted by the Mafia. We have no idea where they may have taken him and we cannot explain how we came to be involved in helping Alberto to enter the UK illegally. On top of all this, we cannot be sure how much the English police are aware of our movements since we left England."

They gathered together some personal belongings which they put into a couple of bags, including their passports, keys, cash and clothing, along with the iPad and the radios, as they prepared to leave the yacht.

"I suggest we go ashore at Helford Passage and meet the courier as arranged, and then we can return to my house to decide what we do about this. We don't have much of a chance of getting Alberto back alive but I must do something." She was desperately anxious and at a loss as to what would be the best course of action. Probably the hardest thing to accept in all of this was the way these people had exchanged her husband's freedom for an agreed amount of gold, which represented a considerable sum of money, only to snatch him back again when he was almost home. Mrs Colarossi failed to understand why the Mafioso had not staged their dreadful operation in France, or even in Italy, rather than allowing her husband to think that he was returning to a new life in Cornwall and that he was reunited with his wife at long last. Why would they be so heartless and cruel? Mr West thought this was so cold and calculated that there must be some motive which was unknown to them. He was still dazed by the sudden brutality of it all. One moment they were dropping anchor at their home port, after travelling across most of northern Italy and all of northern France by road, and sailing across the English Channel through severe weather during which they had narrowly avoided a serious collision, only to lose Mrs Colarossi's husband at the final hurdle. The poor woman must be devastated at this.

Reaching the edge of the woodland as the trees thinned out, Fabio was reading from a map that he had produced from his jacket pocket. Alberto stood waiting and held by the two gunmen while Fabio checked his directions. They were on the move again within a matter of minutes, now following a minor road that seemed to be heading west. It was late afternoon by this time and Alberto could tell by the position of the sun that they must be going roughly in a westerly direction. He was attempting to keep track of where they were in relation to the point at which they had left the yacht, and also how close they were to the nearest village, which he knew was Porth Navas. He remembered this place had been further upriver from Helford Passage, and it was on the back roads to Gweek at the head of the river. According to Fabio's map there was a wooden gate somewhere on the right hand side of the road and that was where a rough track led to the house they were looking for. Finding the gate, they stopped and Alberto was blindfolded for the walk to their intended destination. It was necessary for his captors to climb over the gate so they dragged Alberto over with them. He carefully made a mental note of the road, the gate and the track as the blindfold was tied tightly around his head, taking him into a world of dark disorientation. The handcuffs were hurting unbearably and this pain was not helped by the violent tugging of his arms by the two gunmen, who insisted on dragging him along at a brisk walking pace which was akin to military marching. As far as Alberto could tell, they were on some sort of rough farm track that had an uneven surface and several long sweeping bends. It was very difficult for him to sense how it must look and it was quite a long walk. After awhile they brought him to a halt. Without any warning the blindfold was removed and as Alberto blinked in the daylight the handcuffs were also taken off hurriedly.

It was a good ten minutes before Alberto could function properly again. His arms and shoulders ached incredibly, his wrists were bleeding slightly and the feeling was slowly restored to his fingers, leading to that awful sensation of pins and needles as his blood began to circulate gradually. The anger welled up inside him when he realised how he had been subjected to this very same mistreatment at the hands of Cosa Nostra barely two or three weeks previously. Were it not for the fact that he was outnumbered by three to one, and he was the only one who was unarmed, Alberto would have killed them with his bare hands and thought nothing of it. As it was, he was forced to await his fate, whatever that might turn out to be. He did not have long to wait. They were standing in the grounds of a large house and immediately in front of them Alberto saw a green tarpaulin that was covering some sort of machine or vehicle. The property looked as though it was not quite finished; the doors and windows were boarded up and he noticed there was a heavy chain on the front door. Fabio walked over to the tarpaulin and he began to untie the securing ropes at the corners, before pulling the cover off what was underneath. Alberto was not expecting what he saw. It was a helicopter. While he was taking in the sight, the gunmen suddenly brought both of his hands in front of him and wrapped his injured wrists tightly in duct tape. One of the men slapped a strip of duct tape across Alberto's mouth. At least he would see where he was going. Fabio took him by his arm and led him to the waiting helicopter, while the gunmen climbed into the front seats of the cockpit. One of them was the pilot and the other was the co-pilot. Alberto found himself next to Fabio in the rear seats. So this was how they got in, and this would be how they were getting out.

Picking up her phone aboard 'Moutine', Mrs Colarossi received a call from the courier driver who was calling from Helford Passage.
"Hello, what do you want?"
"Mrs Colarossi, I have a car waiting for you in the car park behind the Ferryboat Inn."
"Good, we are waiting for the ferry to pick us up from the boat."
"We have a problem Mrs Colarossi. There is a Police car in this car park and I have seen two Police officers at the beach. They are watching the pontoon jetty where the ferry comes in. What do you want me to do?"
"O.K., you must drive to Porth Navas Yacht Club, and we can ask the ferryman to take us there. Let me know if you see any Police at the yacht club."
This was not a problem for them as it happened. She knew that the Helford Ferry would quite often take passengers to different locations on the river, usually for a slightly higher price than the standard single ticket. Both of them took off their outer layers of sailing clothes and dressed in smart casual wear, as they went up on deck with their bags ready.

It wasn't long before the ferry boat appeared, coming towards them from the middle of the river. This time the boat was approaching from the right direction and reassuringly it did have 'Helford Ferry' displayed on each side of the hull. The ferryman was friendly and helpful, gently drifting up alongside the yacht and offering his new passengers a hand to support them as they stepped down to the smaller vessel. Mrs Colarossi paid him the required fee and she and Mr West took a seat at the forward end of the boat, under the roof of the cuddy. Turning away from the anchored yacht, the ferryman set off across the river, making for Porth Navas Creek. Although Mrs Colarossi was feeling more confident and even a little optimistic, she could not help thinking of her dear Alberto. Where could he be now? What were those men doing with him? Why did they want him back? All this was running through her mind as they steadily crossed the Helford. Sitting beside her and having much the same thoughts, Mr West was also worried about what they might find at the property in Gyllyngvase. Surely if the Police were watching Helford Passage they had to be keeping watch at Mrs Colarossi's residence also?

They waved to the ferryman as the little boat pulled away from the jetty. Surprisingly, Mrs Colarossi was able to get a signal on her phone so she contacted the courier driver to get an update. The driver confirmed that he was parked at the rear of the yacht club and he could not see any Police activity. Mr West led the way to the car park where they saw the black Audi estate car that was waiting for them. Leaving the yacht club they drove in a north-easterly direction, using the narrow rural lanes to Falmouth, rather than taking the north-westerly route that would join the main A394 road. Both the courier driver and Mrs Colarossi were in agreement that despite the main road being a considerably faster route, albeit greater in distance the single track roads with passing places would allow them to avoid unnecessary hold-ups or complications. It was decided by the courier company not to send a van to pick up the passengers this time because it was not possible to unload the empty casket from 'Moutine' while she was at anchor. As the deceiving rogue driver Fabio had pointed out, there wasn't any real need to move the casket back to the house at Gyllyngvase immediately, when this could be arranged at a later stage. It was also easier for the driver to negotiate the winding lanes and blind bends with a more compact vehicle like the estate car. Mr West raised the issue of Police activity near to the mews complex.

"I am concerned that the Police might be watching your house. Do you think it is likely?"

"I'm sure it is highly likely Anthony, but we have to gain access by some means."

"Why?"

"What do you mean, why? What are you suggesting?" She hadn't thought otherwise.

"Well, think about it. Is there anything that we particularly need there? Why risk any sort of confrontation when we could go somewhere else?" Mr West had a place in mind.

"I suppose we could leave it for a few days before we go to the house but hang on, what about my car?" Mrs Colarossi suddenly realised the Ferrari was inside the garage at her house. She wanted to use the car from a practical point of view, despite hating the thing.

"I really don't think you should drive around in a bright red Ferrari, drawing attention to yourself. We have to lie low until we can be certain that we are not under suspicion."

Her lawyer was being realistic and she could see that what he was saying made perfect sense. Mrs Colarossi then assumed that Mr West was proposing to use a local hotel.

"Do you have a particular hotel in mind?"

"How about we use my house in Mabe Burnthouse? My office in Falmouth doesn't have any living accommodation but I do have my large empty house that would provide us with everything we need, or would you prefer to stay at a hotel?" His smile said it all.

"I know your game Anthony West! Oh, alright we shall go to your place, but don't get used to the idea. What would your ex-wife think about this?" Mrs Colarossi had known for some years that Mr West's wife had walked out of their marriage and gone off to the United States with a wealthy tycoon who bred racehorses. Since then Mr West had been in no hurry to remarry, which was in part due to his business relationship with a certain Mrs Angelina Colarossi.

"My ex-wife as you call her will not be returning to England so you have nothing to worry about on that score, I can assure you." Saying this, Mr West gave the driver directions to his home and he suggested that it would be worth driving along the road past the Gyllyngvase property. It was now early evening and there was a procession of cars filing slowly past the gates of the mews complex that was to the left hand side of the road. On the right, among the parked cars that lined the seafront they noticed a marked Police car with two officers inside. They paid no attention to the black Audi with the rear side windows blacked out.

Maurice the French detective had finished his lunch and he was thinking about the people who were seen getting in and out of the van throughout its journey back and forth across northern Europe. He sat at a desk in the upstairs office and sorted through all the photographs. There were many photos and he had already examined them over and over again, hoping to spot something that he may have missed previously. In some of the shots he noticed two men who were the drivers; while other shots showed two men and one woman, and some shots showed three men and the woman. One of the men in the photos was not a driver. Maurice was trying to work out which of the people were getting in and out of the rear cargo area of the van, and those who were in the front. All at once, he had a photo in his hand, which seemed to show one person going onboard the yacht at the jetty, one driver was at the wheel of the van, the second driver was standing off to one side appearing to smoke a cigarette, and then he could make out a woman standing close to the side door of the van, and….. yes, there was another man partly visible as he began to step out of the cargo area. Maurice rubbed his eyes and scrutinised this one photo more closely. Mon Dieu! There must have been five people on the suspect van at some point. Four men and one woman! Who was this fourth man? Rushing out of the office and down to his car, Maurice decided to examine the CCTV footage at the marina one more time. Bursting into the manager's office the detective quickly asked to see the camera footage and he was shown to the small room where they kept the monitor screens. Maurice sat at the table with his photos clutched in one hand. A member of the marina staff switched on a spare monitor for him and started to run the stored video footage. Staring at the screen, Maurice studied every movement in detail, as he had done once before. This time, when it got to the point where the people in the white van were about to board the waiting yacht he got the staff member to freeze frame the video footage at several instances. There it was! The mystery man was leaving the vehicle. As the video continued, he could be seen walking quickly from the jetty and onto the boat, while two of the people had gone off to the office building with the marina manager. Maurice was rather pleased with himself. It was because the manager had also been walking among the people around the van and on the jetty, the detective had missed this one additional passenger. The unknown man was only visible on one single photograph, and then only partly visible, while he only appeared for a minute or two, once in the entire length of the CCTV footage for that day. This was new evidence. Maurice was aware of the two drivers, both Italians, and he knew that the other two people were Mrs Colarossi and Mr West from England. He was by now extremely curious as to who this mystery person could be. Mon Dieu! His colleague over in Cornwall must be told. Monsieur Cook would need to be aware of this revelation as soon as possible.

The phone rang on D.I. Cook's desk and he put down his cup of tea, eyeing the biscuits that were only a mere arms length away. A voice on the line informed the detective that it was an incoming international call. What he heard next was a stream of French phrases spoken by someone who was very excited.

"Bloody hell man! Is that you Maurice?"

"Derek, Derek, I have found something very, very important. I cannot believe it myself!"

"Alright, calm down Maurice and speak slowly and clearly, please."

The French detective was buzzing, but he did manage to explain what he had discovered having closely examined the photographs and the CCTV recordings. Maurice described to D.I. Cook the photograph of a man beginning to get out of the van, and the scrap of video footage that he had found, showing the same man leaving the van and boarding the vessel.

"This means that we have four men and one woman inside the van when it arrives at the marina. One of the men is the driver that we arrested as he was trying to leave and he is now in custody. His name is Pietro Di Napoli and his story was looking good, but now I'm not sure. I want to ask him more questions before we let him go. The other driver has the name of Fabio but we don't know his family name. We know that Mrs Colarossi and Mr West travelled in the van and they are both from Cornwall in England, which you know already. What I cannot tell you my friend, who is this other man? I don't believe he was in the van when they are driving to Milan, and yet he is there when they are driving back to L'Aber Wrac'h. It is a mystery Derek and that is all I can say."

D.I. Cook thanked his colleague over in France, and after congratulating him on his excellent detective skills he ended the call. His tea was cold naturally, so he ordered a fresh cup from reception and resumed his pacing of the office floor. Who on earth was this mystery man that Maurice had spotted? Could he be the key to the whole operation, if indeed it was some sort of operation?

Chapter Sixteen – Landing

Putting on his coat, D.I. Cook stopped off at the reception desk to speak to the officer on duty. A request was sent off to the Gendarmerie in Brest for them to send copies of the photographs that had been obtained by Maurice's team of officers, along with the CCTV footage from the marina in L'Aber Wrac'h over to the Falmouth station. The detective reasoned that if this 'fourth man' was onboard the suspect vessel, then he would be attempting to go ashore from wherever the yacht succeeded in docking. D.I. Cook had been confined to his office for long enough and now he was eager to get out in the field. He pulled out of the Police station entrance, intending to drive to Mrs Berry's bungalow, but his progress was interrupted by a radio message. Apparently the Helford Ferry had picked up a man and a woman from a yacht that was anchored off the south shore of the river, and taken them to the jetty at the Porth Navas Yacht Club. The officer on duty said that these two people fitted the description of Anthony West and Angelina Colarossi.
"Where is the ferryman now?"
"The kiosk at Helford River Boats called us to report that the ferryman has radioed them to say that he recognised the man and the woman, having seen the wanted photos at the pub. The ferryman is returning to the kiosk at Helford Passage."
"We already have four units on surveillance so I shall drive to Porth Navas myself. I want you to call the unit at the Helford River Sailing Club and have them meet me at the yacht club in Porth Navas. Also, call the unit at Helford Passage and get them to interview the ferryman. Leave the units that are covering Gyllyngvase and Falmouth Harbour where they are for the time being." The detective had to be decisive and he needed to move quickly if he was going to stand any chance of finding these people.

Passing by the narrow road that would have brought him to 'Polgwyn', D.I. Cook continued along the lanes that would lead him to Porth Navas. He could bring James and Judith in on what was happening later if need be. Arriving at the yacht club, the detective parked his car and strode into the clubhouse where he found the steward at the bar talking to a member of the club. Pointing to the photos that were displayed on the notice board near to the bar, D.I.

Cook enquired if these people had been seen around earlier in the day. They were the photos of Colarossi and West that also appeared on the walls of the Ferryboat Inn, as well as various other pubs, clubs and village stores in the Helford area. Shaking their heads, neither the steward nor the man at the bar had seen the two suspects.
"Excuse me are you the detective from Falmouth?" D.I. Cook turned round to see an elderly chap sitting at a table with his pint of beer.
"Yes, we believe this man and the woman were brought here on the ferry today, have you seen them?"
"No, I didn't see them, but I did see something strange."
"How do you mean strange?"
"Well Sir, I was walking here on the footpath when I saw four men."
"What did they look like?"
"They looked like foreigners to me Sir, dark skin and black hair they had. I reckon they was carrying fishing tackle cases and they was going into the woodland. Didn't have much to say they didn't, in fact they didn't say nothing at all, not even a good afternoon."
Thanking the gentleman, the detective walked back outside and looked around. He could not really investigate further until his officers from across the river turned up. The elderly chap who had mentioned the foreign looking men in the forest came out of the clubhouse door to offer a suggestion. He showed D.I. Cook where to get onto the footpath if he was interested in searching the woodland.
"They didn't look like fishermen to me Sir."
"Thank you, I will have a look at that but I have to wait for backup. You've been very helpful, thanks again." Returning to his pint, the gentleman left him to it. Once the patrol unit had arrived the detective soon recognised this path as being the one he had followed to Bilbi's new build property on the other side of the forest. He was torn between going after the two people who had got off the ferry here, and following up this sighting of the four suspicious foreigners. Deciding to position one of his officers at the yacht club that would remain with the patrol car, he set off with the other officer along the forest path.

At this advanced stage of the investigation the detective found himself being pulled in all directions. What little resources he had at his disposal were stretched to the limit, which was making the management of this long running case extremely difficult. These thoughts were running through his mind as he walked the path with his fellow officer. He kept coming back to this mystery man who Maurice had unearthed. Then there was the recent report of two people taken ashore at the yacht club and the description seemed to fit that of Colarossi and West, but why only two people?

"What's this Sir?" Crouching down to pick up an object that he had spotted on the ground the officer held up what appeared to be a discarded cigarette packet. Handing the packet to the detective, he searched among the undergrowth to see if there was anything else of interest. D.I. Cook examined the packet, which was white with a gold crest on it. He saw the words 'Muratti Eleganza Rosso' in red, blue and white. There was more writing at the bottom which said 'Nuoce gravemente alla salute'

"I would say these are Italian cigarettes. Perhaps the foreigners that were seen on this path dropped this?" Putting the empty packet into his pocket, the detective led the way to the road as the path ended abruptly. For a moment he stood there thinking. Would these foreign gentlemen go to the right, or maybe they went left? D.I. Cook always relied upon his gut instinct when dealing with such an important fifty-fifty decision. The walk along this very road had led him previously to the entrance gate of the driveway leading to the unfinished building project that Edward Bilbi was responsible for starting.

"The chain and padlock have not been disturbed Sir, so there haven't been any vehicles in or out since we secured the site." Both of them climbed over the gate and the detective told the officer to radio their unit back at the yacht club.

"Have them bring the car round here and open up this gate. Then contact the unit at the ferry kiosk and I want those officers to find the yacht 'Moutine'. Get them to use the ferry boat and I want to know who is onboard that vessel. Catch me up when you've done that."

D.I. Cook set off at a brisk pace on his own, leaving his officer to organise units over the radio. Halfway along the rough track there was a sudden distinctive noise. Rising sharply from the area of land that surrounded the property, a powerful black helicopter was taking off in a hurry. The quick thinking detective snatched his mobile phone from his pocket and he only had time to get one photo before the aircraft was well out of range. Standing with his feet spaced wide apart, he tried hard to get the fast disappearing helicopter in focus and hoped he wasn't shaking too much. He was already at the scene by the time the officer joined him, out of breath and sweating profusely.

"I would cut down on the chips and burgers if I were you constable. What do you make of that?" Spread out on the ground in front of them was a green tarpaulin of considerable proportions and several deep ruts where the heavy machine had been standing moments ago.

"Why land a helicopter here Sir?"

The detective noticed a half finished cigarette near to the tyre marks. When he compared it to the empty packet from out of his pocket, he was not surprised to discover the name 'Muratti' clearly shown on the side of the paper.

"I did get one photo with my phone, but I don't know if it's any good. Might have been too far away and I couldn't hold the damn thing still!"

Down at the entrance gate, the officers had removed the padlock and chain with the correct keys, and they were driving at speed up towards the property. While his officers checked the access to the property D.I. Cook was fiddling with his phone to see if he had managed to get one decent image that was of any use.

"The locks are still intact on the front door and on the tunnel entrance Sir; doesn't look like anyone's been inside the house."

"Right, let's get back to the station and have a closer look at this photo. We need to put out an alert for all local airfields as soon as possible. I know there is something going on here, but I just can't work out what it is yet." This was both intensely frustrating and challenging for the detective, mainly because he was so close to moving one step nearer to solving this case, and yet somehow he was failing to keep pace with the plot as it grew into a constantly evolving morass of twists and turns.

From the operations room at Falmouth Police station, D.I. Cook and his team wasted no time in processing their most up to date information. The single photograph taken with the detective's phone camera was enhanced using the best computer available to them in the building. Considering the speed at which the image had been grabbed, the quality was reasonably good. The black helicopter was caught just going out of shot and over to the right of the photo. Examining the image, the detective and two officers worked out the first four characters of the serial number that were painted in white letters on the side of the helicopter.

"You can see 'G-EM' but there would usually be some numbers after the letters Sir."

"Yes, I think you're right. I would have expected some numbers and it's a pity the front end of the helicopter is off the edge of the picture. We were lucky to get this much really. Right, let's put out an alert to Exeter Airport, Perranporth Airfield and Culdrose Airfield. Give them the four characters that we managed to photograph; inform them it is a black aircraft and tell them the precise date and time it was seen taking off from Porth Navas. It is most important that the helicopter is not given clearance for takeoff if it lands at any of these three airfields."

Shortly, D.I. Cook was expecting the unit covering Helford Passage to report back with their findings, once they had been able to locate the yacht and also to determine who might be aboard. He had allowed the two people believed to be Colarossi and West to go ashore and then slip through the net. The most likely address for them to appear seemed to be the mews house belonging to Mrs Colarossi at Gyllyngvase but so far they had not turned up there. Later, it would be necessary to question Bilbi further on the British side, and likewise on the French side it would be useful to gather any further information from Pietro the driver about the number of people involved.

It was coffees all round and plenty of overtime for the detective and his team.

"We need to get a result on this case, and it looks like we are going to be working late, so I would appreciate as many of you as possible on duty this evening if you don't have any pressing engagements at home. Thank you." D.I. Cook sat back with his coffee as the sun was going down, the lights came on across the ceiling of the operations room and he gave some thought to reorganising the surveillance units. An incoming radio report revealed that the suspect yacht 'Moutine' had been found anchored off the south shore of the Helford, close to the entrance of Frenchman's Creek. Several officers had boarded the vessel and found no-one onboard. Curiously there was a casket inside the cargo hold, but this was found to be empty. The same officers were in the process of conducting a more thorough search of the cabin area, which included checking charts, logs and instruments. The detective immediately realised that assuming there had been four crew aboard the yacht, and if the information regarding the two people who were seen going ashore from the Helford ferry was accurate, then he was looking for two more persons unknown.

"We have an incoming call from Perranporth Airfield Sir."

"Put the call on the loudspeaker please, Constable." The team listened intently.

"Message for Detective Inspector Cook of Falmouth Police; we have received a request for permission to land a helicopter at Perranporth Airfield at twenty hundred hours today, for a UK registered aircraft with a serial number of G-EM80. This aircraft has been granted permission to land and is now on the ground. We understand that you are wishing to detain the occupants of this aircraft and we await further instructions."

"This is D.I. Cook speaking. Have your ground staff approached the helicopter?"

"No Sir, we have established radio contact only. The pilot of the helicopter has informed us that he is carrying two passengers and two flight crew."

"Have any of the persons onboard attempted to leave the helicopter?"

"No Sir, the aircraft has stopped the engines and all occupants have remained inside the aircraft as far as we can see from the control tower."

Hearing this, the detective ended the call and asked the airfield controller to notify them if there were any developments. He then issued orders for the units that were covering Falmouth Harbour and Gyllyngvase to go directly to Perranporth Airfield as a matter of urgency, and he also requested the attendance of a backup unit from Truro Police station. D.I. Cook picked up his phone and called a senior officer at RNAS Culdrose to see if he could obtain more detailed information about this particular helicopter. He gave the navy officer the serial number and he referred to a database on his computer system from which he provided the detective with details about the type of helicopter and its country of origin. This aircraft was an Agusta A109, currently registered in the UK and built in northern Italy. Interestingly, the Agusta had a limited range of not much more than five hundred miles, and was therefore more suited to flights within the British Isles rather than International flights. D.I. Cook asked the officer at Culdrose what European city might be within reach of the helicopter and his reply was that Exeter to Paris and back was within range, or possibly a one way flight to Geneva but that would be absolutely on the limit of its capability.

No sooner had the detective finished talking to the officer about the range of the Agusta helicopter, than a call came in from France. It was Maurice on the line and he was even more excited than he had been during the last call, if that was possible.

"I have interrogated the driver, Pietro and this time I have made him talk. I explained to him that if he wants to walk out of this Gendarmerie then he must give us something we can work with. I am saying that I will charge him with obstructing a police officer in the course of his duty and this will keep him in custody for longer. Now the Italian is talking to me."

"You haven't been getting too heavy handed have you Maurice?"

"No Derek, we don't treat a suspect like you do in Scotland Yard, this is Bretagne."

"This is hardly Scotland Yard my friend; I can assure you that we have a more traditional style of policing here in Cornwall, now what have you got for me?"

Maurice proceeded to summarise his most recent interview with the Italian courier driver, and as he did so D.I. Cook had to slow him down several times, the Frenchman's voice gathering pace as he reeled off this new information. Maurice explained how Pietro had admitted carrying an extra passenger for the return trip. There was a man who was picked up in Italy and he was taken to the harbour at L'Aber Wrac'h where he was put aboard the yacht for the journey to England.

"That is good so far Maurice, but what is the man's name?"

"He is Alberto Bandini and he is the husband of madame Colarossi."

"Wait, let me stop you there. Mrs Colarossi's husband is deceased."

"No Derek, this man Bandini is very much alive and as you and I are talking, he is almost certainly on English soil. According to monsieur Di Napoli, this man was taken from his home in Cornwall by the Mafia and he was to be executed in Verona because he wanted to leave the organisation. The driver said that nobody leaves the Mafia, well not alive anyway. Bandini's wife later agreed to pay a ransom for her husband's release."

"How was the ransom to be paid, did he say?"

"Yes Derek, in exchange for Bandini's release the Mafia did not ask for cash, the ransom was to be paid in gold. The wooden box in the van was used to transport the gold and the exchange was arranged in Sirmione using different vehicles. For the return journey the second Italian driver was picked up as the van passed through Chamonix, on the French side of the border and Pietro tells me that Fabio was one of three people who boarded the yacht to cross La Manche." The French detective was consulting his written notes as he was speaking.

"What do you know of Alberto Bandini?"

"Well I have to say Maurice we don't have a great deal on him. We do know that he was one of three men who were the crew of the yacht 'Moutine' when an accident some years ago claimed the life of the skipper and owner of the vessel. The man we have in custody is Edward Bilbi, and he was also a member of the crew who went to sea on the day of the accident. Bandini became the new owner of the yacht after the previous owner's loss of life and when the Italian supposedly passed away suddenly, his wife Mrs Colarossi became the owner of 'Moutine'. She entered into a shared ownership agreement with her lawyer Anthony West, and also Edward Bilbi, for reasons unknown. At the moment we do not know the whereabouts of Colarossi and West as they have gone into hiding in the Falmouth area, following their arrival on our shores. Alberto Bandini and his wife are both wealthy property developers, with assets in the UK and overseas. We have a legal team examining their files, which I understand are extremely complex."

D.I. Cook went on to describe what was happening at the airfield in Cornwall, involving the helicopter on the ground and how the detective and his team of officers had traced the concealed landing area at the property owned by Bilbi shortly before the aircraft was able to take off for the airfield.

"We have not established the identities of the people in the helicopter as yet, but three of our units are due to reach the airfield any time now. I have been assured by the officer in the control tower that the helicopter will not be given clearance to leave this airfield, if they request to do so."

"I think we both know who could be inside that helicopter, don't we Derek?"

"Well Maurice, we are only guessing, but I would be very surprised if Alberto Bandini was not one of the people inside, yes."

Nothing more could be done from the operations room, so the detective allowed his officers to go off duty, apart from P.C. Hammett who drew the short straw for special duties.

"Come on Hammett, let's get over to Perranporth and see what we've got." Just when he thought his working day couldn't get any longer, the constable found himself roped into attending a potentially dangerous incident with the D.I.

Pulling into the driveway of Mr West's imposing detached house, the courier driver stopped the car outside the stone steps that led up to the front entrance door. His two rear seat passengers stepped out and Mrs Colarossi handed the man some cash which she had produced from out of her leather bag. The light was failing and Mr West rummaged through his pockets for his house keys, while Mrs Colarossi watched the red tail lights of the Audi as it swept away into the darkness. Once inside the hallway Mr West flicked a few switches and they went through to the sitting room. She could only recall having been here once before, and that had been when Anthony's ex-wife was away in London on business.

"How about a nice drop of brandy, Angelina?" She sank into a comfortable armchair and kicked off her shoes. There had been enough travelling in recent weeks. Time to relax.

"Have you got any food to go with it, Anthony?" The lawyer poured two large glasses of his finest Hennessy and placed them on a polished mahogany side table next to her.

Sitting beside Alberto in one of the rear seats of the helicopter, Fabio leaned across him and tore off the duct tape that was covering his mouth. Alberto gasped for breath and let loose a stream of Italian expletives. Fabio did not remove the duct tape that was binding his wrists which annoyed Alberto. When he did eventually find his normal talking voice, he tried to determine what was happening.

"What are we waiting for?"

"You don't need to know."

"Are we taking off soon?"

"No."

The two Mafioso in the front seats had switched off everything, so there was silence in the cockpit. Alberto could see the stationary rotor blades drooping limply outside. In the dim light around the area of the airfield where they were parked he could see only tarmac and grass. Darkness fell while they waited and he saw the lights come on in the control tower which was quite some distance away. Then two lines of white lights lit up the edges of the main runway to the right of the taxiway where the helicopter was standing motionless. Looking at his watch, the pilot told the co-pilot to switch on the radio receiver. Five minutes later a call came in from another aircraft. As the co-pilot was using headphones and speaking into the headset microphone, Alberto only heard the receiving end of the radio conversation.

   Arriving at the airfield from Truro which was only seven miles away, the first of the patrol cars drove up to the control tower. One of the two officers went into the room where the air traffic controller was sitting at his desk watching the green glow of a radar screen. One of the police officers from the Truro unit remained in the car to maintain radio communication with his base control. D.I Cook had issued the order for all units not to use blue lights, as he wanted to contain the situation from the perimeter of the airfield to begin with. He instructed them to use the radio channel for his patrol car as the base station at Falmouth was not manned. There would be a slight delay before the units from Falmouth Harbour and Gyllyngvase reached the airfield, so initially it would be the Truro backup unit that was the first point of contact at the scene. The detective was also delayed by traffic and he radioed the operations room at Truro to ensure that further backup was available if the situation escalated. They confirmed that armed officers could be at the scene very quickly if the detective required them.

   "It's usually very quiet here at this time of day officer, and if there aren't any incoming or outgoing flights booked we close for the evening and go home. This airfield is used by the local flying club mostly, and also we have flights stopping off en route to the Scilly Isles, the Channel Islands and Ireland too. During the Second World War there were some twenty-four RAF squadrons of Spitfires based here between 1941 and 1944, so we have a lot of history here."

"What can you tell me about the aircraft that's out there now?"

"Well Sir, this is a bit odd actually. I got this call earlier, from a UK registered aircraft with a serial number of G-EM80 and a chap with an Italian accent requested permission to land. We had already received a call from Falmouth Police well before the aircraft was on our radar and we followed instructions to allow them to land."

"Are you sure the pilot is Italian, and not Spanish?"

"Yes I'm sure because he said 'ciao' a couple of times. I'm sure he's Italian."

"How many passengers are there, did he say?"

"Yes, he said two crew and two passengers. That helicopter is just sitting there on the tarmac; engines off, lights off and even the radio is off. They haven't asked to refuel and so far they haven't asked for clearance to leave. As far as I am aware, the people are still inside; no-one has come out."

They didn't have long to wait before a blip appeared on the air traffic controller's radar screen. An incoming call on the radio signalled the approach of a second aircraft that was represented by a small green light, moving steadily inwards from the edge of the screen. This was unmistakeably an Italian voice and the police officer listened to the exchange of radio chatter as the ATC responded.

"Perranporth EGTP, ciao. We are Piaggio Avanti serial number I-RHFX arriving from Milano. Requesting permission to land, we are ten miles west of EGTP, over."

"Good evening India-Romeo-Hotel-Foxtrot-Xray, you are clear for landing on zero-five runway; you need to follow a heading of four-eight degrees. Wind direction is westerly two-seven-zero degrees and wind strength is twenty-one knots, over."

There was a short pause while the pilot and navigator of the aircraft coming in from Italy checked the figures given to them by the ATC on the ground.

"Negative, Perranporth EGTP, we do not wish to follow that heading. The runway zero-five requires that we land heading north-east, and we have cross wind of twenty-one knots from the west. We wish to follow the heading of two-seven-zero degrees, so we are downwind at the approach. Please advise runway number for this heading, over."

"Roger, India-Romeo-Hotel-Foxtrot-Xray, you may use runway two-seven, repeat two-seven; this runway requires caution, it is short length at seven-four-one metres, over."

Confirming that he was bringing the aircraft in to land at runway two-seven, the pilot signed off. The air traffic controller explained to the police officer that most of the flights into Perranporth used runway zero-five, which was longer at nine hundred and twenty-three metres. Approaching the airfield directly from over the sea, this Italian pilot would have to touch down at the threshold of the runway near to the top of the rugged cliffs and then reduce speed rapidly to avoid an overrun. It was more usual to land at this runway from the opposite direction, so that the approach would be from inland, crossing over a minor road. This was denoted as runway zero-nine, due to the heading of ninety degrees from the east.

Judith preferred to listen to the radio rather than have the television switched on, and she had enjoyed the play that was on for just over an hour. This was followed by the nine o'clock news on the BBC Radio Cornwall channel. James was sort of half listening to the play and falling asleep some of the time. He stretched out on the comfortable sofa while Judith made a pot of tea. She was in the kitchen when James heard Perranporth Airfield mentioned on the radio news. There was a report coming in from a BBC correspondent about a developing situation at the small airfield that was just north of Truro on the coast. Judith came back into the room as the correspondent on the radio announced that he was speaking to Detective Inspector Cook of Falmouth Police.

It was rather odd to hear D.I. Cook's voice on the radio as he proceeded to explain what was unfolding not more than twenty miles away from where they were sitting. James and Judith listened with interest while sipping their tea. The detective began by describing how a black Agusta helicopter that is registered in the UK was seen taking off from an area of land surrounding an unfinished building project near to Porth Navas. Later the same day, this aircraft was given permission to land at Perranporth Airfield where it was established that two crew and two passengers are aboard the aircraft. D.I. Cook said that the identities of the four persons had not yet been verified, but it was believed that one of the passengers may be a man by the name of Alberto Bandini who is of Italian origin and has an address in the Falmouth area of Cornwall. The detective went on to say that Mr Bandini is wanted for questioning in connection with an offence of money laundering, but details cannot be disclosed at the moment. When the BBC reporter asked if any of the persons had been seen to leave the helicopter, he was told that all four persons are inside the aircraft. D.I. Cook added that a second aircraft has also requested permission to land at this airfield and this has led to a disagreement regarding which runway should be used. The reporter asked the detective if anything was known about the second aircraft, and was there any evidence to suggest that there was a connection between the two aircraft. The detective thanked the correspondent and he assured him that as soon as there was any new information about this ongoing incident, this would be announced.

"That's all very odd, don't you think Judith?" Getting to his feet, James set down his teacup and Judith changed the radio channel to classical music. Turning down the volume she pondered for a moment. The detective had mentioned an unfinished building project near to Porth Navas. Surely he wasn't talking about Edward Bilbi's property?

"Why would a helicopter be taking off from the land at Edward's house, James?"

"I have no idea, but it's clearly not possible that Edward himself would have any knowledge of this because he is still in police custody. That gives him the perfect alibi."

"You do remember who this Alberto Bandini chap is, don't you James?"

"Oh, was he one of the crew on your husband's yacht?" James did remember D.I. Cook speaking of him previously.

"He was indeed, yes. The detective told us that Mr Bandini bought 'Moutine' through the Falmouth yacht broker shortly after I had lost Jack. Within a year of buying the boat this Mr Bandini passed away suddenly and the ownership of the vessel was transferred to his wife, Mrs Colarossi."

"How can Bandini be inside this helicopter that has landed at Perranporth airfield if he has passed away?" James failed to see how a dead person could be suspected of money laundering. "There must be a lot more to this and we haven't been told all the facts."

Judith agreed with him and usually she and James would drive to Falmouth Police station at some stage for a meeting with D.I. Cook, or the detective would visit 'Polgwyn' for a more informal discussion.

"Well James, as it is nine-thirty at night and it's pretty obvious that Mr Cook has his hands full with this complicated standoff at Perranporth, I suggest we keep well away and let's see what tomorrow brings."

By the time James came into the kitchen early the next morning, Judith was already sat at the table with a bowl of porridge. She invited him to sit at the table while she got up to make the coffee. James helped himself to cornflakes which Judith had set out for him.
"Shall we go upstairs after breakfast and listen to the news on the radio?"
"You can if you want to James; I'm taking Pluto out for a long walk."
"No it doesn't matter; I want to go with you." James did find it rather surprising that she wasn't particularly interested in what might have happened at the airfield during the night but he wouldn't choose to stay indoors listening to Judith's radio while she was out walking on such a lovely day. They had a nice breakfast without any conversation on the subject of the detective's long running investigation. After clearing the breakfast table and organising Pluto's collar and lead, they set off from the bungalow at a brisk pace.

Judith walked in front with the dog at her feet and James fell in behind her. He kept a couple of paces between them at first, and then drew alongside her as they crossed the large field on the other side of the lane. This was their favourite footpath to Durgan and it was always a joy to follow the coastal path that took them out towards the sea, with the Helford river widening as it opened out to the estuary beyond. It really was a splendid morning. Arriving at John Badger's seat, they both sat down to take in the view across the river and Judith looped her dog's lead around the armrest of the wooden seat.

"I was thinking about all this business with Edward and the yacht when I woke up this morning, and do you know James, if I am honest with myself it is something that I simply cannot get involved with. Whatever Edward has done, he is now going to have to face the consequences and he will be dealt with by the magistrate's court. Nothing that I can say or do will make the slightest difference to the outcome of his case and he is just not my responsibility when all is said and done. On several occasions I have somehow become entangled in some of the things he has been doing, and each time he ran away and left me to pick up the pieces. Now it seems as though this whole affair has blown up out of all proportion. Other people have come in and used 'Moutine' for the purpose of carrying out criminal acts and she has been taken over to France with who knows what onboard. Jack never knew these people. He would never have allowed such a thing to happen. When I think of what they might have done with his beloved boat, it makes me feel very sad James, it really does."

Judith began to cry.

He wanted to put his arm around her shoulders and tell her that everything would be alright.

The sun's warmth bathed the two people sitting there. A dog lay quietly at their feet, his soft brown fur ruffled by the sea breeze. Above them the branches of old oak trees swayed and creaked like the spars of some long forgotten sailing ships. You could barely distinguish between the sound of the leaves rustling gently aloft, and the white crested waves that were rolling ashore from the blue-green water to the golden sands.

Through her tears Judith could see a two masted yacht that was slowly making her way out to sea. Unbeknown to James and Judith, the police officers who had conducted a search of the vessel while she was at the anchorage near to Frenchman's Creek, further upstream on the Helford, were now moving 'Moutine' to Falmouth Harbour where she would be much less accessible to any of the suspects.

"Where is she going James?"

"I'm sorry Judith, I can only guess...."

"She is going to look for Jack...."

The End

Made in the USA
Charleston, SC
29 January 2016